THE GROWING-TREE

by Gwen Mariani

DORRANCE
PUBLISHING CO
EST. 1920
PITTSBURGH, PENNSYLVANIA 15238

Dorrance Publishing Co
585 Alpha Drive
Pittsburgh, PA 15238
Visit our website at *www.dorrancebookstore.com*

ISBN: 978-1-4809-5132-7
eISBN: 978-1-4809-5109-9

For my "Granny,"
whose creative and soft spirit is always with me.
You are sadly missed and joyfully remembered.

ACKNOWLEDGEMENTS

First, I would like to thank my husband and two sons for giving me the solid foundation I needed to be creative and to fulfill this dream. I would also like to thank my mother, sister, and all of my friends who have supported and encouraged me to keep writing and to share my work with the world.

Thank you to editor Doug Henderson, whose insights and guidance over the years has helped this project grow to its potential.

Finally, I would like to thank all of you who will take the time to read this beautiful piece of creative writing that truly came from the heart. May you find yourself as a strong, independent individual ready to reach beyond your limited canopies to bask in the sunlight.

INTRODUCTION

Nature reflects Life; Life reflects nature
As we grow through the strength
of our roots.

CHAPTER 1:
ON SHAKY GROUND

With solid ground beneath our feet, our destinations are endless.

[The previous year]

I watched Aunt Lil and Aunt Betsy exit the house without a word. Signs of the family picnic behind me faded to clusters of voices drifting through the open sliding door. I questioned the sight of my mother's sisters descending the driveway with only the echo of the front screen door closing between us.

"Why are they leaving?"

My mother, Ruth, was busy avoiding the question as she consolidated appetizers to small dishes.

"Mother, why are they leaving?"

"I don't know what to say, Lizzi. They wouldn't have come if they had known."

"Known what?"

"That Jake and Emma would be here."

"Why wouldn't they be here? I invited everyone as usual, including Uncle Teddy. Who didn't show?"

"You know things have been difficult for your Uncle Teddy the last year."

"I understand this is hard for him, and I thought if Jake and Emma came he could see the kids here."

"You know this isn't what he wants, Lizzi," Ruth said, her voice scolding. "What he wants is to see those boys on his own terms."

"Well that's not my decision to make."

"No, but you don't have to support Jake and Emma in this act of separating him from them. They are his grandsons after all."

The moment became still, and all I could feel was the silence between us. It came with a burden of sadness for her, sadness for her and for her siblings who were forever bonded through their rocky childhood. In this silence lay the reminder of the past that held onto them with relentless control.

"And what about Chris? He didn't show either. He couldn't let his kids come play with their cousins today?"

"Oh, you know your brother. He loves Uncle Teddy. He is just taking a stand."

"Against who? Me? My Boys? My boys lose out because adults can't get along for one day," I said, feeling the questions burn within me like a hot flash insisting on being acknowledged. "Because they are what? Testing my loyalty?"

"Yes, Lizzi, loyalty! Loyalty to family. Jake is Uncle Teddy's only son, and he wants to see his grandchildren. Is that too much to ask?"

"He could have seen them here."

A slight crack formed in my sheepish demeanor.

"I don't think it's right," she admits.

"Which? Jake not allowing Uncle Teddy to see his grandkids, Uncle Teddy and Chris not showing today, or that everyone holds me accountable for fixing this whole mess."

"Well, you are not making it any better."

I felt forty-four years of personal growth vanish in an instant. The need to be a good little girl again rushed to the surface, wanting to make it all better for her, or at the very least, not any more difficult. She must have felt my regression for softer words came as she handed me a salad.

"Look, honey, they feel the way they feel. Go back to your picnic. You have guests waiting. It will all be fine."

I returned to the outdoors where my family gathered. While breathing in a tear, I knew I was standing in the wake of their turbulent past. Many emotions were buried long ago but still resided in the tender ground we counted on. I felt a wave of insecurity reach up and consume most of my familiar foundation. Here was the family I loved, growing with a younger, stronger generation and weakened by the passing of my grandmother, Gigi, just two years earlier. Her absence had left a hole in our connection to one another, and miscommunication had built a wall of anger and resentment to replace her.

All of this is my life, is my family, and it has initiated a deeper search of who I am and where I stand.

CHAPTER 2:
RESTLESS

Restless is the voice that sways our beliefs.

The truth is, it wasn't fine.

The truth is, it is not fine.

Time has fallen away. A year has passed with a growing separation of family and an all too familiar disconnection gathering within me. Thoughts of them are often and with those thoughts I find myself questioning the very foundation of my beliefs. Each other is all we've ever had and now there appears to be no place to turn for the answers.

The morning hours are the roughest as I often struggle to wake while pushing uneasy thoughts from my mind. These family issues linger in the distance, affecting me still with a strong call from somewhere not quite seen.

A morning breeze pushes through my open window. The salty air brings a welcoming peaceful smell. My dogs have taken over Jeremy's side of the bed and the boys will soon be readying for school. With my eyes still closed, trying not to drift too far away, I can faintly hear a bee buzzing in the distance. It enters like it was called to wake me and moves about my bedroom with sporadic rhythm searching for something intangible. It clearly has lost its way.

No doubt blown off course by last night's storm and most likely drawn in by the fresh cut flowers Jeremy sent me for our eighteenth wedding anniversary. I understand its detour. It senses nature and the smell of freedom nearby, but it is unaware of where it went wrong. It finds the open window and begins thumping against the screen unable to break the barrier that holds it back. A slight panic sets in, but it relentlessly doesn't give up. It is desperate to escape, even though the cold chill of the morning may be a little too much for its tiny body to stand. I start to feel for its enthusiasm and agitation.

I hop out of bed, for only a moment, and push the corner of the window screen out enough to shoo him to freedom. I feel the bee's relief as it disappears into thin air. For a moment, I wish I could go with it, but the softness and warmth of the comforter lure me back into bed. The dogs are also unmotivated to start their day.

A few minutes of quiet is welcomed before forcing myself out of bed. The shower runs steady with Jeremy inside. I am tempted to join him, but the fleeting thought is overruled by responsibilities, the call of coffee, and a walk in the backyard before my day begins. I throw on a sweatshirt over my pajamas and walk barefoot down to the kitchen. The aroma of freshly brewed coffee hits me before my feet hit the last step. I grab my favorite *Mom* mug the kids gave me for Mother's Day a few years ago, pour a cup of coffee, and head outside with the dogs in tow. Four in all, three Labradors and a bloodhound make up the pack. My little soldiers they are, my little friends on days when the loneliness creeps in and threatens my world.

It's a beautiful morning with the clouds scattered in white puffs and the breeze blowing gently off the nearby shoreline. It is trying to be summer, but the crispness of spring still fills the air. Newborn leaves dance with the swaying trees and nature chirps in harmonious tones to complete my surroundings. The bustling nature stirs as the squirrels scurry away from the dogs in pursuit of them. The plush blades of grass between my toes ground me as the wind blows away my restless thoughts.

Last night's storm has passed, but it has left a lingering of calm. The grass still shimmers with light cool dew that awakens my bare feet. I will take these moments of peace that come after the storm and before the day begins. In moments like these, nature summons my thoughts to the surface.

I listen to the breeze in the treetops and remember back to a time when all was well—when my relatives weren't so distant, when all of our relationships weren't so scattered. My memories of the past carry a peaceful feeling, yet sadness seeps in in the wake of the emptiness that now lies between us. My home is my sanctuary, and I am blessed with a happy marriage and two growing children. At thirteen and fifteen, they are finding their way. The journey to get here has not always been easy, and now I know I have lost something along the way. With my extended family's absence, I find myself constantly on edge for I am uncertain of where things went wrong.

There is more than just family missing these days. My beliefs in where I stand with them and my importance among them have become my questions, and have been answered, painfully, with their silence. Their opinions have collided with one another, as I have also stayed silent. I can't make a choice between them and this leaves me with a heavy heart. I am left to wade in my inaction, collecting the whirlwind of thoughts that pass through me daily. I stand in the quiet of their storm that has been a lifetime in the making. I am beginning to embrace the unnerving calm between strikes of lightning and rolls of thunder. There is a pause of loneness while the winds settle and the clouds break up. I am starting to see that as the air clears, this is my time, my chance to reposition myself and reassess my place in this life and amongst my family.

I take in a deep breath of fresh air and release the urge to fix what I cannot control. I can only walk in the face of scattered clouds and feel the rays of sun as they try to warm the air.

I enjoy watching the dogs at play and take a note from their page of contented freedom. Like children on the playground, their personalities are all different.

I begin to think of freedom and what that really means. As we walk the large yard, I note the absence of fences and the presence of only stone walls for barriers. The dogs are free to leave, but don't. They are free in their own minds to love the moment. I take a sip of my coffee, join the pack, and enjoy nature at its fullest.

I could stay out here forever.

The boys should be awake by now and expecting my help with breakfast, so I call the dogs to my side and head back. May has ended and spring fever has taken over. If we don't stay on task, they will surely be late for school. Just as

I turn to head back to the house, I hear a call from inside. It is my youngest, Justin, looking for me.

"Mom! Where are you?"

I take a few more steps as I giggle at the dogs at play. I look up to answer when suddenly I feel heavy and my foot sinks beneath me. My heart drops from fear of the unexpected and the feeling of the hollowness below. I catch my balance and turn to see what has jolted me from my peaceful walk. A hole appears in the ground where grass once grew. Like a trap door, it hangs limply into a dark crevice. I lean over, peering down and ask out loud, "What is that? What on earth could have happened here?"

"Mom?"

The stress in my son's voice shakes my thoughts and matches my level of discomfort over my discovery.

"I'm out here," I scream back, disrupting the silence that surrounds me, but my voice is stolen by the wind and never makes it back to him.

I walk back to the house leaving the uncomfortable thought of unsteady ground behind…for now.

"Mom?"

I do not answer this time, but the dogs hear his call and head in to get their morning pats and hugs.

CHAPTER 3:
OLD WOUNDS

The past lives within us, holding our beliefs safely in its empty space.

Leaving the backyard behind me, I set my coffee down on the nearest counter where it is sure to stay and get cold. The boys are preparing their breakfast and arguing over the toaster. Justin is distracted by the dogs' good morning licks and nuzzles, allowing Jonathan to use it first.

"Where's your father?" I ask after a few good morning exchanges.

"Getting dressed," Jonathan responds while getting out the orange juice.

I head upstairs feeling a need to share my anxiety about the hole I found. I find Jeremy in our bedroom tying his tie in front of the tall mirror. I sit on the bed behind him.

With his hair combed back neatly, he is clean-shaven and wearing his favorite pinstriped suit. We are an awkward pair as I sit in my lounge-wear, owning my disheveled appearance. The length and thickness of my dark brown hair highlights the paleness of my face from a long winter. With my thin lips, no makeup, small brown eyes, and the puffiness that comes with the morning, I can see my mother in me more with every year. My small frame has taken on a few pounds over the years, but the large sweatshirt does nothing for the figure I have left. Those days of rolling out of bed looking cute and ready for the world are long behind me.

The rigidness of his morning routine is always a reminder he will be leaving me for the day. I notice how handsome he is in his suit as he pushes his tie up to his neck. I think this often, but rarely find the words being expressed. Today is no different, for I have something else on my mind.

We make eye contact and acknowledge the moment through our mirror images. Almost reading my mind, he finds my silence an invitation to inquire about my thoughts.

"Good morning, honey. What are you doing?"

I think for a moment to respond differently, but the only words that come out of my mouth are, "We have a hole. Did you know we have a hole?"

"What?"

His eyes shift back to the task at hand. He is clearly confused and disinterested in my answer.

"A hole—in the yard!"

"Where?"

"In the backyard."

"Really?"

"Yes."

"Oh? So?"

"So, why would we have a hole in the yard?"

"Oh, it's probably just a sink hole."

His casual response and lack of concern annoy me to say the least. Labeling it with a name seems to be enough for him. I look at him blankly, and he feels the need to continue:

"Probably from the storm. All that rain must have washed something away."

"That can happen?"

"These houses were built twenty years ago. When trees were cut down many of their roots were buried and left to rot. It's bound to happen. All this rain may be washing away what is left."

He turns and walks away.

"That's it?"

He returns with his shoes in hand. He sits on the bed beside me, undisturbed by my news as if his day will just go on. He clearly isn't seeing the devastation.

"It's a hole in our yard!" I repeat, not knowing how else to show the depth of my concern.

"What else do you want me to say, Lizzi?"

He tightens his tie in the mirror before leaving the room. I follow him down the stairs. The boys have finished eating and are now headed to their rooms to get dressed.

"So what do we do?"

"Nothing," he says while walking away. I realize he does not fully understand my discomfort with the situation. He turns to find me right behind him, smiles, and kisses me lightly on the lips.

"I am sorry, honey, but I have to go."

I stand motionless as he continues out the door. He must feel the apprehension in my silence causing him to stop a moment.

"Call someone if it will make you feel better. Have someone look at it. I will call you later."

I watch him leave, feeling a little abandoned with my newfound problem that just decided to rear its ugly head this morning. A glance at the clock gives me heart palpitations, knowing the morning is slipping away. I need to focus.

The next half hour is filled with packing lunches and backpacks. The boys make the bus. It pulls away leaving me to my day and thoughts.

I find myself with a fresh cup of coffee peering out at the backyard from the deck as my full-bellied dogs lounge at my feet. Only winks of moisture shine in the shadows while the sun burns off the last of the cloudy haze and the morning dew. I always enjoy these moments, the simmering of nature's chatter awakening the world to a new day. This is usually a beautiful awareness when accompanied by the feeling of freedom and safety, but at this moment, I still feel a little shocked that my comfortable surroundings are compromised and flawed. I mean, I know my home has flaws, but I thought I knew them all.

The thought that this hole has been growing beneath me, just waiting to trip me up, has taken me aback. This feeling is unusual and uncomfortable, at least here. This is my home after all. This is a place that I have looked after, worked on, and worked around. It is a place where my life is lived, where comfort is the goal, and safety is assumed. Unbeknownst to me, something has been eating at the foundation of these beliefs.

My thoughts are restless. I try to process why this is happening. As I re-think how I could have missed the signs, fear creeps in. My breath shortens, for I feel trust has been broken. What I *thought* to be my foundation of balance and truth is now in question.

A short move from the porch chair to the top step, which leads to the back yard, tests my comfort zone to the idea. I hold my mug with both hands to protect the last bit of warmth that is left. My mind wanders as I contemplate what to do next.

The phone rings—a startling noise— jolting me from my thoughts as if a skeleton has reached out and touched my shoulder. The caller I.D. displays a familiar number, but I hesitate to answer. I find the phone still in my hand as I go back outside. I place it on the porch table where it rings freely.

It is Auntie El again, my grandmother's only sister, calling to fill me in on family sagas. I usually love to hear from her with her quirky ways and peppy voice, but this morning I have something deeper on my mind. I am sure she will find another family member to call as soon as I don't answer. Besides, I don't think she really cares who is listening to her as long as someone does.

She is sweet and harmless, one of the only tethers I have left to family. It is comforting when she calls, but the gossip can get the best of her when the story is juicy and worth repeating. Her mind is forgetful and scattered lately. Not quite herself at times, she is unaware that her age is showing. Just last week she was telling a story, in a gossipy sort of way, and she was halfway through before I realized she was talking about me. I never did bring it to her attention. The story was true, after all, with a little spin on it, of course. I found myself re-sponding with phrases like: "Really?" "You don't say!" or "She did not?"

"Oh, yes, she did" would be the response and the story would get larger from there.

I laugh to myself because she is almost eighty-nine years old, and her lack of filter is mostly charming, truthful, and to the point. I normally play along, except lately it has been hard to hear all the words; all the noise that everyone is making about every little issue, stemming from no one dealing with the big ones. Mix in the attitudes and personalities, and what we have ended up with is a perfect storm.

The phone has rung six, seven times by now, and the thought of being a sounding board for the drama today just isn't in me. I have my own issue that has come up from the depths of nowhere, and I must dig up the strength to deal with it.

I walk away from Jeremy's voice on the answering machine fading to the background with my thoughts of Auntie El. I don't miss the chatter in my ear for the words in my head are busy taking over. I head to the spot in the yard that is causing me such anxiety. Not sure exactly where it is, I tread lightly. As I get closer, it lets itself be known as the ground beneath my feet gets softer and threatens to break lose.

My yard of green grass is seemingly sturdy, but is somehow threatening the solid ground on which I live. I thought I had a sharp awareness of my surroundings, but now this flaw has landed itself center stage, blemishing what I thought to be safe.

I have always found that a new path to be taken is an adventure and that it will eventually bring me somewhere I am meant to be. With that belief, the ground beneath me must be solid to reach my destination.

I stand above the sensitive area.

So, what do I do with this? Why has this situation arisen and shown itself in such a way? Why is this happening?

My acknowledgement of this problem, in all honesty, has brought an answer of "Got ya! This is what you get for standing still." I realize in this moment that staying in one place too long can only bring on the recognition of real details. I wonder why, with all the work that has been done, how this could creep up on me. I should have noticed. I should have known. I should have felt it long before it threatened my family, my animals, and the beauty of our home. Instead of looking forward, now I must concentrate on looking down and back so I can understand how this could happen and how to secure a solid ground.

I feel attacked by my insecurities as I stare this issue in the face. A piece of my life was compromised long ago and is now demanding attention. In self-defense, I take my shock and dismay, retreating to the sanctuary of my home. Maybe putting some distance between this subject and myself will help me get perspective.

The transparency of the large picture window separates me from the full view, while the divided panes do nothing to stop my growing disappointment. From here, I see wide-open space, full of nature appearing to be free of disruption and stress, but I know differently now. My ground has opened up, and what I took for granted has proven not to be a secure truth. I can feel it now, giving way from deep in its core. It festers at a soul level with aggravation until avoidance and denial seem to be the solution. Finally, I turn to the comforts of my home, ignoring this issue altogether.

CHAPTER 4:
LINGERING STORMS

The wind and rain twist within me, swirling up memories from the past.

The night came and went, as did my morning routine. No mention or questions about the hole from Jeremy. The weather threatens the day with a tame drizzle. Storms linger on the horizon as the news calls for scattered showers.

The windy rains come and go in this small New England town and, some days, the inconsistency of the weather's mood is enough to send me over the edge. Just as I begin to depend on the sun to brighten my day, it is swallowed up, leaving me alone in my murky thoughts.

Clouds are sometimes friendly enough by cooling the air or providing color and distractions in the sky, but the angry ones—the dark rumbling kind that are filled with explosive energy—gather too often lately. I can feel them twisting within me, echoing through my core of insecurity, reminding me with their muted moans that they are in control of my sunshine. Furthermore, something deeper has been calling to me lately as I compensate for the weather. Something I thought was dead and buried, calling from a place in my foundation, determined to be dredged up with the clashing of the storms.

Today, the phone is a welcoming distraction from my thoughts. I answer without hesitation. It is my Auntie El. She is in a talkative mood, as usual. She wants to remind me that the anniversary of my grandmother's death is just a few weeks away.

"I would like to put a memorial in the local newspaper, Lizzi, what do you think?

"That would be nice, Auntie. I will see to it."

I still find it hard to think of her as *gone*, even after three years.

My senses have been fooled by the time that has elapsed because I feel her presence every day. I carry her with me in thought and prayer, knowing her spirit still guides me during moments of question.

Wasn't it only yesterday that she sat with me, listening to me talk about silly things while drinking hot tea and pushing her glasses up on the bridge of her nose as she looked at me with wise, soulful brown eyes? She always understood. She always knew what to say.

She was my granny, my Gigi as we called her, and family has not been the same since she left us. She was the center of my fond memories as a child. She was the warmth and comfort that all children should have in a grandparent. Gigi was the kindest of souls. She was sweet, soft-spoken, and lovable. A round, large woman, her giggle shook her whole body and her soft smile and sparkling eyes were enough to comfort anyone she spoke with.

Gigi's imagination and creative nature was what I remembered so vividly. My creativity was my connection to her and that which I honor most. Many days my brother, cousin, sister, and I would find ourselves together at Gigi's spending time making crafts. Whether it was an old egg carton, or paper plates, she always had something in mind. Egg holders separated into individual cups with pieces of yarn added to the center made a perfect flower. A pipe cleaner for a stem completed it beautifully. Paper plates, when colored in and cut just right, made the perfect pinwheel. A button slid onto the head of a bobby pin, then stuck through the center of the pinwheel and through the tip of a straw allowed perfect movement as we blew on them. Gigi could make anything, and I loved spending time just creating something from nothing. It was amazing how creative she was. To this day, a random box of items gives me a burst of ideas.

During the summers, we would find ourselves at Gigi's cooling off with water fights. The weapon of choice was dish-liquid bottles filled with water. With the right amount of squeeze, right in the center, a stream would squirt out and reach halfway across the yard. Of course, while refilling with the hose, one of us would find that it did a much better job and the water was much colder, sending the rest running, screaming and soaked.

The evenings with Gigi always included popcorn—and none of this microwave stuff. Good old-fashioned popcorn. A little oil in a large pot as one of us poured the kernels in. Gigi would say, "Enough, enough!" with her slight giggle, knowing it would overflow. The lid would go on and the pan would be shuffled back and forth over the small flame of the gas burner. We all stood there watching impatiently, waiting for that first pop. It would feel like forever, but once it did, we could smell that butter-soaked corn, making our mouths water.

Gigi would remove the lid to check the kernels, and with that chance to escape, the popcorn would shoot sky high and rapidly like fireworks, out of control. She would jump back, lid in hand so not to recover it. Her screams of surprise were amusing as we all screamed in laughter at the snowy display. It happened every time. It was one of the funniest sights to see. Us running around trying to catch the flying corn as Gigi pretended to be scattered and surprised that this was happening, but she made it happen just to put the fun and excitement into making popcorn.

Mornings would bring more stovetop cooking with oil frying homemade batter to a golden brown. The small circular shapes of dough were then dropped into brown paper bags filled with powdered sugar or cinnamon. We would shake them vigorously until they were coated thick and sticky. Each bag could hold up to three doughnuts, and they disappeared as quickly as the bags were opened. I can still smell the sugar and cinnamon as the oil fried bubbly and hot. The paper bags were a vision in themselves: wrinkled, soaked, and sagging with grease spots dusted with the white powdery sugar. It's those kinds of images that pop out of my childhood, coating my memories thick and sticky with happiness.

When life was chaotic and stressful, Gigi's house was the retreat for us children, the place we all gathered, the place of play and creative thinking. She was a collector of many trinkets, old and new. She would always say, "I will never know when I will need that." Newspapers piled high in the corners, washed-out jars and containers gathered on the counters, and baskets were filled to the top with random items like yarn, buttons, pieces of broken jewelry, empty spools of thread, and old keys.

I sometimes wondered about those keys. Where did they come from? How did she come about them? What did they open? A door? A padlock? If so, where were their mates? This was enough to send my imagination soaring. Maybe a secret box held passionate letters from an old boyfriend? Whatever the truth, it was fun to imagine the stories behind them.

This is what I loved about Gigi's house and her collective spirit. There was so much to explore and so much stuff to let my mind wonder about. For hours, I would go through boxes and ask, "Where did this come from? Whose is this? Can I have this?" Many days I would come home with a treasure from the mounds of boxes and objects Gigi collected. The jewelry boxes were the best; when she would let me in them, that is. Those were a rarity to find and even rarer was to be allowed a glimpse into their magical world. I loved all the colored stones, the golden and silver chains, bracelets of all kinds, and even the pendants that found themselves separated from their partners. She would just say, "Stay out of there. I need to go through that someday, and then you can pick something out."

One silver pin always caught my eye. About three inches long, it had a lacey design and came to a point at each end with a deep blue sapphire stone mounted right in the center.

I remember asking about it one day as I shuffled through one of the many drawers in her bedroom. She said, "You can have it when you are older, dear."

"You promise, Gigi? You promise?"

"Yes, now put it away for now."

 Gigi and Lizzi

I had forgotten all about the pin that I had admired so much as a child. Early one afternoon, about a month before my wedding, I stopped by to visit Gigi. I entered her small first floor apartment, a downsize from her small cape that she had raised her family in. A small place we all thought would keep her collections to a minimum with less space available.

After one knock, I pushed the door open as far it would go. It only opened enough for me to stick my head and one shoulder into the living room area. A clear garbage bag of what seemed to be blankets and pillow shams block its path.

Gigi's collections had again taken over. Stacks of items, newspapers, clothing, and boxes filled her innocent space, becoming pieces of her. The essence of their importance had dwindled to a distant eyesore and an agitation for visitors.

I heard her scurrying about her bedroom, shuffling things around the way she often did.

"Gigi, are you home?"

"Lizzi, is that you?"

I heard her voice distant and muffled, but cheerful and welcoming. I entered slowly, conscious of the items that cluttered the living room. A quick assessment of the area screamed Gigi with every pile. A closer look clarified her thought process with all the craft magazines together, a basket of yarn, a box of winter clothes ready to be stored away, and a bag of cans by the door cleaned and ready for recycling. These were the items readily nameable and out in the open. The array of shelves stacked full, knick-knacks that lined the windowsills, and the random newspapers that lay about were all just the silent complicated backdrops of her life. From past experience, she would only acknowledge them in passing with a *just move those, darling. I need to bring those to Goodwill,* while pointing to a bag of old clothes sitting on a chair.

More times than not, I had believed her only to find them later on still occupying the space closer to the front door as if they were trying to walk out on their own. Other times I would offer to take them for her, but after a long drawn out conversation about her doing it herself, and how she still needed to go through them again, the conversation would exhaust the gesture, resulting in them staying where they sat.

On that day, I passed by all the items and found my way into her bedroom where there was a pile of clothing on the bed next to a box that was either ready to hold them, or was just relieved of them. I called to her loudly to bypass her belongings and shifted my sight around a large dresser piled high.

"Gigi, are you in here?"

"Yes, Lizzi, don't come in. This room is a mess."

"I hope you don't mind me just stopping by."

"Of course not, dear. Actually, I have been thinking about you. I will be right out. Why don't you start us some tea?"

I tripped over a shoebox on the way out of the room. It barely moved. Only the top flipped over with my impact, and surely would have hurt had I been walking faster. It was filled with rolled pennies, a collection surely started long ago and slid under the bed for safekeeping. Without a word, I recovered the box with its ripped corners and slid it back into its hiding spot.

"Sorry for the mess. I have been going through some things lately, and they're getting the best of me."

Her voice echoed from behind a large wardrobe box that never got thrown away when she moved in three years ago. She claimed it made a great extra closet.

"No worries, Gigi. I will meet you in the kitchen."

The rooms were small and the hallways narrow, but Gigi was good at stacking items high and finding corners for excess stuff. The kitchen, only a few feet away, held a refrigerator, a kitchenette stove, and a table big enough for two that was home for her mail, newspapers, and magazines. The stovetop was the only surface left for its intended purpose. I filled the kettle and placed it on one of the two burners.

Making room on the table, I stacked mail and coupon flyers to the side. Gigi entered the kitchen with her squinted smiling eyes twinkling through her glasses. Soft small curlers wound up her short gray hair, lumping up a paisley silk scarf wrapped around her head. "I am glad you came by. I have something for you."

"You do?" I returned to clearing a spot on the table.

"Just set those aside. I'm headed to the grocery later and will need those."

After moving a bag of washed-out soup cans from the chair, I sat and watched her gather mugs from a lower cabinet, milk from the refrigerator, tea bags from above the stove, spoons from a drawer, and a tin of sugar that was kept behind her medicines and stacks of drying plastic containers on the counter.

She moved about her collections with an ease that made it all seem like a full extension of her already large figure. Her baggy housecoat in a light pink floral pattern draped over her, reaching down to her large veined calves, while worn terrycloth slippers in pale yellow covered her feet. Comfortable in her own skin, her welcoming energy gave off neither embarrassment nor apologetic undertones. Her surroundings were like a maze she could not escape, as though these things that belonged to her, owned her through past decisions. This part of her life gathered momentum as each item by itself was harmless, together they created a stagnant landscape for life. However, within these walls she was happy and comfortable, and a home she had made.

It was these moments alone with her that I treasured most, as she was nothing more, or nothing less than herself. She was my Gigi, a grandmother, nothing more. In these moments, she was not her past, not someone to question or to analyze. She was the connection I longed for. All the other perceptions of her past and choices fell away, disappeared to a void that time and thought couldn't follow. We just were grandmother and granddaughter in admiration for the moment, and I felt it. During these moments, I felt her see me, see me for who I was, and she loved me for that and I her.

The kettle's whistle screamed louder until Gigi pulled it from the flame and clicked the burner to off. A multi-colored crocheted cozy protected the table from the heat as she placed the kettle between us. Tea bags were ripped open, the mugs were filled, and the cool milk dulled the steam. Sugar sweetened the taste.

"How are the wedding plans coming? Everything set?" she asked while opening a plastic cool whip container full of chocolate chip cookies. "Have one. I just made them yesterday."

"I think so. I have my final fitting next week."

I nibbled lightly on the cookie for this very reason, not wanting to be rude.

"I'm happy for you, Lizzi."

"Thank you, Gigi. Sometimes I can't believe it's really happening."

I stirred the tea although it didn't need it. Glancing back up at her brought a lump to my throat for I always felt comfortable enough to share my deepest thoughts with her, and the subject was surfacing my feelings quickly.

"What is it, dear?" she asked trying to catch my eyes with hers.

"I don't know. I just get so overwhelmed with the thought of everything. Sometimes I want it all to slow down and stop so I can think straight and make sure I am making the right decisions. Have someone tell me I am making the right choices."

"Well, that is the big question, isn't it? And we never really know for sure until it's all said and done."

"When is that?" I ask.

I try to laugh it off but the question is all too real.

"I can only tell you that even when it seems as though life is going wrong, time has a way of pushing us through. You need to trust yourself with what you know right now. Know yourself the best you can. That will guide you."

"How do you know? How do really know for sure about anything?"

"Oh honey, it will come. Just because it's hard doesn't mean it's wrong. Life is hard sometimes."

Her gaze was distant, almost as if her thoughts had touched a memory too strong to ignore.

"I don't want to make a mistake."

"Oh, mistakes are our teachers, dear. Mistakes can be our blessings."

I felt as though I had surfaced an old wound, but she continued without a pause.

"You will find that happiness comes after some mistakes are made. Life is funny that way. Through our struggles, we find ourselves."

"It's just all so scary at times."

"Yes, it can be. But you would know if it wasn't right."

"Would I? Sometimes I wonder."

I stir some more.

"Did you always know? I mean, when things went wrong, did you regret much?"

"At times. We all make choices that don't turn out the way we thought, but at the time we are making them, it all seems to be okay or else we wouldn't have made them. Our intention is never to fall, but sometimes we do anyway. Sometimes we have to find our way. All I ever wished for myself was to have a happy family. That is what every mother wants. I want you to be happy, Lizzi."

She pushed her glasses back up her nose, settling them on the fullness of her cheeks. Her words connected to something deeper in me. They connected us as women, not just grandmother and granddaughter. It made me want to know her fully, intently, and individually as a woman.

"Are you happy, Gigi?"

Her eyes moistened just a little.

"What is it Gigi? Did I say something wrong?"

"No. It's just—"

"Just what?"

"It's been a long time since anyone has asked me that."

Her pause caught me off guard, but I asked again.

"Well, are you?"

"I have my family, all of you, and I can't want for much more at my age after all this family has been through. And to watch you all grow and know there is more for you, all of you, is what makes it all worth it."

"I worry. I worry that I will lose myself. Did you feel like you lost yourself when you got married?"

"Times were different then, especially for women. We were brought up to conform to our husbands, to conform to the men in our lives. That is what we did. That was what was expected. We were taught that a man in your life made you worthy. That is not true, and you must never believe that, Lizzi. Women can have whatever they want these days. You can have, or do, whatever you desire."

"What if I am not completely clear on everything I want? It is all so much to decide on right now."

"One step at a time, darling. You have a good man there, Lizzi. Don't question that. You've had your share of disappointing relationships. It's time you step into the life you deserve. The best advice I can give you is don't let life happen to you, Lizzi. Don't let life swallow you up and don't let other people's choices hold you back. Love people, but love who you are, too. I know Jeremy loves you, but his love can't be what you hang your hat on. Don't let time pass you by. Do you hear me, Lizzi? Live your life with him, but live your life always. That is your opportunity."

She reached across the table, taking my hand and making sure she caught my eyes with hers this time.

"You have a great life ahead of you, Lizzi. Don't ever question that. I am excited for you." She smiled with an offer of one more cookie, "Just don't forget about your old Gigi. You will still visit me? Yes?"

I smiled back knowing the moment had passed.

"Yes, Gigi. Always."

The next cookie was sweet and melted deliciously with every full bite.

"Hopefully, I will live long enough to see some great-grandchildren."

"Oh, I see where this is going. No pressure, right? Let me get through this wedding first and then we will see."

I smiled at her, knowing we were connected, knowing life was happening before me and that I wanted to remember every word. As I etched them in my mind along with her smile, she pulled a small square package from her pocket and placed it on the table.

"What is this?"

"Something for you."

A gift sat between us, wrapped in a brown paper bag paper that she had drawn flowers on with markers and colored in with crayon. Purple yarn had been wrapped around three or four times in each direction, and a small pom-pom gathered loosely in the middle of the square.

"For me? What is it?"

"Open it and see. I found it the other day. And I can't think of a better time for you to have it."

The yarn slid off easily. I peeled off the tape instead of ripping the paper, admiring her artistic design. The box itself was a yellowish-white from age. It opened easily. There in a light bed of cotton laid the silver pin from years ago. My heart paused and memories flew back to childhood. Before I could find words, she said, "You always loved that pin. Do you remember?"

"Yes, of course. I can't believe you still have it."

"I told you that you could have it one day. And I thought this could be your something old and something blue."

"Oh, Gigi, I love it. It's perfect."

I take it from the box and feel its delicate form, thinking the sapphire is a deeper blue than I remember.

"Thank you, thank you, thank you." I rushed to her and hugged her tightly. She was soft and smelled like lavender lotion.

"You're very welcome. I am glad you like it."

"Like it? I love it. It will go beautifully with my dress."

"You're going to make a beautiful bride, Lizzi. It will be a wonderful day. Try to enjoy every minute."

I still have that pin in a special place. I take it out now and then just to hold it and remember. Life has been complicated at times, even hard, but I am blessed with children that Gigi did live to hold and know.

I think of her often. It is hard to believe she is not here. Sometimes I imagine us being friends of the same age. I think we could have connected on a whole different level, and I missed out on that side of her. Even so, when I was a child she was the soft place to fall and the quiet listener all grand-daughters need.

My thoughts of her are so clear, so *real*, that I know she is with me. Talking to her relieves my anxiety on those rough emotional days. I even dream of her, but in my dreams, she only smiles. I am so comforted by her presence that I don't need to speak to her. Only after I awake do I wish I had at least said, *I love you*. I believe every one of us in the family feels the same way. We all have our special memories of her. When Gigi was with us, she kept us together. We all gathered for her and knew that our years with her were limited, so even in the heat of family problems, we always forgave each other in honor of her. When she left us, we became emotional orphans, wobbling on our feet, barely able to walk or connect on our own. The time that has passed has not healed us, and we are still hobbling, unable to lean on each other for support; instead, we are falling, unable to rectify ourselves.

Will it ever get better, Gigi? Will it?

After Gigi passed, our family spent less and less time together and our tolerance for each other became minimal at best. I know she would be heartbroken over the scattering of the family, and I feel her pain. There are times when I think of how it was when she was the center of our world. I long for the comfort of those days of having a close family, but I recognize now that closeness came with thin boundaries. As one we gathered, but little was done by anyone without others knowing and having opinions about. One unit, one entity, one thought process, this was my family, my childhood, my memories. As the matriarch, Gigi was loving and kind, our whole world. Under her care were all of us—her kids and her grandkids—one big group looking to her, caring for her, living around her. She was as much a part of my life as my mother was, and my uncles and aunts were more like brothers and sisters to me.

Now we are struggling in her absence. With her passing came a shifting of generations. A younger generation maturing to parents, bringing spouses and children into the family fold, and the older generation moving into grandparent roles with less control. A shift in family dynamics, a shift in the roles we had all played for years came to an explosive head as these new roles were distrusted. New ways of thinking were resisted, and we all fell quickly.

This family storm stirs up the wind of change while casting shadows on the lives we have built. The rains will come with growth, and true growth can be painful. I am comforted to know that nature evolves all of life. Unfortunately, we don't all move at the same pace. Sometimes we have to leave others behind to catch up someday. For now, I need to shelter myself and my children from the debris of unkind words and actions, allowing time and growth to protect us.

Many moments alone, I pray for Gigi's forgiveness for I do not have the strength to fix everyone and everything. I hope she can see that life changes, and I must change with it. I want her to know that I must leave behind old wounds and the negative thinking that came from them. My children deserve to be planted in fresh soil, to grow without the limitation of past generations. Our closeness under her care brought many fond memories, but it came with all of their pain and anger attached, and I felt it, knew it, and absorbed it. My own growth has been hindered and I must choose differently now.

Auntie El's voice draws me back to the moment. Her speaking of Gigi warms me in ways I cannot explain. Even her voice is like Gigi's. Sometimes it soothes me to imagine I am listening to Gigi herself. Words are difficult to come by as I think of her and the disintegration of the family.

I hear Auntie El's words, "I understand, honey." but somehow, Gigi's voice comes through.

Do you, Gigi? Do you? I want to ask out loud but silence comes over me as tears well up in my eyes.

I barely hear Auntie El say, "Lizzi? Lizzi, are you there?"

I choke out a weak, "Yes, I'm here."

"I understand this can be hard for you, but what do you think?"

"About what?"

"About the memorial."

"Yes, of course. I will call the paper today."

"And Lizzi?"

"Yes, Auntie El?"

She speaks in the softest, kindest voice that finally sends tears streaming down my face. "She loved you, you know. She loved all of you. She would never want the family to be separated like we are."

"I know, Auntie, but I don't know how to fix this mess," I say, barely able to form words at this point.

"I know, darling. Sometimes things have to find their own way into the light."

Auntie El and I hang up, although I don't actually remember saying goodbye. I can only think of Gigi and how her spirit shined through all that had happened in her life, and now the family has fallen apart without her. We all felt her love. She made mistakes, but her intentions were not malicious, and our relationship was purely the energy of grandmother and granddaughter, overriding all actions of the past. I never saw my roots as painful. They are just the facts of my existence. Now I see, through the generations before me, that the sadness has not only carried over, but festered. I am afraid those storms of the past have finally come to wash my foundation away with their sadness.

Slumped in my overstuffed chair, looking at the silent phone, my tears are drowned out by a bursting cloud and matched by the trickling streams of rain on the windowpanes.

I feel a warm glow embrace every cell in my body as she hugs me from above.

Gigi, I love you.

CHAPTER 5:
WHISPERS OF PAIN

Whispers of pain are fading echoes from the past, waiting to be heard and healed.

The shifting sky brings on another day. Something calls to me from a distant place, maybe from the past, maybe from the future, I am not quite sure, but a peaceful feeling resides there. This is a passing sensation as I open my eyes to the relentless breeze forcing its way through my bedroom window. It howls and whistles good morning. The bustling leaves shake off their dew like a wet dog does his swim, happy and replenished. A warm snap has awakened the bees and tulips. Kind as nature can be, it teases time with these moments to awaken us while testing our fortitude with future moments of chill, disappointment, and struggle. As the dusk and dawn piggyback the afternoon warmth and the crisp, dark sky, they will soon blend into a sea of sunshine, starry nights, and easy transitions of warmth, allowing all that is alive to fully expand, burst, gather, and flourish.

I am drawn back to the safety of my dreams. Snuggling down, I drift in and out of sleep. Like this day, and so many others, I lie in the morning air with the day ahead and my mind deep in the past. I fight my thoughts, but my sleepy weakness is no match for their drag. They gather beside me, crowding my bed and forcing me to participate. These old rusty moments are coated with time and ooze an arrogant swagger that owns me. The voices have clearly burrowed in and taken up residence, insisting on rehashing the events of last year.

The picnic itself was nothing out of the ordinary. I host one every spring. Maybe the absence of its planning is what is causing my restlessness, for to do so could cause a clashing of personalities once again. I should have known that emotions were running too high and were too fragile to withstand the gathering after my brother, Chris, called me a week prior. He has always kept our relationship on the edge of civility, but this time was different as he tested my patience with every word. His emotional unrest was clear, but I have always found it hard to breach his rough exterior.

 Lizzi and Chris

There was no hesitation in his voice, only blunt unwavering confrontation. "About the picnic. Who's coming?"

"Everyone, as far as I know."

"Oh, I see."

A silence hovered through the phone.

"You're coming, right? The boys are looking forward to seeing their cousins. It will be fun. The pool is open, so don't forget your suits and towels."

"Lizzi, are Jake and Emma coming?"

"I believe so."

"Well that is a problem for me. I don't understand what they are doing."

"I don't know either, but they must have their reasons. I am hoping Uncle Teddy can see the kids here for the day."

"You think that is going to change anything? Jake has not spoken to his father in months."

"That has nothing to do with me. They need to work this out on their own. Without family getting involved. Whatever happened is between them."

"Has Jake told you anything?"

"No, and I haven't asked. But if I had to guess, I would say the family constantly interfering in his marriage has something to do with it. Same with the lack of boundaries. No doubt it's probably rubbed Emma the wrong way."

"Interfering? Is that what you call people caring?"

"Caring? Is that what demanding everything be done your way is called?

You can't push your way into someone's life, and neither can Uncle Teddy. No matter how much we have all accepted it in the past, it clearly isn't working this time. Can't you see that?'"

"All Uncle Teddy wants is to see those kids."

"Yes, on his terms, his way."

"So?"

"So, there has to be respect in there somewhere, don't you think?"

"Well how about respect for his father?"

"Respect goes both ways. And I think Uncle Teddy needs to give it to get it."

"Why are you sticking up for them?"

"Look, I am only saying that I understand frustration with family, and that I don't think forcing your way into someone's life works. Everyone needs to stay out of it for a while and see if it simmers down on its own. Maybe they will come around."

"Your family needs you to stand up to Jake."

"Not my place, Chris. I think there are too many people involved already. Besides, Jake is family too! Maybe everyone needs to see that."

"Well, Jake wanted a fight and he got one."

"I really don't think that is what he wanted, but I guess if you think so, it must be true."

"Well, that's the way I see it, and you have picked the wrong side here, Lizzi."

"Just come to the picnic and get Uncle Teddy to come too. It just might be the ice-breaker they need."

"I don't think so. As far as I am concerned you have made your choice."

Choice? What choice?

I shake the conversation from my mind and roll over to watch my furry friends cozied up with one another. They rest in heaves of breathing calm, oblivious of my unease. I decide to leave them to wake gradually.

My morning begins with coffee and an easy breakfast routine. The bus pulls away softly in the distance. Jeremy is running late and is the last one to leave me this morning.

"What are your plans for today?" he asks curiously.

"I thought I would work in the yard. Maybe start opening the pool."

"Still no plans for a family picnic this year?"

"There is no word that things are any better."

"We could have it anyway and see who shows," he suggests.

"I don't know. It's all so complicated."

"Actually, it's not. Your family just has made it that way."

"Well, what am I to do?"

"Nothing I guess. Let it be for now. We can try again next year."

"Yeah, maybe."

He starts out the door and asks, "How about that hole? Did you call anyone?"

"No, not yet. Maybe I will today."

I watch him pull out of the driveway. The truth is I am ready for nicer weather. It is the middle of June, with another school year almost behind us. The signs of newness are all around me, and the fresh morning smell holds promise. A few moments alone and the quiet of the house is soothing, yet I still feel the undertow of family swirling beneath me, trying to pull me under.

Conversations in the last year tug on me until I acknowledge them and give them attention. I find it strange that there was a time that these rifts and behaviors would have seemed normal, but then again, one has never lasted this long before, and I have never been forced to participate either.

The following weeks after the picnic were quiet, too quiet, really. There was a shift I could not explain, one that held me in disappointment for the ones I loved. A phone call with my mother a few weeks later drove home the depth of the situation, and I found that the wounded dynamics of family was no longer an us against them mentality. We had finally turned on one another.

 Last Summer—Lizzi and Mother Ruth

"Good morning, Lizzi."

"Good morning, Mom. How was your luncheon with the girls yesterday?"

"It was nice. Everyone is doing well. You know Donna, the woman from my knitting club. Her youngest daughter is having another baby. This will be her fourth."

"Oh, she must be very happy."

"Yes, she is hoping for a granddaughter this time."

"That's very nice. I am glad you get out with the girls now and then. Are you still having lunch with Aunt Lil and Aunt Betsy next week?"

They meet at least once a month and most times I am invited, but there has been no word from either of them since the picnic.

"I believe so. They have been a little scarce with the phone calls lately. I need to check in with them."

"I have tried to call them. I have left both of them several messages, but neither have returned my calls."

"Well, Lizzi, they are having a hard time with this whole situation with Uncle Teddy, and I am not sure they are ready to talk to you."

"Really? What does that have to do with me?"

"They really feel Uncle Teddy is being wronged. He is really hurt over this and they feel protective of him."

"I understand that, but how is being angry at me helping anything?"

"They just feel that if the family took a united stance that Jake would change his mind. You could make the difference. They don't understand why you have turned against everyone."

"I haven't turned against anyone. Isn't that the real problem here?"

"They just feel that if Jake were to listen to anyone, it would be you, and your lack of concern for the family is hurtful."

"I am sorry, Mom. I don't see it as my place to get involved."

"Well, I understand them. I feel for Uncle Teddy, too. It is difficult to watch our brother struggle."

She hesitates, but continues with conviction.

"They believe you should at least care about how I feel, care about how this is affecting me."

"I know this is hard on you, too, but they think I don't care about you?"

"Well Lizzi, this is our family. You should care."

"I do care. I just don't think pushing Jake away by threatening our connection to him and his family is the answer."

"They feel you are choosing against them, against us, and against your family."

Today, I am caught between this generational tug of war with the ones I have only known as my mentors and supporters, and the growing process of myself and cousin who struggle with finding an independent voice and foundation for our children. My inner battle lies between what I know to be real and true for myself and family, and understanding the loyalties that our previous generation holds for one another. I am caught between how I see life unfolding and the knowledge of the past that has laid the foundation for us to be here. This fracture has grown with the weight of every word and has tampered with the heart of the family, the family I thought I knew. This slight crack in our family tree has weighed so heavily on the older generation that it has broken the very unit which I have depended on my whole life. Since that conversation our family has continued to splinter. A sad withholding of connections, as I see it.

Our family structure has never been traditional by any means, but I have always assumed, even to this day, that eventually these clouds would clear and the winds would settle so we can all cohesively blend back together.

My insecurities have hijacked my thoughts today as I work in the house. The yard, pool, and hole will have to wait for better mental circumstances. Today, I have recognized how far I have to travel to come to peace with my beliefs. I must try to move beyond the limitations of others. All of this is something I must look at, something that is in need of attention, focus, and acceptance. I can only assess the damage, collect the good, and move forward for the purpose of giving my children positive steps to follow.

The vibrational current of a family's past, a father and son's inability to connect, and a lack of understanding and communication, has brought this family back to the pain of its roots. This allegiance to family at all costs has awoken a defensiveness that holds us hostage. These emotional whispers hold the deafening echoes of the past, because they are not as much heard as they are ingrained, waiting to be recognized and healed. Could it be that the past is in need of healing so that the future can flourish beyond repeating the past, beyond the pain?

Like most families, our footprints lay deep and overlapping, patterning our past and echoing a collective call. I find it a challenge to break free and allow my own footprints to trail off, creating lasting independent impressions of my own.

CHAPTER 6:
FAIR WEATHER

In the light of the morning hours, the day shifts to an awakening of life's possibilities.

The season is shifting. I can feel it. The sun has won the battle over the clouds for a number of days. The clouds that run free today are tame and content to move with the breeze. They float sensuously through shades of blue, and I can sense their surrender. The air is clean and thin, giving the birds and other wildlife a playful arena. All visiting showers have gifted us the rewards of awakening flowers, perky, tall, and blooming, even the trees and hedges shine a more lustrous green in the morning light.

The morning mist evaporates in the sunlit hours, and the evening shades soothe the heat of the day. A perfect balance nature has provided during these earlier summer days. As fragile as life can be, nature always seems to find a way to remind us that all is meant to be, no matter how difficult it sometimes is.

The school year has ended and June will soon be gone. Jeremy has left for work. The boys are sleeping in waiting for the sun to invite them to the pool. I have found my way to a fresh cup of coffee and a seat on the front porch swing. As I rock gently back and forth, I reaffirm to the world that this is my favorite part of the morning with a deep relaxing breath. Here I am, sipping on my coffee, sitting peacefully in solitude with a day of possibilities ahead.

For a few days now, my mornings have been blessed with calm, and I have enjoyed them for all they are worth.

This is a time of transition in the change of seasons and school schedule. Now, instead of the crazy, early morning routine of the kids grabbing breakfast, backpacks, and whatever else needed to catch the bus on time, the mornings have quieted. Slow awakenings and long cups of coffee fill my mornings, giving me time for reflection and thought.

My quieter afternoons of menial tasks and errands will be pushed aside, bringing long hours of heat, picnics, packing coolers instead of backpacks, cooking outdoors, and sandy-beach living. The mounds of jeans to be washed will be replaced with shorts, t-shirts, sandy towels, and coconut-smelling bathing suits. Summer camps and sports activities will help move us through the weeks. All of this will fill my months ahead, but for now, I can fold into my swing and feel the blessings of my surroundings.

The squirrels are awake and busy this bright morning. I watch them race up and down the trees in play. Around and around they go. Many sit perched in the grass, hands to their faces, nibbling a morsel they have found. The dogs seem uninterested in them and snooze nearby unaffected. These bushy-tailed creatures busily dash through the trees in pursuit of gathering, for the cold days that are sure to come again. I see their happiness and the spring in their steps, almost as if this day is a gift so they can gather much and prepare for more. They see through the temptation of basking in the beauty and see it as nature providing an opportunity to get busy with hard work. They are reminding me that days of calm are those when much can be accomplished.

I try to ignore my analysis of the scurrying ones by turning my face to the sky, eyes closed. I try to rid my mind of thoughts, for once they start to fill my head, my day has begun. A deep breath clears my lungs and calms my mind just long enough for one more moment of peace.

I rock back and forth in the swing, swaying my thoughts away like a baby being calmed after waking too quickly, but the thoughts creep in and my mind goes where it always does as I watch the wildlife move to nature's call.

I gaze out at them, feeling the shame and fear of idleness, wondering where my days have gone. I have allowed my thoughts to swallow up time while avoiding the work that needs to be done. I feel a sluggish weight from deep down pulling me to the hole that has claimed a part of my life, a part of my world. Lying there innocently in my backyard, it remains to remind me of the space it owns.

Now, bent to nature's will, the ground gave up and surrendered a piece of itself. The hole, empty and lifeless, has shown me where growth has stopped, where time and avoidance have caved in on themselves. Instead of facing it, I chose to wallow in a protective distance, in a defensive standoff behind my closed doors. I even sit comfortably in the sanctuary of the front yard where the view remains untarnished.

This fair weather before me is leaving nothing to distract my mind, nothing to fog my thoughts. It is inviting me, all this open space, back out to play. I see the irony as the clarity of the weather shows me how this issue is clouding my head. I have not found a way to deal with what is on my mind. It has been weeks since stumbling upon the sinkhole in my foundation, and yet, it is not the only issue still lingering.

Likewise, my distant family has been collectively silent as a whole. The deliberate interactions have stopped altogether, clearing my head of chatter so I can reconsider my position within my family. The only words I hear are filtered through my mother and Auntie El who are both loyal to all and play both sides of the fence very well. Never stepping too long on one side, they avoid forming real boundaries or enemies.

Any words cast my way are construed as bait, as an invitation to play along, or maybe a chance to change my mind and come back to their flow of thinking. It has been hard to keep my composure at times while simply choosing not to discuss anyone at all. This seems to ignite the sparks of bitterness and prove their point of my disloyalty even further. Words like "uncaring" and "selfish" are thrown my way.

Unfortunately, my nerves have been struck and my reactions have not always been desirable. Treading lightly and standing steady are difficult to balance when the ground is thin, so to be left out of the drama certainly does have its benefits. The absence of their words has cleared my head, leaving an emptiness of its own, for me to ponder the truth.

Oh, where the mind goes when there is nothing to fill it! I think it is the empty space that the words once filled that brings me to an awkward feeling of excited comfortableness. Oh, the possibilities. *Swing and sway, I rock those thoughts away...* As I sit swinging in my morning calm and deepening thoughts,

I realize I have had no interest in addressing either issue while retreating to my comfort zone of staying busy with kids, animals, and daily errands. These activities have kept me from facing the work that awaits me. Time has been passing me by, and I have compensated for the insecurity that I feel.

This hollow space has intruded on my life, on my home, and is making me question my surroundings and the life I have built. It is dredging up old feelings I thought I had let go of long ago, making me ask *where did this vulnerability come from, really?* And *how did it find me here?*

It is funny to me that this void I have found, this hole (*or has it found me?*) as empty as it may be, is filling my head with many questions. In reality, the finding has been by neither. It has been lying in wait all along, waiting for me to notice that I, too, have obviously buried and covered up a piece of my past, leaving it to fester. As time has passed, the ground can no longer hold that which is not true and strong, as with my avoidance, neither issue has righted itself. They have only continued on the path of destruction.

I know, logically, time heals and changes only what is tended to. I understand my moments of wallowing have gotten me nowhere. Although I still struggle with myself on what to do, I know life has presented an opportunity for me to reconcile an issue of great depth. I am tempted to only enjoy the beauty in life during which I may be passing on the chance to gather knowledge and insight, like the squirrels do for a cooler day, as I prepare for the future. To face it or not face it: this choice is upon me and awaits my decision. I can only imagine the turmoil that will be stirred up with this contemplation.

Right now, fear and anxiety for the unknown is all that grows within me. *Where will it take me? Can I do this? How do I get to the bottom of this?* I must dust off these old familiar fears and see them for what they are. I realize in this moment that I have attempted to respect my fear by treading lightly around the areas, afraid to disrupt the tenderness of it all. Avoiding the hole and my family protects me. In the last weeks, I have been living cautiously, not placing weight near or allowing activities around it, or them, for it may shake loose any stability that is left.

With this emptiness digging deep into my thoughts, I realize the control it has over me. I find the dogs' playful runs make me nervous, so I keep them close while keeping family at a safe distance. My attempts to control all of my surroundings have created avoidance. *Out of sight, out of mind* seems to be the idea. I have moved my morning strolls to the front yard where the beauty to the passerby is still intact. I, too, sit only wanting to see the beauty before me while behind me the thoughts pull me back.

I swing and sway, back and forth, trying to slumber the thoughts that are awakening within. However, they have been given light, and like the child who has been woken, they now scream for attention.

My life has continued while ignoring it thoroughly with fear at the forefront. I am avoiding the issue while living with the knowledge of its existence, keeping a light distance so not to examine it too closely. Size or details are not the concern. Its presence is enough to stir up emotion.

Actually, ignoring this all together is acknowledgement, for every time I compensate, I give the fear strength and energy. *For me to avoid it, I must be acknowledging its presence, right?* Again, the confusion of this emptiness filling my head is creating much disruption and aggravation for me. It's not the issues in question, but my thoughts for them that are the culprits in these moments.

What is it, really? It is emptiness where something once was, Right?

It is not bad, nor good. It just is. It has been created by nature, by nurture, by the doings of others and cannot be controlled. It has been placed in my life, placed where I will have to deal with it if I want to enjoy all I have worked for, all that has been blessed to me. This cannot take that away. I will find a way to accept what has happened and move on.

Move on? What is that?

Swing and sway, rocking those thoughts away... Guilt will come with that, for sure. Guilt is no stranger. It accompanies most of my feelings. This is no exception, for I have benefitted from the sacrifices others have made. This is what I was taught. Many sacrificed so I could be and have. I should be forever in their debt and gratitude, and know my place. Those sacrifices became part of my crooked, self-doubting growth. With great sadness, I find guilt attached to enjoying the beauty of this large yard. It is one of the details that attracted us to this very house, the wide-open space, the emptiness of it all. Now, I question this emptiness and the process of how it got here. *Would I have been as attracted knowing the truth of what was buried beneath? Knowing the destruction of the trees that fell? Knowing scarifies were made only to be remembered one way or another?* Here, too, as in my family, I am to be reminded daily of the pain that was endured so that I could have joy.

Overwhelmed with thoughts, questions, and mixed feelings of confusion about this problem, I realize I am refusing to enjoy this area, and I am the only one creating fear for it. Actually, no one would ever know of its existence if I don't point it out.

Why face what everyone else is willing to ignore? Swing and sway, rocking those thoughts away...

I have tried to take that approach. Despite all my efforts and energy put into avoiding the hole, now and then I stumble outside my comfort zone, landing me too close to the damaged area. The last time this happened, I noticed more of the ground had started to give way. A larger hole appears now amongst a patch of brown grass. There, lies proof that my avoidance did not stop it from deteriorating from within. It never does.

The awareness of needing to make a decision sent shivers up my spine, and I quickly backed away, retreating to the safety of the indoors once more.

I then sat in the safety of my walls, floor, and roof. Boxed in by my fears and insecurity. I suddenly felt the gap had narrowed between avoidance and truth and wondered just how much of my beautiful view had been tarnished by the actions of the past.

Remembering the timid actions of that day collects questions of uncertainty and what I am creating. Paranoia visits quickly and aggressively.

Will I be afraid to venture out anymore? Am I stuck in the comfort of safety from the fear of what it truly is? Has my life reached smallness due to narrowing my field of enjoyment? Has the outdoors, which has brought me much happiness over the years, become a place of insecurity from the insensitivity of others in the past? Has avoiding sensitive areas narrowed my ability to reach out beyond my walls? What is it, really? How big and how deep could this go?

I think, too, of the many moments I have enjoyed the landscape built up around me while watching over and caring for my yard. I see it differently now, almost awkwardly annoying. It bothers me to my core how something so old and deep could tarnish the view of my horizon.

It is unnerving during these long thoughts that this weakness is from the deterioration of a strongly rooted tree cut down in its prime and covered over so to give the appearance that such devastation never happened. Knowing that people have caused this trauma in the pursuit of their own agendas creates disgust for them, not for *it*. Even though they may not have realized at the time how their lashes would cut so deeply and scar such a beautiful place, it still amazes me. I sit in the creation of the devastation and wonder. *Did they know the deterioration would continue long after they had moved on only to be left for someone else to fix?*

The child within me knows of these pains and how they can dig in and fester. She knows how they connect us to others and how they cannot be dug out without leaving scars, especially when nothing has been put in place of them. They cannot be hacked down and covered over for appearances because their roots are still intact. They can only do one of two things: they can take root and grow again, or deteriorate, leaving an empty space in our foundation.

The words "no more" begin to flood my thoughts.

No more will I allow my walls to close me in. No more will I fear what I enjoy. No more will my path be blocked. No more will sensitivities or a soft spot be a disability, controlling where I tread. No more will appearances give me false security. No more will I retreat from past mistakes. No more will I question the strength and solidarity of what can be.

All of this tires my mind and plays out another hour of restless inaction. Restless are my legs as I swing and sway faster and faster, breathing deeper and deeper, feeling the need to take part in the present, in my future. To recreate what has been given me, to collect and gather, like the squirrels before me, the knowledge for the situation and take control of what is next.

This fair weather is clearing my head and the breeze is blowing away the fog. I know now what I need to do. I will see this as a gift, an opportunity to find solid ground. This is a chance to work hard and gather for another day.

For the purpose of healing, I am motivated to deal with the issue at hand. With an open mind, I will enter into this unknown territory and search for clues on where to begin. I need to find the core of my agony and face it head on. I know this is going to be a dirty job, but I am determined to dig deep, work hard, and muster up the courage to know it, to own it, and to move past it.

I will see this through.

Venturing out of my comfort zone, I leave the porch and the view of the undisturbed behind me. The swing is left empty, fending for itself, swaying with the momentum that has been created and rocking itself to sleep.

Swing and sway, rocking those thoughts away. . .

CHAPTER 7:
PUSHING AHEAD

Oh, what thoughts a hole can dig up!

I cross through the house where I quickly slide into a pair of flip-flops before exiting to the backyard. They are the most protection my toes have on a normal summer day. My footwear shows little initiative for the pursuit of this mission, but still more traction than the usual bare feet. The dogs are awake and follow loyally. With laid-back ears, fury bounds and barks scare away any creatures that may have gotten comfortable during our absence. I can't help but smile at them, my friends, tough, ferocious, and cuddly.

The sun is creeping up the edge of the sky, squinting through the last of the hazy clouds, which pattern the sky with brush strokes and feathery wisps. The shadows are slowly retreating from the sun where they will hide during the noon light. Stillness vibrates within me. The breeze has dulled as this piece of my yard—where my journey is heading—seems farther away than I remember. I march in solidarity, trying to remain stern and focused as the dogs follow behind me in a go-ahead-you-first glare. I sense they are right, but push ahead anyway.

My approach is slow. I can feel it near, but my accuracy is uncertain. The birds chatter noisily as I get closer and the wind rejuvenates in the treetops. Youthful leaves flutter in the breeze, whispering amongst themselves as they peer down like spectators of a suspenseful event. A hawk screams in the distance. Her echoes ripple through the sky. With her presence known, she either has caught her prey or is in search of one.

Maybe it is *me* she is looking for.

I have often felt the fear of being prey in this world. After all, those are the two main roles in life, aren't they? *Exciting, isn't it, this thought of predator versus prey revealing itself in a wondrous suspense?* I wonder which one I am as the hawk soars nearby, and I stalk the weakened, damaged part of my life. *Am I the predator, strong and able, ready to pounce and conquer for the sake of my future? Or am I the unsuspecting prey bouncing through the last of the meadow, headed for certain death?*

Where does the answer lie? In strength? Who has it and how much? And where does it live? Below? Within? Mine seems scarce at the moment. Did I ever have any in the first place? I know I did once, but over the years, I tucked it away not to offend, and now I am hoping it will show itself. *Or has it, too, been weakened from the lack of acknowledgement?* I realize strength comes during unexpected times, like when the heart has been broken and pain washes over you, capturing all that you are, or when fear creeps up on you crushing you down to the ground. Strength is what helps us stand up and struggle through. My strength is here, *somewhere*, pushing me ahead.

This morning's walk is long and awkward as I glance ahead to spot any flaws in the grass. I can see the brown patch prominent and larger than I remember. The dogs finally prance ahead as if knowing our destination. I call them back in a slight panic, not knowing how weak the ground really is. They halt just outside the brown area with their noses to the ground and tails in the air as if sensing the void beneath. My approach is slow and calculating as I test each step with a small light-footed bounce. The ground is soft.

I feel as though I am being watched, and I realize the hawk is perched in a tall tree at the edge of the yard. She peers down on me as I examine the hole in the ground. I look up at her, but the sun shines directly into my eyes. I squint from the glare, and she flies off into the distance. I turn my attention back to the hole and realize I am not the weakest here. The hawk moves on as I move ahead.

This is an opportunity to study my fear, give it a name, a face, an opportunity to bring the details of its existence to light. Needing a little extra encouragement, I think of my Gigi and feel she is watching from above.

Please help me, Gigi. Help me stand strong in the face of this challenge. Help me to see the life within this world which I am called to live. Help me to find the sturdy ground I need to move forward on my journey.

With courage, I stand above the dying grass where a part of it has given up and fallen to the pressure of nature and gravity. I pause a moment, noticing how the damaged section is spreading. Strange how negativity grows, contaminating its surroundings. A small hole remains where live, rooted grass once flourished.

This is where my work begins with awareness and acceptance for its existence. Knowing it will not go away unchallenged, I am ready to fight for what is mine. Failure stops here.

The hole gazes up at me like it is begging for help and attention. I remain frozen, staring back at this pathetic site. I take a moment in silence. I feel I have abandoned a piece of my life. Strength collected here once. The smallest of blades and roots gathered together with the tiniest specks of dirt to support the weight of the world above, but damaged, neglected, and left unattended to, it now crumbles and cries out for help.

This gash in my life, in my foundation, is a distant wound no longer isolated or contained.

What is my part in this destruction?

Yes, my fear has kept me from seeing the truth.

Did that fear contribute to the damage?

Like so many things once set in motion, they collect momentum until someone or something stops it. *Could anything, or anyone, flourish under these circumstances?* Generation after generation of heartache has embedded the insecurities so deeply that the pain had no other choice but to thrive in the wounds of the past. All too familiar is this pain, and once damaged to this extent, *what in life could heal without the proper attention?*

Time was its friend, but healing it was not given. I feel for the loss of time, for the loss of appreciation and character. This is a part of my life that deserves quality, time, and energy to be rebuilt to true stability, strength, and beauty. It is meant to be brought back to solid wholeness.

When the cuts are deep and the wounds are this clear, it is all too familiar, and it leads back to my family and all they have endured. All their pain has swirled up around me my whole life. A generation of bonding through heartache and struggle, their born insecurities that only they can claim is dragging down all that surrounds them, much like this hole. They tried to gather like the small blades of grass to support and protect us, but with all their efforts, time and nature has released pressures that cannot be withstood.

Like this hole, family roots gathered here once only to deteriorate over time.

As children my mother and her siblings—six altogether, three brothers and two sisters—were bonded through the shocking events of their father—my grandfather—choosing to leave the family and start over with a younger woman. This left them young, in poverty, and full of insecurities as they fended for themselves and protected their mother, my Gigi. Anger and embarrassment were prevalent, and hope was lacking while they hid and joined in their pain. They mastered defensiveness at a young age.

They have successfully covered over their uncertainties while growing beautiful families with healthy, adult children who make decisions for themselves and for the good of their young, but now their pains have gathered too long, festering to a gaping hole waiting to swallow us up.

Most of our generation is all too aware of the pain that was endured, but still they raised us to be strong and tough while pushing ahead without needing help from others outside the family. We have grown to be independent, and we are, choosing not to repeat the patterns of the past. We move ahead like the grass above refusing to cover up the hole any longer. Our parents see this as an attack on their very being, a reflection of their legacy of being left behind, instead of a testament to their parenting skills and family structure. The truth is, without the strength they gave us we would be unable to move forward without them. *Isn't independence exactly what every parent wants for their children?*

My family's pain is real. There is something eating away at them. They are hurting in ways that time alone cannot heal. The pain is festering like the rotting wood beneath the surface.

"Dig it out," I say.

It is the roots of old beliefs and old memories holding us down. The time has come to replace it with goodness.

"But a finger needs to be pointed," they say. "Who is to blame for this catastrophe? Nature? Nurture?"

Putting a name on it will not make it go away. Blaming the one who finally put the last ounce of pressure on a falling rock is like blaming nature for making it heavy or gravity for being an element in nature. Wounds are being opened, and the pain throbs, but it comes from devastations of long ago, from pain that was patched up at the surface and left in their foundation, *my* foundation. These wounds lay dormant, weakening the world above until finally, the weight of life's simple actions brought it all crumbling down on all of us. *Why?* Because a person who was unaware came along and stepped too close to this sensitive area, and we were all effected because we are all part of the same collective unit. Like dominos, we have fallen one after the other. Now my foundation is suffering, and I must deal with it *my way*, not theirs.

The hole is *there* and the hole is *here*, and healing one way or another will begin, starting within me, in my foundation. There is no room in my foundation for bitterness, pain, past devastations, or petty anger. Not in my home. Here it has come to heal. I will make it new, healthy, and strong again. They are welcome to enjoy the beauty and walk the sturdy ground, but they cannot put my family and home in danger of falling into the destructive anger of it all.

Elements of nature or human's misstep causing this ground-breaking event moves on without a second thought, moving on like the winds, never understanding the past they have stirred up. They continue on their own path while the hole is stationary waiting for validation, waiting to be dug out and replaced.

Seeing and feeling the devastation doesn't change what it is. It only narrows and limits my thoughts. I have validated my family's pain for years by tiptoeing around issues, subjects, and people, and I have held my tongue many times when they did not. This is the hole I dug for myself and now I am mocked for doing the same for others.

So, here it is! A physical hole: tangible, pliable, and something I can finally put my hands on. At the surface, it is small in comparison to the world above, but I can feel the energy below echoing with hollow darkness, and with the acknowledgement of its presence lies work to be done. I accept what is visible to the eye: a tiny glimmer of buried issues. It is large enough to peek through, and I see there is unknown territory to be explored. To ignore its presence is to surely have a rude awakening one of these days. The darkness demands attention as I pray for the strength, courage, and clarity to attack it head on.

CHAPTER 8:
LEANING IN

These thoughts are growing roots of their own.

The hole lies before me, the sun is wide-eyed and glaring down at me, the wind has calmed like a hush falling over a crowd, and I feel the pressure of expectations. Slowly, I approach the center. Leaning down to get a closer look, I balance myself above the small opening. I see darkness and try to focus my eyes, but I only manage to hear it calling to me. Echoing from the bowels of this lonely place, it knows me by name.

"Lizzi! Lizzi! Is that you?" I hear it beckon.

My heart stops and I jump back. My dogs have abandoned me and are now standing on the stone wall looking out at the field beyond. Relief and silliness wash over me as I see Mr. Hansen, my neighbor, shuffling across the field. He is sporting the typical denim overalls, t-shirt and work boots he wears all year round. The only change to his daily wardrobe is his hats. For the summer, it is straw, the same straw hat he has had for years, ragged and dirty with one edge unraveling and frayed. For the winter, it is a black-knitted ski hat, and for the fall and spring months, it is an array of baseball caps with no specific color or logo. His house is behind ours with a large field separating us. I speak to him once in a blue moon. I mostly see his straw hat bobbing up and down behind his fenced in green during the summer months.

Mr. Hansen is a gruff man with aged and weathered skin. He has a hearty stance of solid intimidation for a smaller guy. On first appearances, he projects a glare of annoyance that will set a person aback. But once that tough exterior has been breached, he is just a sweet man with a deep voice and few words.

I first met Henry "Hank" Hansen when we moved in three summers ago. I saw a man working in the gardens across the fields and decided to introduce myself. I took the long walk through tall grass to find him busily weeding and digging out a vegetable garden. I had made it to the fence of his garden without disrupting his activity, and since he was elderly I wasn't sure of his hearing. I waited awhile, which seemed like forever, afraid that I would scare him by blurting out a greeting of any kind. I cleared my throat gently to let him know I was there. Without looking up, he finally said, "Did you walk all this way to watch me or do you need something, young lady?"

Shocked and a little embarrassed, I replied, "We just moved in across the way."

I pointed to the house beyond the stone wall.

He looked up at me, squinting his lined eyes, tipped back that same straw hat a little, and with some annoyance that it was his turn to speak, said, "Oh? Who's *we?*"

"My husband and I and our two sons."

He glanced over at the house and gave out a little grunt. In silence, he disappeared behind some greens and yanked out a large rooted weed, tossing it into a nearby wheelbarrow.

"I'm Lizzi. Short for Elisabeth."

Unimpressed, he bent down and went back to gardening.

"You have a beautiful piece of property here Mr…"

"Hansen," he said, still not looking up.

I waited a moment for more, but it didn't come.

"Well, I will let you get back to work. Hope to see you around. Stop by anytime you'd like. We are just across the way."

I awkwardly pointed to the house once more. Realizing he was not paying attention, I decided to leave.

I was a few yards away when he yelled out, "Do you like fresh squash, Lizzi?"

I turned, surprised.

"Yes, of course."

"Good," he said, then lowered his head back down to the dirt.

That was my first introduction to Mr. Hansen. I didn't see him for weeks after that, except for his hat, that is. Then one day, I found a large wooden bowl on the stone wall filled with fresh squash, zucchini, and cucumbers. I returned the bowl with a thank you note and some homemade banana bread.

An occasional wave and bowl of vegetables left on the stone wall is the extent of our relationship. When we do speak, it is from our own sides of the wall. Those are rare days to spot each other outside, but it is friendly, and I feel good about that. I like him, and today, the stars have aligned for us.

"Hi, Mr. Hansen. How are you today?" I yell loud enough for him to hear me.

"Oh, just fine, Ms. Lizzi. And you?" His deep voice carries the distance with little effort.

"I'm okay. What brings you across the field this late morning?"

"I haven't seen you around these last few weeks. I was hoping to ask you a favor, Ms. Lizzi."

"Sure, what do you need?"

"I'm going to Florida to see my daughter, and I was wondering if you'd keep an eye on the house."

The dogs have crossed the stone wall to greet him. They bounce around, excited to see the visitor. With his hat in one hand, he pulls a few biscuits from his pocket with the other. His grey hair is short, but slightly curly, and still covers his head nicely for a man in his late seventies.

Day-Z in her deep, bellowing bloodhound call, howls at him over and over until he pats her.

"You sure are loud, girl. I can hear you all the way over at my house most days."

He leans down to slip her a biscuit.

"I'm sorry. I try to keep her quiet."

"Oh, don't be. It's kind of soothing, a familiar sound. She reminds me of my first dog, Old Buck. He was a hound, too. Not good for much but chasing down those rabbits. You could hear him howl through the woods for miles." I think I see a slight smile as he rubs her head and lifts her chin up to look in her baggy eyes. "How things come back to you when you least expect it."

He releases her with one last pat between the ears and she quietly accepts his acknowledgement with a wag of her tail.

"So, you're headed to Florida? When do you leave?"

"Tomorrow. I'll be gone a week. Not much to do but water a few plants and throw some food on the back porch for a stray cat that comes around. You sure you don't mind?"

He has stopped in stride just on the other side of the stone wall.

"Not at all."

I smile gently his way to reassure him I am glad to help.

"The key is under the back-porch mat. I'll leave a list on the kitchen table," he says while stretching his neck and leaning my way to see what I'm standing over. He hesitates, but then begins to cross the wall slowly, cautious of wobbly stones. "What do you have there?"

"A sink hole, I think."

He joins me with his hat back on his head and his hands on his hips.

"Yep, that's what that is alright. A good size one, too."

"Yea, you've seen these before?"

"Oh, sure. Nothing you can do about them. They are bound to pop up," he says, taking a deep breath as he looks around. "They cut a lot of trees down when they built this neighborhood. Some quite large." After a moment of thought, he continues, "Storms can sure dredge up the past."

"What do I do?"

"Dig it out. Fill it in. It's all you can do."

After standing for a moment in silence, I notice his gaze has become distant.

"Are you all right?"

A scowl and a brief sadness cloud his eyes.

"Of course."

I think for a moment that I have crossed a personal boundary, but then he continues.

"I just haven't been on this side of the stone wall since they built back here."

"Really? Why?"

"It was just so sad, is all."

His tone changes in a way I cannot explain. Softer, more real.

"All this property, all those trees, all so some out-of-towner could make a lot of money."

"I didn't realize."

"These woods were where we played back then, building forts, camping out, just walking for hours, napping under the big oak. Those were good times long ago."

He shifts his gaze to the ground, clears his throat, and starts to walk away.

"Mr. Hansen?"

"Yes?"

"Who's *we*?"

He turns and looks back, scanning the area behind me with moistened eyes.

"Me and the Missus. We were childhood friends before we dated and married. We used to meet under the large oak. Right about here if I remember correctly. It was our place."

"I'm sorry. I didn't know."

I feel tears filling my eyes.

His tone changes back as he removes his hat, scratches his head, and takes a good look around my spacious yard.

"That was years ago. No reason to be sorry. Just a hunk a'wood," he says, motioning his hat downward as if to wave the thought from his mind.

I nod, not knowing what to say.

He climbs back over the wall without looking back at me and loudly offers, "If you need to get some dirt for that hole, my truck is in the garage. She is an old girl but has never let me down. You're welcome to her. Holes need to be fixed. The keys are under the seat."

"Thank you. I'll be over to check on the house. Have a nice trip."

A wave of his arm with his hat still attached and landing back on his head is his casual way of saying he heard me. I watch him slowly make his way back across the field. My Buddy thinks of following him, but I change his mind with a quick clap and call of his name.

I watch the image of him shrink smaller, disappearing into the tall blades of grass.

Many days, I have wondered what his story is. I have gathered some details from the local people and neighbors, but some say he is a mystery. He's not very talkative, and he keeps to himself. Not exactly a people-person. He is known as Hank to most. From what I have heard, his wife died ten years ago from a stroke or possibly from heart problems. They lived there for thirty years together and his parents lived there before that. It was the house he grew up in, and he moved back when his parents couldn't take care of it any longer. That's all I know indirectly. He has never spoken of his wife before. I never wanted to ask. I know he has a daughter, but I have never met her. It all seems too personal for a man who seldom looks up from his garden.

With the world the way it is, *why do family and personal issues have to be such a secret?* I see this older gentleman living alone with no family around, and he finds a way to move on, keeping the peace within his boundaries. He minds his own business, finds no need to wallow in the past, and just lives his life. And here's my family, with numerous relatives nearby, claiming loyalty as their reason for keeping the distance while concentrating on the past. That has only torn us further apart, and here I am, only a few hours into my day, and my emotions threaten the calmness and clarity of my thoughts.

I turn and realize I have been left with this problem once again. I guess this is mine alone to deal with. I stand above it, looking down, wondering, *what is the next step when you are afraid to step forward?* It is too real now that someone else has seen it for truth. Life isn't real until you share it with a friend. When it's only in your head, it can be written off as crazy, overly sensitive, or paranoid, but not today. This is a moment of truth for the life it has taken on.

Even so, that little distraction was enough for me to consider the odds of ignoring it a little longer. *How bad could it get? A hole in my foundation? Is that horrible? Would it actually collapse on me one day?* Besides, I had managed to survive without knowing it was there or questioning how it could be better. *So why should it be addressed now? Maybe this is just the course of nature?*

Oh, what thoughts a hole can dig up!

If I take on this task, will I fix it completely, or will I just make a mess of the situation? With my family, the problem started with simple miscommunication. A daughter-in-law forgets about a play-date with Grampa, or isn't home when he visits or calls, leaving one to believe it was an intentional avoidance. A man insists on picking up is grandchildren at inconvenient times, and it becomes a pattern of disappointment. He starts to question his welcome, his right, his own son's respect. Word gets around the family who starts demanding action. A new father stands his ground as his father refuses to understand. Life triggered actions and actions were repeated as boundaries were made and tested on all sides. *Left to its own course, could it have been corrected? Did stubborn intervention become our downfall?*

All I know is that it explosively triggered generations of past issues. Like the surface of the sinkhole—manageable, it might seem from the onset—it ran deeper than anyone would ever suspect. It uncovered layers of personality conflicts and allegiances with one another. What started as a we-can-fix-this situation turned into many he-said-she-said and who's-on-whose-side confrontations.

Oh, Gigi what happened? How did we get here?

Nature has taken its toll on both the hole and my family, decaying and washing away what is not necessary while opening up an old wound to be healed if attended to.

I am looking at this area differently now with concern for the outcome. *What will come of this? What will be the turning point? Where is the bottom? Where is the baseline to start growing strong again? How far do I have to dig?*

These thoughts are growing roots of their own.

I sigh.

Deep down, I know I cannot live in fear of treading on my own path. I know that future progress means energy spent digging out the truth, at least my own.

My racing thoughts have drained my energy, and I feel heavy. An image of the ground giving way beneath me and swallowing me up overcomes my senses. In an instant, I find myself backing away in caution, believing even my approach could create the disaster of my worst fears. I have danced around this for so long. As suddenly as I retreat, logic wins, and I remember how I have come close to this before and it never gave way. Tiptoeing on eggshells and the burden of carrying the weight of others has created feelings of falling.

My fears have always kept me from facing conflict, *but why?* My fear has always been a comfortable friend. Even when buried, I can feel it lying below the surface, ingrained in my personality, enabling me to passively accept the discomfort. Don't question, don't fix, and don't even acknowledge it. This has always worked for the whole family, for the unit, and my place in it, *so why question where this has gotten us? Who am I to question the natural deterioration or progression of life? Maybe this is how it is meant to be, tender and unsafe, so we will stay away and tread lightly forever? Surely, many families do that, don't they? Why should we be different?*

Who am I to find myself greater than what has supported me for so long? The tender spot has never given way. It has been a comfortable flaw in the course of my life. *Who am I to fix a part of nature?* It has been the sensitive nerve that has never snapped. The one that never quit, the one that lays quiet, just waiting for someone to notice that it feels the weight of the world above and that it needs to be attended to so that it can be strong enough to handle the years ahead. So here I am, ready to acknowledge it, ready to face the fear, ready to call its bluff of collapsing as it lies there threatening to fall beneath me, waiting for someone to lend it a hand. I stand here noticing as this deterioration is turning into my progression.

I believe that if it wasn't meant to be fixed, it wouldn't have shown itself to me. It would have just sucked me into its devastation without warning, and I would be in it and under it. Instead, I am looking down on it, analyzing and contemplating its existence. The ground beneath me holds its own, even with the damage below. My world must come with some strength for it to have come this far, and with that thought, I know it has been waiting to be discovered, uncovered, and recreated to become the solid, sturdy ground it was born to be.

I take a deep breath. This hole will be taken care of one way or another. I approach it once more, but this time with intrigue and curiosity. I will look into its strength to find answers, not just question the problem. I need to know its true depth, its true-life force, and how to regain footing here. Taking action is the only way to begin, and I realize I will need help reaching the answers. Perhaps a stick, maybe a branch will do, and then I'll be able to gain insight into the depth of the issue in front of me. I will poke at it a little and see if it reveals the truth once and for all.

CHAPTER 9:
BREAKING AWAY

To the edges of life, we search for our boundaries, where within, a supporter and friend may be found.

My midmorning mission has consumed my thoughts, placing me on the edge of my comfort zone. Here in my big backyard, I feel alone and abandoned with a need to find a friend for this journey. *Who likes company more than the confused seeker in pursuit of better days?* I go looking for a companion, a friend to travel alongside me and to help me reach the bottom of my issues.

A quick turn about the yard points me in the direction of a patch of pine trees, familiar landmarks that trim my view from a distance in soft-bushy spikes. They are the frame for the picture-perfect yard, a constant reminder of the space we inhabit and where it ends, while filling the air with color and infusing the wind with hints of pine.

I consider them friends, and although so easily dismissed, they are consistently comforting. Tall, proud, and intimidating up close, they reach high in the sky marking clear borders for all to see. They are my guardians in green watching over us, letting those who enter and those who leave know where they stand. Year round they project their presence, reminding all, especially me, there are clear boundaries here.

I head toward my tall friends, hoping to find a fallen branch or stick amongst them, one sturdy enough to assist me in assessing the damage. These lonely edges of my home, while desolate and still, dark and forgotten, buffer all of what we enjoy and exude a life of their own waiting to be explored.

They call me to where they settle, to where the tree trunks grow wide, the branches hang low, shadows linger all day and the leaves pile old and thick. Isolated, like a part of my life, the ground collects with what has been pushed aside. Although separate and forgotten, they are part of the whole and bring together what is needed to create the bigger picture. These edges, these boundaries, give barriers and perimeters to protect the space within. This is where I will find something strong and hearty to extend my reach and to stand by my side. So, beyond my center, I will search for a sturdy, supportive friend.

After all, a friend, a supporter, is important in times of question and self-questioning. We all need someone to at least stand by us and brace us during times of weakness and doubt. We all long for a friend in this big world of uncertainty. One who can withstand the pressures of supporting us when we fall or when the weight of the world knocks the wind from our breath, a supporter who is willing to assess the situation from the outside when we are caught up within. This is my wish so I may test the foundation of which I live.

My dogs follow me with no caution for this pursuit. They prance around me, shuffling amongst each other in a playful way. One bounces ahead of the other, swinging his head, while another barks and bows to the call of play. Growls are endured with wide jaws and teeth showing over a neck or a paw, but no motion to bite is implied.

One rolls over submitting to the motion and more noise comes. Just as it gets heated, a third party enters the play. The dominant, controlling blood-hound, Day-Z, approaches with her ears squared off and lifted. Her controlling nature doesn't allow her to know if she should stop such action or join in. In a statuesque pose, she stands over the one who has been grounded. Day-Z is 120 pounds of proud intimidation.

I know if she joins in that the other two will retreat not knowing if she is setting them up for a real bite of control. I laugh to myself for I know people like this. They join a situation under one set of circumstances and then they forget the rules of play and go for the jugular, wondering in the end why others choose not to interact the next time.

Many times in my life, especially lately, family has engaged me in casual conversation only to pursue their interests with the subject of picking sides. I, too, had to accept that some people change the tone of their intentions once I have joined in. I have trusted them—time and time again—to relate nicely and keep their fangs at bay, but blood has been drawn too often. So, I too, have learned as my labradors have, that there are certain temperaments that are too innate to change, that it is better to walk away and take your joyfulness elsewhere.

I move ahead and leave the dogs to their own pursuits for my own search carries on. A strong stick may be the goal, but my inner strength needs to be dug out as well. I know I have the strength, but I also know that it lies dormant and buried in the dark edges of my past, waiting to be revived. My strength revealed itself years ago as it pushed me through, allowing me to reposition my life. Unfortunately, a shameful attachment came with the necessity for that strength to which I immediately disowned both with the memory. At this moment, the memory floods back fully and heavily to remind me of how strong I can be. My sister Jeanie played a pivotal part in the outcome.

Jeanie

Jeanie, my half-sister really, is only four years older than me. My father's oldest daughter, she came to live with us when I was ten years old. By the time I hit my teenage years, she had taken on a protective role. She became a guiding force whether I liked it or not. Always trying to keep me on track, her attempted supervision was mostly met with disgust and rebellion. I cannot say how many times she dragged me out of a party because I hadn't come home. She would methodically weed out my boyfriends by having her friends scare them off if she felt they were a bad influence. She also drove me to school during junior high to make sure I went. Mostly though, she was my confidant, my friend, and the one I turned to. Even today, I wonder where I would be if she hadn't been there to help me navigate the hard times and difficult decisions. At this moment I think of her, for the strength I search for now, outside of myself, is one that she helped me find within, years ago.

Jeanie is headstrong and independent. In her own life, she is focused and goal-oriented. She has worked her way through night school to finish her degree and runs a successful business on her own. This was outside the norm for the women in my family and was often met with scorn and attitude when she was not around. At the time, I did not understand why this was, but today I see how her actions were pulling on the structure of what our family knew, making them uncomfortable at the sight of her moving on without them.

Controlling Jeanie always seemed to be an underlying objective. I often got caught in the crossfire. Jeanie and I spent most of our free time together after school and on weekends, and this did not always sit well with the adults. One time in particular comes to mind.

We had spent the afternoon at the library one Saturday afternoon and had accepted a ride from one of Jeanie's friends when we were done, rather than calling home as we should have. We stopped at the mall and then for ice cream before heading home. It all seemed innocent enough.

My mother was furious when we showed up and grounded us both, but it did not end there. When my aunts heard what had happened, they had other opinions about the influence Jeanie was having on me. They convinced my mother that I shouldn't be allowed to hang out with her anymore. As such, school and meals were the only times we were allowed to interact. Our separation, me riding the bus and us going to separate bedrooms after dinner only lasted a couple of months, but it became clear that the intention was not strictly for our own good.

My young mind was confused and cautious around family members after that.

Where did that come from? Was it jealousy of our relationship? Was it true concern? Was it control? Or, was it the fear of me becoming independent and strong, just like her?

Once Jeanie had graduated, I fell into a crowd that was less than desirable. Drugs, alcohol, and parties became the escape from my family and myself that I wasn't looking for but found easily. By the time I was eighteen, Jeanie was in night school and starting a career.

She was clearly choosing her own path and making her way without the approval of family. We stayed close, but our age difference started to take a toll on our relationship. A string of bad relationships led me to a worse decision, and my life came crashing down around me. I moved south, with a man who said he loved me, who pushed me into a corner with little options and few choices to get back on track. Steve, a few years older with an illusion of stability, caught my eye and held me in his trap of emotional control. A job offer for him in North Carolina spurred the thought of better, but a change of scenery was all I got.

At nineteen, the break from family, even then, seemed to clear my head, but the insecurities were too ingrained to be left behind. The distance only brought me closer to my unwavering convictions to fix another human being. Breaking away from family was not my plan, but the further away I physically got, the more their disconnection felt intentional, leaving me uncertain of where I belonged, if anywhere. Without the comfort of a home to turn to, I tried to make it better for us, for Steve, though my caring and isolation only triggered his incisive control. I eased deeper into my self-loathing. Back home, uncertainty was always welcome, individuality was feared, and joy was mocked, especially when it was not collective. As this was the lesser of two evils, I remained with him, blurring my sense of reality even further.

After eight months away, I felt an inner calling to go back home for Christmas, a visit just long enough to test my resolve to leave again. The drive was long and filled with anticipation. I was quickly immersed back into old feelings as if time stood still and the distance I thought I had gained disappeared instantly in the face of family. This home was a place I was a part of, a place I floated in and out of easily and comfortably, a place I somehow belonged to and yet felt a strong desire to run from. I felt the shame of what I knew about myself, and disconnected because of what my family didn't. After the time away and my own difficulties, I believe now that the only connection we truly had was the inner sadness within us all. I had come home, *yet had I ever truly left?* This family oozed with uncertainty from years and places I knew of but had never been. Insecurities ran through us like moisture through the sky. No matter the weather, these clouds recycled old wounds, absorbing residual pain, and held on to them to extinguish passions at the slightest inkling of happiness, even if only perceived as so.

 Lizzie

Steve and I were the last ones to arrive at my mother's house on Christmas Eve. I walked ahead of him in the driveway. We were running late because he insisted on checking into the hotel first before heading over. As we approached the front door, he reached for my wrist.

"Remember, we are not staying all night."

"Okay, okay. You told me already. I get it."

"I mean it, Lizzi. I only agreed to come because you were homesick, so let's not overdo it here."

"Gee, Steve, can we get inside and say hello before you are ready to leave?"

"I want to know you hear me."

"I hear you. Now please let go of me."

I shook my arm from his tightening grip. We entered to a sea of people and mindless chatter. I found the cold weather refreshing while we were outside and a blessing once we were in. My turtleneck and long sleeves were acceptable warmer clothes to others while confidently hiding my body. The discomfort that came with long hugs was easily absorbed inward and ignored. My thinness was noticed immediately but only remarked on with jealous snips.

If only the thought of the young, thin traveler who finally got away was as special as they perceived it to be, and if only they knew the truth, then a true welcoming of one of their own back into the fold would ease any defensiveness of new and separate experiences. It would then be a welcoming of the familiar back home instead of judgment based on the unknown.

My mother's house was bright and festive and smelled of baked goods and pine. The familiarity gave me an immediate feeling of withdrawal. Packages waited under the tree to be opened. I placed a small shopping bag full of gifts next to them and noticed all the usual ornaments dangling from the tree. They sparkled in remembrance of happier times but held no weight to changing today. I had returned to the place I began with no further gain to account for. I had escaped, but it seemed that I took myself with me. I took back control only to give it to another. At that point, I had only returned carrying my own new experiences and pain. Suddenly, I feared for my chances of ever succeeding. I worried that I would be forever haunted by their limitations, or worse even, my own.

Steve hovered in the background acknowledging everyone in his pleasant accepting manner, a side to him I mostly saw in moments of tears, flowers, and apologies. *He was being accepted.* With that thought came a wave of comfort for the evening and a fear that he truly fit in to that which I wished to escape.

I vaguely acknowledged the presence of the men in the kitchen joking and laughing heartily. Steve was stopped in the gauntlet of people and offered a drink, which he accepted quickly. I entered the attached room where Gigi and Auntie El sat together. My younger cousins sat on the floor before them playing with newly opened toys. I headed straight to Gigi and her outstretched arms. She was a beacon of light for me as she centered this family gathering. Her light shined through the dense static of what was. This was the first true acceptance I had felt in months. I leaned over to kiss Auntie El, and from behind me, I heard my Aunt Lil say, "The golden child is here. Everyone, move out of the way."

I turned her way, but she and Aunt Betsy just laughed.

"Oh, have a sense of humor," someone said loud enough to quiet the crowd. My mother ignored their behavior, grabbing me for a quick hug and kiss on the cheek.

Gigi broke the tension by taking my hand.

"Don't bother with them. They are just a little jealous."

Jeanie swooped in for a hug. She excitedly pulled me aside to get the full details of my travels, for our phone conversations had been short and vague with Steve monitoring every word.

With a slight move of my head coupled with the right lighting, she pulled my sweater away from my neck.

"What the hell is that?

I gathered the turtleneck back up against my skin and pulled away.

"What? Nothing."

The feeling of Steve's hand around my throat, the back of my head hitting the wall and his infuriated screams came flooding back. His rage had reached a new level with the mention of my moving back home. Humiliated, as if she had watched the whole scene play out before her, I swallowed back the tears, unable to look at her.

"Lizzi?" she leaned in with a whisper. "What is going on?"

"It's no big deal."

"Damn it. I knew something was wrong."

"He's been under a lot of stress lately. The job he went there for is not what he thought."

The truth was that it started before we left. He claimed that he needed a change in is life. He promised we would be good together if we could get a fresh start. With little convincing needed, I attached myself to believing that I could help him, change him, be what he needed to be kind.

"Are you kidding me? Tell me you are staying here and sending him back alone."

"I can't, Jeanie, he needs me right now. As soon as this new contract comes through he will be fine."

"Look at me. He's not going to change. It will always be something."

"And where am I going to go? Back here to this house? To live here again? Come crawling home for everyone to talk about? I don't think so."

"Stay with me. Come live with me until you get on your feet."

"No! Now stop talking about it. I will figure it out. If it happens again I will come home." Her face was too disappointed to look at. "I promise. Okay?"

"No, Lizzi. It's not okay!"

She searched my face with her watery eyes for some sense of connection, a connection I wish I could have given her, but there was a numbness that had taken most of me away, and my sense of self had disappeared months ago. Steve's behavior heightened so rapidly after the move that it knocked me off balance. Every time I started to get my equilibrium back, there was another incident. His drinking was out of control, and no matter what I did, it wasn't getting better. I forced myself to be strong and convicted in my stance in helping him.

Jeanie allowed me to change the subject with a false withdrawal of her concern.

The evening continued with a restlessness I could not escape. Lost in my own world, I wanted to run and scream, jump out of my skin. The sight of the food that filled the large dining table turned my empty stomach. Polite excuses of a big lunch on the road were thankfully accepted as eating had become a pleasure I was no longer able to allow myself. I had learned that with it came weight that was instantly ridiculed. I had never felt so separate from all that I had known in my life. With no sense of direction and no place to fall, I teetered on the unknown, slowly fading from the familiar voices and stories. For a moment, Steve came and stood by my side, his hand on my back, a small rare jester of affection that I was pleased Jeanie and the others could witness.

The night moved on, and Steve's drinking picked up. Jeanie watched us with an intent disapproval. All others, aunts, uncles, and cousins exchanged in small talk and laughter, oblivious to my own denial. Gigi and Auntie El sat amongst the crowd in a timeless connection to one another. I eased into an outer calm, defaulting to a safe invisible presence while my insides remained raw and twisted. I even fooled Steve, but he was triggered by the sight of me melding into family. He signaled me from the other side of the room to join him.

"What do you think you are doing? You have been ignoring me all night."

"I'm sorry, I didn't think—"

"You never think of anyone but yourself. I am done here. Let's go."

"But it's only nine o'clock. We haven't even exchanged gifts yet."

"Look, I agreed to come back here for the holiday, but that doesn't mean we have to spend every waking moment with your family."

I turned to walk away but he pulled me close to him with a tight grip of my upper arm and a harsh whisper in my ear.

"Say good-bye," he said. "We are leaving."

The air felt confining, and I found it hard to breathe. A dash to the bathroom to a confined space somehow gave me room. I shut the door and sat on the edge of the pale, yellow tub as small black and white octagon floor tiles stared back at me.

I inhaled deeply and stood to get a good look at myself in the mirror. Leaning over the sink, I gagged at the thought of the truth and where I had come to be. A flash of heat burned my face. I ran the water cold, cupped my hands to splash the tears and redness from my eyes.

A loud double knock startled me and I tried to clear the tears away. Jeanie pushed the door open without an invitation.

"Are you okay?"

She saw through my demeanor, quickly sliding through the door closing it behind her.

"What is going on here, Lizzi? What have you gotten yourself into?"

"I told you, nothing. Christ, would you mind your own business for once?"

My head pounded. My thoughts came too quickly to make sense of them. I sat on the edge of the tub again, rubbing my eyes hoping to mold my brain into clear thinking.

"I'm sorry Jeanie. I don't know what to do? It just keeps getting worse."

The tears came uncontrollably, and I felt I wouldn't be able to breathe much longer.

"Look, you need to pull yourself together here. You're worried about giving them something to talk about, but you're clearly a mess."

I had no energy for a response.

"Why are you doing this to yourself?" she asked, "You don't owe him anything."

I heard her, but her words were all jumbled in my mind.

"Look at me. Talk to me," Jeanie demanded as her compassion struggled with her frustration.

"I don't know how to change this, how to change him," I answered. "I tried to leave, but he just went crazy. He talked me into just visiting for the holiday. He said I was just homesick and that this visit would make it better, but it's not better, Jeanie. Not here, not there, not with him, not without him. I don't know where to go from here."

Steve must have seen Jeanie follow me into the bathroom. He came to the door, knocking and asking forcibly, "Lizzi? You in there, sweetie?"

Jeanie quickly locked the door. I couldn't breathe through my sobs.

Steve tried the door. Agitated that it was locked, he hit it with the palm of his hand, yelling, "Open the door, Lizzi."

"I'll be out in a minute, Steve. Just one of my migraines starting again. Jeanie is helping me find some Advil."

He tried the door again, "Let me in, Lizzi!"

With no response, his voice changed to a persuasively-calm tone, "I just want to help."

Jeanie pulled the door open, forcing him back a step, "I think you have done enough. Don't you?"

He tried to push by her, but she pushed back.

"What did you tell her, Lizzi? Let's go to the hotel. We can stop and get you whatever you need on the way."

"Just leave me alone for a minute, Steve," I said, trying to hold my composure.

The palm of his hand hit the door again, harder this time, and Jeanie jumped back.

"I think you should leave us, Jeanie," Steve replied. "I want to talk to Lizzi alone."

"Not a chance," Jeanie said, holding her position between him and the doorway. "I think you better leave now before all those men out there find out what a real coward you are. Lizzi will be staying with me."

He ignored her and tried to get me to look at him, but I couldn't.

"Lizzi?" Steve started to panic. "Lizzi, is this what you really want? I love you. I told you I can change. I promise. Lizzi? Please?"

I looked up at Jeanie, unable to move, frozen between moments of nausea. Confused beyond recognition, I said, "I think you should leave."

Jeanie's face turned pale. She remained shocked as Steve pushed the door open and stood in her face. Smirking he said, "See, bitch? She understands me. She knows I love her."

"No, I mean you, Steve," I said firmly, "I think you should leave."

Jeanie breathed a sigh of relief and stepped closer to him stating, "Oh, she understands you, alright. I think you are done here."

One last rush toward Jeanie with a stomp of his foot ended with a maddened expression. With a closed fist this time, he took one more swing at the door.

"Don't bother calling me when you come to your senses," Steve said while walking away

Only my brother, Chris, noticed him leave in a huff, which piqued his drunken interest. Swaggering to the bathroom, he stuck his head around the door as Jeanie went to shut it.

"Trouble in paradise, Lizzi?"

His laugh was cut off by Jeanie shutting the door in his face.

"Come on, I am only kidding!" Chris yelled through the door. "Tell me what happened."

His words were met with silence for too long to be any fun. By the time I got myself together and came out, Steve was gone and Chris was back in the kitchen where most gathered.

I made excuses for Steve's early exit. I said that he wasn't feeling well and that I would be staying with Jeanie for the night. Most accepted the story, but my brother eyed me closely until I acknowledged him. He just shook his head and turned away without a word. Presents were exchanged and dessert was served. I avoided long goodbyes as if I was headed back to North Carolina, because I knew I would be seeing everyone sooner, and more often, than they were expecting.

I hugged Gigi goodbye. I tried to pull away, but she held me a few seconds longer whispering, "You are awful skinny, dear. Put some meat on those bones."

I giggled and smiled as I tightened my squeeze. I inhaled the sweetness of her. It melted away my internal chatter. I knew I was doing the right thing.

"I will, Gigi. I will."

I called the hotel the next morning only to find that Steve had left town with not a word or phone call. His abandonment, even under the circumstance, felt oddly attractive. I tried for weeks to reach him but he refused to speak to me. I struggled with his silence for weeks only to be consumed in an emotional rollercoaster for months to follow. Calls came from him after mine had stopped, some ranting and threatening, others crying and begging. The former were the easiest to ignore.

It took me over a year to fully find the strength that Jeanie insisted I had. These are times rarely spoken of, times even Jeremy has only heard echoes of. He only knows them in story form, of course, not felt or painted with the emotions that give them life. These memories lie silent but still own a piece of me. They lie at the edge of my past, hidden from the sight of today, buried in the underbrush of my beautiful boundaries. Within these memories is where my strength was awakened, tested, and left, hoping I would never need it to that extent again, yet, here I am gathering the courage to even acknowledge I may need it once more.

All these moments that linger on the edges of my memory, left as debris of the past, and known as my foundational work frame in and support what I have become, and found myself to be. These moments lay hiding just below the surface. Here, I will search my darkest moments. There is the strength I know I have, lying and waiting for a chance to be pulled from the rubble of the dark and quiet, to be useful and shown for its part in my future.

I am brought back from this memory safe and sound with the dogs playing nearby. I watch the bloodhound, Day-Z, begging the others to trust her by dropping to her front paws and shifting back and forth in a playful stance. The Labs ignore her thoroughly and walk off. The trust has been broken long ago. Her play is known to turn controlling and painful. This I know of and feel in my bones for their position. I wish I could trust. I wish my past didn't reflect, or remind me that I can't, thoroughly.

They certainly remind me of the dynamics at play. Their personalities hold their positions in the fold, unwavering and clear. Mysti, a black Labrador, is the lady of the pack, the oldest and most sophisticated. She walks quietly along the stone wall within sight of me at all times. Buddy, a yellow Labrador, and Penny, a chocolate Labrador, resume their play somewhat close to me, rushing the area where Mysti is poking. The bloodhound still follows them and watches closely as their play picks up. Their bouncing ensues as they side-swipe Mysti, leaning into her.

This is a slight attempt to engage her in their play, but she is not impressed with their dog behaviors and continues to stroll as if she is not invited. Mysti also knows Day-Z is nearby with her eyes on her, waiting for a reason to pounce.

Day-Z forgets the two that bounce by as she continues to watch Mysti. Day-Z knows her superiority over the other two because they accept her mood swings, but Mysti is the one to break. Mysti has no use for the hierarchy that Day-Z feels so strongly about. Mysti refuses to acknowledge her presence at all. Day-Z intently stares her down.

I can read Day-Z's mind through her intense glare. She thinks of jumping Mysti in a harmful attack, but a quick, loud call of her name distracts the thought momentarily.

"Day-Z! You leave her alone."

She looks my way with her scolded, wrinkled, droopy-eyed face and a sigh that relaxes her ears, showing her disappointment. She looks at the other two, now playing across the yard and thinks of joining them again, but then decides it is too far to go to end up not participating. She places her nose to the ground, and with her ears dragging along she sniffs until a scent is picked up, probably a passing squirrel from earlier. This will keep her busy for a while. I'm reassured that the deviant thought has passed, knowing these moments and interactions are necessary for all to find their place amongst the crowd. Whether it is a pack or family, we learn to relate within the boundaries that are set.

Just as I come to the low hanging pine branches, the playful two rush up and trip me. My startled scream echoes. I catch my balance and they run off, resuming their play, without even the smallest apology.

The leaves under my feet layer in a crunchy, damp mix as I enter the darkness of forgotten debris. I think there might be something hardy that was tossed aside during the last major storm.

When the winds get strong, the nearby trees battle it out, clanging their branches together like swords, and many fall to the sacrifice of nature. The yard is usually scattered with these fallen soldiers. In large numbers, they are gathered and thrown to the edges where the darkness hides, so I enter in search of a fallen one.

As I duck down to avoid spiky green tips, Penny sneaks up under me, taking full advantage of my closeness to the ground, and rushes to jump and bump-kiss my nose and lips. Any harder and she would have sent stars rushing to my head, but this is something Penny is very good at. She can jump and land a kiss on the least expecting guest without as much as a push from her.

Again, in surprise, I scream at her, "Penny!" knowing if I play along, another will come quickly. In response to being scolded, she noisily rolls unsuspecting Buddy onto his back who is poking around nearby. The two toss around in the leaves, uncovering debris beneath them. Penny suddenly hears Day-Z howling at something in the yard and runs off to inspect her find.

Buddy stays with me as I kick around a few piles of sticks. They lay scattered and eerie like a pile of bones in a lion's den. Buddy decides to help me, pulling on one stick in particular until it breaks loose of its entangled grave. He drags it out with small short tugs, feeling prouder as each jolt reveals more of the large stick. Finally, it is fully exposed. I laugh as he struggles to carry it.

Longer than either of us expected, he can't seem to get it off the ground in one piece. It always leans heavy to one side, dragging on the ground. For one brief moment, Buddy has it in his teeth, balancing it carefully while the branch hangs almost three feet to each side of his mouth. With a proud bounce, he begins to run into the yard to show the others his prize, but it sends him tumbling, tail overhead, as one end catches the ground. He quickly regains composure by standing and shaking the leaves from his ears. He is a little dazed and confused on how he landed there. I giggle out loud and ask him if he is okay, but he ignores me and rushes off to bark with the others.

Curious about the branch that has sustained such a rugged exit, I walk over to see how stable it could really be. There it lays, crooked, weathered and sturdy in its own temporary landing. I lift the branch to my side, feeling its weight and knowing its thickness in my fist. I take it out of the dampness, further into the light. I examine it thoroughly. A notch lands perfectly for my grasp, and I stand with it upright like a staff beside me. My eyes follow it from the ground up, and I lift it once, pounding it into the ground, shaking off all loose bark, dirt, and moss. Not weak or hollow, it stands strong. I brush it off gently following every curve with my hand, noticing every scar and all its character in every inch.

My eyes trace its height as it points to the sky. I see the beauty beyond my physical reach. The mature oaks and maples that share this space with my friendly pines stand tall and sophisticated. They watch me intently as I hold one of their fallen in my hands. They are living examples of what stood in the hole I have found, which is now only an impression of what once existed.

I scan the view above trying to decipher where one tree ends and another begins. Their crisscrossing branches within their green leaves invade each other's space while living harmoniously in nature. They are linked together because of where they were born. They show a tightly-woven family left to battle it out in moments of turmoil and storms. It is impossible to tell where this branch fell from for it is one of many, and they all look the same from where I stand.

Are we all this commonly seen amongst a crowd or family? Are we all blended so tightly? I guess it doesn't matter for when we are separate and alone; individuality has to stand out. Feeling this heavy branch in my hand, I cannot imagine it being a part of that massive collection.

Do all the branches, at closer look, look as individual and have such character and strength? Is this one really different or just recognized only when separate from the whole? How would we ever know?

My new friend stands beside me, a sample of strength. From one of the many above me, or from my sorted past, exactly where it came from does not matter, for it is here, solid and hearty, appropriate for the job to be done. I believe my search is over. I have found a supporter in the mesh of castoffs and fitting it is.

I know my story and from where my strength developed, but now I wonder about this branch. *Why would it choose to leave behind, or above, the collective it came from? Why did it break free from the only world it had known? Where did it find its strength? Did it grow too big, too heavy, too differently, or too awkwardly for the massive tree to withstand? Did it not know it was throwing everything off balance?*

Was it an acceptable casualty for the tree to part with a piece of itself so not to risk the unbalancing of the life it knows? Was the tree itself unwilling or incapable of growing new branches to balance the growth of the ones that already existed? Or did this branch swing and sway too much, while enjoying the winds, putting extra pressures on the core of its ecosystem—ego system? Or did it jump as to commit suicide from the shackles of its controlled base? Only to find it was stronger than it knew and survived the fall?

Did it know that it would never be grounded while attached? Or know it would never know the feeling of freedom unless it fell, or have the chance to soar unless it jumped? Did it just decide that growth was impossible if it were to stay still while fighting the urge to move with the wind, fighting the urge to disrupt the pattern it was raised to follow? Or, did it just become larger than what its life source expected it to be? Finding its space too crowded to be recognized as unique?

How many others linger in this balance, waiting the opportunity to grow and leave?

Whatever the answers, this branch is with me now. By disconnecting itself from the only life it knew, this beautiful, unique, solid, grounded staff becomes a lifeline for me, a friend in my endeavor.

It feels strange to be out here alone in the light finding my way to a healthier place when Jeanie has always been the one to see me through, to show me the way to steady ground, but today, I have found a new friend that will extend my reach, strengthen my independence and see me through the darkness. It is strong and independent although it has broken away from the tree it was born to, although its source of birth has betrayed its existence by letting go when the weight of true growth overwhelmed its core. Like me—it survived the fall. It waited out its purpose. It is now an ally in testing and finding my true foundation. A supporter I have found in this piece of nature.

My stick and I proudly walk back across the yard enjoying the light that shines down on us as we both leave the darkness and questions behind. I suddenly wish Jeanie were here. If anyone would appreciate the beauty and irony in this moment, it would be her.

CHAPTER 10:
GROUNDWORK

The open space of emptiness may be the only solid beginning we have.

The morning is flirting with noon and will soon be immersed in it. The house seems abandoned from my view, but I know better for my boys are in there somewhere. They have yet to research my whereabouts this morning, which leads me to believe they are still sleeping or happily lounging in front of the television without Mom pestering them to go outside in the fresh air.

My first thought, as I stare at the walk back to the house, is to rustle them up and make them get moving. This distraction of guilt is for their non-active roles this morning, but now that I have found a friend to help excavate my issue, I don't wish to put it off any longer. I cannot stop until I know the full depth of what I am dealing with and find grounds for my obsession. No. *Determination* is a better word for this mission. I am determined to do the groundwork necessary for a safe, healthy, solid foundation.

My stick and I will explore what nature has shown to me. It is nature's way to be curious, *but what if I am discouraged with my find?* I stand between the house, which holds my children and the hole that reminds me of a deeper family issue. I am torn about what they should know, be told, or experience at their age.

My children are unaware that their extended family members are at odds, and I would have it no other way. This is a personal journey for me. They need not know of adult conflicts nor the pressures my family has placed on me. My family will have to leave the children out of the chaos this time for I will not allow the pattern to repeat itself. They are children I have given comforts and have few worries. I have kept them from the details of adult complications and don't wish for them to be involved.

Like a lioness and her cubs, when the eye has been shifted to include her young in the fight, the fight has truly just begun. I will work hard to protect them, to fix this, to control what has crept up on us and make it a peaceful part of our lives and not a memory of dysfunctional family drama. At their ages, there is no need to know why certain decisions are made. They can just enjoy the outcome of them. This is not here for them to live through and feel every grueling detail. I was raised in the wake of adult dysfunction and will not repeat that pattern for my children. I will protect them from this even if it means digging out my past alone.

Here I stand, trying to understand how people, who are my family, could in one moment cut me off and walk out of my life. *Is this the extent in which they will go to get their own way? To get me to go their way?* I cannot follow them this time. I will head down my own path not letting their actions take over any part of my life. Any part of my children's lives.

I *have* spent too much time wallowing in the disappointment. I *have* tried many times to reconnect, but efforts have fallen on turned backs, and although my mother and Auntie El are courteous, I can hear it in their voices when we speak that they, too, feel differently now. Their objections to my opinions are subtler, but they have mentioned loyalty or lack thereof, several times. This is not about disloyalty. This is about control, dysfunction, and the fact that it is being repeated in the family and they don't like admitting it.

Nobody is right here, and I will not compound the situation by contributing to crazy warped patterns. I will only support the way of healing by keeping the door open in hopes it will get better. Until then, I will work to rebuild my ground so that I can stand strong and tall. I will gladly stand in my own issues, fixing them for my own future. That is all I can do.

I head back toward the hole, this time to find the bottom and make it whole again.

I imagine Gigi watching over me as I stand to test this weakened space in my foundation. *Are you cheering me, Gigi, from your green and white lawn chair on the sidelines? Or, are you warning me, begging me to stop?*

I don't know, but my curiosity is spiked with my courage coming in a weak second. The stick comes down hard near the mouth of deadened grass. It slides through the ground easily—too easily for my comfort—and penetrates halfway its length. I pull it out quickly, watching more of the surface fall to the darkness below.

Where does the weakness end? Is it only reacting to my negativity toward it? Or is it ready to give in to the power of healing?

I stand back a minute and then poke at it lightly, in a teasing sort of way on the off chance that it decides to attack back. It does not, and I gather interest for its lack of response. It lays limply, accepting my jabs, reminding me of a 'possum I once met, a moment that could have gone bad very quickly.

 Possum

One cool spring morning, the dogs had cornered something in the bushes. I went to inspect the situation. A baby 'possum laid upside down, mouth hanging open, still as could be in the cluster of the hedge roots. Once I pulled the dogs away, I went back to check on the little guy. Nothing, not a twitch came from his seemingly deadened body. Its little eyes stared wide open. He was sprawled out and twisted where the trunks separated. A senseless death, I thought, for crossing the wrong path.

I grabbed a pair of gloves from the garage and went to pick it up. I was inches from this white, long-tailed creature when the saying, "playing 'possum" came to mind. *Ugh! How do you really know when an 'possum is dead or playing 'possum?*

I decided to get a stick and poke at it a little to see if it would move and give me a sign it was alive. Nothing. Its body was limp, lifeless. Not a heave of breath came from its chest. I was still unconvinced. Still scared was more like it. *Have you seen the teeth on those animals?* I went inside and decided to check on him every twenty minutes or so to see if anything had changed, not knowing how long a 'possum would play this game.

After the third try, almost an hour later, there was still no movement. It was still tangles beneath the hedges. Just as I went to grab its tail, I saw a slight twitch of his eyeball. I couldn't believe it. He was alive. I went back inside and when I returned, he was long gone. Nowhere to be seen. That was a lesson for me. *How silly would I have looked telling people I got attacked by a 'possum that I thought was dead?*

For some reason, my little friend in the bottom of that hedge bush comes to mind as I poke the edge of the hole that lays lifeless in front of me. Things are not always what they seem. I might end up explaining how I ended up at the bottom of a hole that I knew was here.

Hesitation has joined me, but I continue to see what it is really made of. I poke the large stick through the gaping hole until it hits something solid. My grip is tight at its mid-section as I lift the weight of the stick just slightly and twist my wrist. I can feel it touching ground to one side, scraping it lightly, while beneath me seems to contain more air than dirt. This only manages to knock away a bit more of the top and another clump of grass falls below. This problem runs deeper than I thought.

Oh Gigi, what has happened here? Where has the stability gone?

I fear for where I stand. The thinness of the ground, even at its best is tiny roots of grass gathered together keeping me from being sucked into oblivion. They are like the smallest of nerves intertwined within us that keep us from unraveling, keep us from giving into the fear that can bury us alive. This thought grabs my attention. I have walked this area many times unknowing of its instability and have carelessly trusted the scenery. These small blades of grass, so intricate and plush, are comprised of false stability and beauty. They tried so hard to be what they seemed, but in the end, could only project trust where there was none.

How disheartening to think the world can be so cruel to give such false security in the form of beauty to only later find disappointment beneath its efforts. As welcoming as our path may appear, the steps we take are really at our own risk.

I suddenly feel lonely in this execution, wanting nothing more than family to turn to.

Oh, Gigi, how do I do this alone?

I see that what I thought to be security and beauty are now being uncovered as dead, faltering roots. As the top falls easily, revealing more and more of its true size, I am angry at those who have scooped out a part of my life, leaving me with this empty hole.

The light from above exposes the gap before me. Sadness echoes in the emptiness of it all. *Why is it that within emptiness we feel a loss? Is it because we see emptiness as negative space, as less than, rather than as a positive area for more good to come? How do we tell the difference between room to breathe and something missing?*

Here I am presented with this wide-open area before me and I have difficulty deciding.

Is it openness or emptiness, spacious or hollow? Oh, Gigi, was space a concern for you? In your collective nature, were you afraid of the emptiness? Was sadness collected there so you collected everything to fill the void of negative space? Did you fall into the hole that society has set for us all; that more is more and less makes us lesser than? Was openness so deeply filled with the unknown that it took your breath away? While the clutter was cozy, comfortable, and full of tangible controllable items? While filled, was your space—your security—your tether that held you down? For, if that space were empty, full of air, would you have floated away like a balloon in the wind? Is that how you felt? I can feel it now. What is it, Gigi? Why do we fear the emptiness? How should we gauge space? Is it only there if it is empty? Is it only valuable if it is full? Gigi, where is the balance? When does the staleness of emptiness become fresh spacious air to breathe and be? I need to know. Help me, Gigi, to figure this out. Help me to dig this out, dig out the corrosion and fully bring it to light. Help me to see it as the openness of truth and not as a missing part of my life. And with it, remove my fear of the void, replacing it with excitement for what it can be.

I look into the open hole that now welcomes the light, hoping I can see and feel all that is special in it. I smile at the sun that shines down on us. I breathe deeply, and I am thankful for all the space that is surrounding me today.

I know there is more to this space than it is perceived to be. I know it needs time to soak in the light and be given a fresh outlook to its position. I will leave it for now, feeling my discovery has clearly made a mark and will hold steady for me until I return.

My walking stick and I cross the yard with the dogs gathering for our progress toward the house.

I enter the quietness of my home knowing there are creatures that await and welcome me. I will poke and prod at them until they show signs of life. Hopefully, coaxing them into the light and the beautiful space nature provides.

CHAPTER 11:
BEYOND THE EDGE

Beyond the edges of teacups, family connects, relationships grow,
and no truer words are spoken.

Entering the house brings a sigh of relief and a welcoming break from my thoughts. There is a slight concern for my courage, which I left at the edge of the hole along with my anxiety. I hope I will have the motivation to go back. I hope I will find my way.

My home greets me with cool, brisk air from the air conditioning brushing against my skin. I understand why the boys haven't entertained the thought of swimming. Crumbs on the counters, the peanut butter left out, and dishes stacked in the sink leave clear clues they have not starved without me this morning. I smile, in spite of earlier somber thoughts.

The phone starts to ring almost on cue as I walk by it. That Auntie El certainly has a sixth sense.

"Hello, Auntie El."

"Good morning, Lizzi. Well, afternoon, really. How are you today?"

A glance at the clock shows it is just past noon. "Fine and you?"

"Oh, you know. *Old people* stuff. Nothing you want to hear about."

This is Auntie El's way of wanting to talk about something. I oblige her with an invitation to complain a little.

"Not feeling well today, Auntie El?"

"Oh, you know, the arthritis is acting up again. Just one of those days."

"Can I do anything? Come help you with something?" It is a selfish offer, really, for it has been a few weeks since I have visited her. I am missing Auntie El and craving her company.

"No, darling. I'm sure you have plenty going on yourself. How are those boys of yours?" This is also a sign that she is a little lonely and wants some company, but she won't come right out and say it.

"They're good. A little lazy today. I need to drag them out of the house, so we could stop by if you want. Besides, I need to go to the hardware store, anyway."

"Well, if you're headed out." I was pleased to hear the excitement gathering in her voice. "Did you say the hardware store?"

"Yes, something you need?"

"Some light bulbs. Can you pick those up for me? And maybe that tall boy of yours can change a bulb or two. I've been letting those things go lately."

"Sure, anything at the grocery?"

"If you're going, I could use some lemon for my tea. And milk. Is that too much to ask?"

"Not at all, Auntie. We'll see you in a little while."

I hang up while Jonathan pounds down the stairs like rolling thunder. "Hi, Mom." He is down the stairs in a flash. I think gravity did most of the work.

"Gee! A little loud?"

"Sorry."

Justin follows behind him, but less enthusiastically.

"What have you guys been doing?"

"Just playing a game," Jonathan answers. "What have you been doing outside?"

"Working on that hole I found."

"We have a hole?" He seems excited. Boys, dirt, and destruction. *Why would I think he wouldn't be interested?*

"Yes, so be careful if you go out there." He is already headed for the door, "It's pretty big."

"Cool, can I go see it?"

"Sure." He runs out the door without thinking any further.

"Be careful." My voice trails louder so he can still hear me. "And get ready. We have to go out."

"Where are we going?" Justin chimes in while opening the refrigerator door. He doesn't seem impressed with some stupid hole.

"A couple of stores. We need to get Auntie El a few things."

"Oh, is that all? Boring!" he muffles from inside the refrigerator. Shuffling noises let me know that he is looking for nothing particular.

"Well, maybe we can stop and get ice cream on the way home." Wide eyes poke out from around the door. "If you're good."

"Okay."

"Go get ready."

He seems happy that his efforts will at least get him ice cream and heads back upstairs.

I quickly shower and change, throwing my thick brown hair in a ponytail. A last look in the mirror shows wrinkles around my eyes and reminds me of my age. I wonder if time has naturally aged me or if life experiences have worn me out. Either way, I hope I don't run into anyone I know.

First stop, the hardware store. The boys are less than excited, but they follow, intent on getting everything we need and moving on.

I love the hardware store. As crazy as that sounds, I find it full of possibilities. Full of pieces—pieces that can go anywhere, pieces that are organized and gathered together in bins and shelves of all different sizes and colors. It's enough to make my imagination run wild. So many different tools that do so much, like a giant box of Gigi's crafts all in one place. It really sends my creativity through the roof.

I am an awkward thinker when it comes to creative play. It comes to me in a backwards sort of fashion. Sometimes I will walk up and down the tool aisle inspecting and holding each one. I look at the box and see what it does and then decide what I can make with it. I confuse the customer service men when they ask, "What are you looking for a tool to do?" and I answer, "I don't know. What can this tool do?"

"What are you making?" they ask.

I say, "I don't know. What can this tool make?" Then they are really confused and look at me like I am a dumb chick in a hardware store. I have created a few interesting pieces. Of course, they don't know that. A long-threaded pipe with the right drill bits to cut through stainless steel. Some tin canisters, a lamp kit and a colander for the shade. Put them together and there—a cool kitchen lamp!

Yes, there's something about a hardware store. I could spend all day planning new projects. But not today. I have a list to help dig me out of this mental dungeon I have created. I need a couple of items to prepare and protect me when I go back to the hole. There is a method to my madness today.

I will collect my smaller treasures in the provided little wire basket. But first, a long handle shovel, which I ask Justin to carry and then a garden rake I hand to Jonathan. They walk behind me moping and bored with our errand. Jonathan purposely shoulder bumps into Justin knocking the shovel out of his hand and onto the floor. The loud bang turns heads and they giggle while apologizing to me. Justin shoves Jonathan back in retaliation. This time Jonathan points the rake handle out like a sword, to which Justin obliges with a swipe and a crack of the shovel handle. This continues to escalate until an unsuspecting customer is knocked into. I am thoroughly embarrassed, demanding apologies, which they do, and vowing there will be no ice cream today.

They only smirk at each other.

Their embarrassment and disappointment only last a second. Their shoving starts lightly again as they accuse the other, "It's your fault"

"No, it's yours. You started it."

We cut through the electrical department, and the spools of wire distract me. All different colors rolled neatly waiting to be unwound. I imagine them long, mixed together in colors and thickness, then twisted and wrapped around a package. Yes, wrapped around a present, tied in a bow on top like multi-colored ribbon, the perfect accent for the new drill we bought Jeremy's father for his birthday. He will love it.

I grab a few small rolls in red, yellow, blue and white. They land in the basket happy to join me, and I can't wait to sit and play, but for now my imagination has to stay spooled up with them.

Back on task, I look for work gloves and Auntie El's light bulbs. We check out quickly. I feel I have left unexplored projects behind and secretly vow to come back for them. Meanwhile, I have my colored wire to be creative with.

The grocery store is next. It is my least favorite place to be. The boys choose to stay in the car with iPads and phones to interact with. I let them enjoy their technological world. It will make my time in the store quicker.

Lemons and milk, and some tea, and some bread, yes, we need bread and bagels, and toothpaste. Yes, we are almost out of toothpaste. Okay, that's enough.

I came to the grocery store specifically for Auntie El. It is a trap, if you ask me. The long aisles that are so thin one has to stop several times for other shoppers who are choosing their items. The more times you stop, the more items you stop in front of, and then, it is more likely you are to think of that item and buy it.

Wow! No wonder we have a hard time getting anywhere in life. There are always ulterior motives being placed in front of us like obstacles in our paths. A polite "Excuse me," can get me past most of the ones here. I wish all issues in life were that easily overcome.

I push on through the aisles full of people. I'm trying to avoid anyone I recognize for they may prolong my visit here. Finally, I've collected all my items in my handy red plastic basket and head to the front of the store where my exit is at least within sight.

Even leaving is a hassle though. This is where they have you, where it is clear that all the bright lights and lures of delicious morsels are just bait. Never enough registers open, they try to keep you in their world. They try to make you feel at home with women's magazines and temptations of candy so you'll be comfortable, stay, and buy more. The longer they can keep you, the more you'll think about why you're here. Then, you'll think of all the items you need to buy so you won't have to come back. The stuff you need to survive is here. This is where you have to come and once you're here, it's got ya! From enter to exit.

We all end up at the grocery store at some point to gather life's necessities, and then we have to find our way out of the craziness. Finding my way out—past the mental and sometimes physical challenges—is always an accomplishment.

I choose the self-checkout register, which makes more sense. At least I am in control this way and only at the mercy of the person in front me. At least they, too, are taking action to move forward, seeming to know the meaning of exit rather than just accepting a place in line where the person in control can't leave anyway.

I escape with only the items I need in two small bags, one for Auntie El and one for me. I scoot through the electric glass doors that don't open fast enough.

The boys don't flinch from their handheld devices as I open the hatch and throw in the small bags. They barely notice I am back.

The drive to Auntie El's house is quiet and smooth on this early afternoon. We arrive twenty minutes later. Her home is bright and welcoming, one that stands out in this small neighborhood. I'm always amazed at her ability to grow the most luscious gardens and planters. Even at her age, she manages what I consider to be the impossible. The first impression of her home is like walking into a cartoon. The plush grass shows off the small bright yellow Cape, bursting at the seams with flowers in her window boxes and along her front walk. Plush and creamy like a wet painting that might run off the canvas if tilted too far forward, the reds, purples and whites pop against the yellow clapboards.

Inside, her house feels cool, but cozy, striking the eyes with more of the same brilliant colors. A deep rosy pink greets us as we walk into the small foyer, leading to a larger living room boarding in thick bright white trim around all the doors and ceilings. A chair rail halfway up the wall transitions to a large floral print wallpaper in yellows, greens, and more pink. The sofa and chair are striped yellow and white sitting on a pure white carpet that would give any mother nightmares. However, it's perfect here and awakens the whole room. Not a thing out of place, the room earns the respect of all who enter.

I am soothed but agitated at the same time. One part of me wants to melt into the room like the perfect picture and never move, but the truth is, *Wow, high maintenance! I could never have this.*

The boys trample through as their sneakers squeak against the clear plastic runner that leads directly to the kitchen. This clearly leads anyone who enters the house away from the untouchable room. I am tempted to step off the runner and mosey into her world of color, but, I too, am distracted by the straight and narrow path placed before me. So, I dismiss my inner desire and follow the crowd.

With declarations of how much the boys have grown, I can hear hugs and kisses being exchanged. I enter the kitchen with the teakettle whistling and the smell of warm cookies being pulled from the oven. They are oatmeal-raisin, my favorite. Baking is the one-shared passion of Auntie El and Gigi. They were different in so many ways, but the thought of children in the house without cookies available was something neither would ever allow.

Auntie El looks a little thin to me for her height. Her short salt and pepper hair tops her lankiness. A long, purple housecoat drapes easily to the floor, covering her body well. Usually dressed to the nines, heals and hat included, this is unlike her at this hour of the day. I feel for her. I am sure fidgeting with buttons and snaps on a day her hands are giving her trouble is not appealing. As she pulls the teakettle off the stove, I notice her stiffened fingers manage a loose grip. I find it endearing that making cookies for her company was worth the pain. This reminds me she was looking forward to our visit today. Although I feel bad she has gone to the trouble, I know she would have it no other way.

"Let me get that, Auntie."

"Oh, I'm fine dear." She turns in time for me to hug her hello. Her smile and blue eyes are bright and happy.

"Sit, we will have some tea."

I place the bag on the counter and remove the milk and start to place it in the refrigerator.

"No, dear, leave it out so the boys can have some with their cookies."

Her kitchen is not big by any means. However, its openness and a small table give it the appearance of being spacious. The off-white tile continues into a breakfast nook. Windows frame in the half-octagon shaped room. A small glass table for two awaits us while two china teacups sit perfectly on their matching saucers. The China pattern stands out in a floral green while the tails of teabags drape limply over their dainty rims.

The water is poured steaming from the pot, and the lemons are sliced and squeezed. A perfect afternoon tea as if I were seven years old again, playing house. The only thing that's missing is my puffy ruffled dress and heels that were many sizes too big. Instead, shorts, a t-shirt, and sneakers will have to do today.

The remnants of lemon and folded rind lay beside our cups. The boys are inhaling cookies and milk only a few feet away at the kitchen table. They smile and chat amongst themselves, laughing about something unknown to me. I relax in this moment observing their innocence, for they are happy and safe.

The view of Auntie El's garden is exquisite. I gaze out the window at the soft brightness. Each flower stands tall and vibrant, making the tea all that tastier.

"Look at your gardens, Auntie. How do you do it? They grow so eloquently."

Her hands are shaky and the cup clatters lightly as she places it on the saucer, "Oh, they are my pride and joy."

Taking the attention off of her, she continues after another sip, "I could ask you the same for those boys in there. They certainly are wonderful young men."

I blush lightly because I am not sure that this compliment is quite deserved yet. They are still so young. "It's not easy."

The tea is still too hot for me, so I blow at the steam escaping the cup.

"No, it's not. I find it's a lot of work and very little praise until they're grown and out of your care."

I agree with her, but the tea burns my lip, keeping me from answering, so she continues, "And then the happiness is in the pride that you feel, not the compliments you get."

I set the tea down to let it cool. "I understand that, but after all that work, how do you ever let them go?"

"With satisfaction that all the hard work has paid off and you've somehow given back to the world and with pride that they will make someone else happy someday."

"That would be nice."

"You'll see, when they are strong, grown individuals. You'll know you've done a good job."

"I'll miss them when they're gone."

"Of course, but the time you spend with them now, the time they spend brightening your days are the ones to enjoy while you have them."

"Times like this?"

"Yes, times like these are special."

"It seems so sad to watch them grow sometimes. To know someday they will grow beyond me and no longer be as close." I try to sip my tea again, but first, I lightly test the edge of the cup.

"Yes, sad in ways, but everything must run its course, dear. A part of them will always be with you, be a part of you. Everything must grow to its potential."

"It just makes everything seem so temporary."

I see Auntie El glancing out at her gardens in pride for their beauty and where they are now. Not wanting to think of a day they will not be here. "It all is, really. Just some more temporary than others, is all."

I can see my boys from where I am sitting and smile for their presence, soaking in their smiles with nothing more than cookies and milk between them. "Why does life have to move on so quickly?"

The tea goes down smooth and warm this time and I look in her eyes, catching a glimpse of Gigi in them.

"It's nature, dear. Something else will come along and fill that space. Maybe or maybe not as beautiful or meaningful, but something and you will know it was meant to be that way."

"I guess. It just feels different when it is moving away from you instead of you moving on from it."

"Yes, this is true."

"I always question if it's right or wrong when changes come."

"We all have moments that we question."

"I question so much these days, Auntie. And I'm not sure where to find the answers."

"If we never questioned were we have been, we would never try to do better."

"That is true, but how do I change circumstances I can't control?"

"You can't, dear. Take my flowers for instance. They are like family, like my children really, while they are with me. I can care for them and treat them all the same, but not all will grow to the same height or beauty. I can question why, but sometimes it is just the nature of them."

"Does your heart get heavy for them?"

"Well, I do wonder where I went wrong. Why they never grew quite the way I wished. And then there are the ones that grow beyond my expectations and move on before I get to fully enjoy them. But I know in my heart that I care for them all the same."

"And when they are gone? Do you think of them?"

"Yes, but I know they will come back next year. As long as I keep the soil fertile. As long as they have a place to grow and be, they will return."

"Not everything that dies off returns to us, though. Relationships sometimes move on forever."

"Yes, true. But maybe they will just come back differently, maybe better somehow. My gardens sometimes need to rejuvenate before they come back stronger and more beautiful than ever. I can only plant the seeds in fresh soil and wait for nature to takes its course."

"Is it exhausting?"

"What?"

"You know, all the work, year after year, and then waiting for them to come back?"

"No, because I know if I didn't, they definitely wouldn't. I enjoy them too much to not be here when they are ready."

"So you always know they will grow?"

"It is of nature for things that are cared for to return to those who love them. They always come back, but you have to be there for them when they do."

"I'm not going anywhere, but I do have ground work to do."

"Well, you work on that and it will all be beautiful, no matter what happens. I can promise you that."

I find myself lazy after the tea, but enlightened by Auntie El's words. I am not sure if we were talking about her flowers, my children, or the family, but maybe she is right. Maybe we can all find our way with a little love and care, along with fertile solid ground waiting for us.

After cookies, Jonathan changes light bulbs while Justin takes out the garbage for Auntie El. She packages up some cookies for us to take home and bids us goodbye at the door. The boys run to the car fighting over the front seat, both yelling "shot gun" in stride.

I kiss and hug Auntie El as if it were the last time I will see her. With watery eyes, I hug her hard because she is the sweetest of family, and someday, she, too, will not be here.

She feels my hug getting tighter and whispers, "Flowers, family, it's all one big garden waiting to be cared for so they can grow. All we can do is tend to it and give them love. Don't give up. They will come back around."

I relax in her arms and thank her for the tea and kind words. I wipe the tears away before she, or the boys, can see them.

The drive toward home is quiet. With soft music playing on the radio and the boys absorbed in their games, I replay my visit, hearing Auntie El and seeing her smiling face. I feel grateful for her.

Beyond the edges of teacups, family connects, relationships grow, and no truer words are spoken.

CHAPTER 12:
FAMILY ROOTS

My rocky memories stack high and wide like a wall separating the past from the future. As I cross over the wobbly stones they support me—ever so hesitantly.

I watch the scenery flash by my window as the double yellow line leads us home. The sun has passed over us while time was well spent with family and conversation. There is a tug and pull of family these days, bringing many forgotten childhood memories to the surface. I know in my heart the family I *know*, are people of great caring, feeling, and love. It is sad to me that somewhere we got lost, as our connections have faded in the wake and division of only two-family members unable to communicate.

I hope Auntie El is right. I hope the ground stays fertile where our roots gather, where we are all connected so that one day we will return to one another, rejuvenated as the beautiful family we can be. I want my children to know the lives they are connected to.

I believe our roots are the hidden connections we all have to life, to the truth, to the earth and to family. With all that we are, all that we do, it begins deep in the soul and in the *soils* of the past. Our belief in ourselves stems from what we have been taught through those roots, that connection.

A tree gathers nutrients through its long limbs that reach deep into the ground. We gather nutrients from the roots of our experiences. A tree will grow and gain strength where it is placed by absorbing the elements of its surroundings. We, too, take in our environment to make sense of the world, and then flourish or deteriorate based on the surrounding of which we were raised.

My family is no different and I have come to understand that all the challenges placed before us have contributed to both our strengths and our demise.

I can only make sense of my family history based on what I have experienced and been told. How I have viewed these stories has changed over the years as I have grown. However, one perception has always rung true for me, our family has bonded through circumstances and decisions made by others, and those experiences have molded us into the family I know.

When I was younger, I often asked what happened between Gigi and my grandfather, whom I only knew as Grampa Charles. Stories flowed through the years of their divorce and the angst that followed it. I had heard that Gigi and Auntie El were always close, but these events shaped their future forever.

Gigi never remarried and Auntie El, already being the caretaker of their mother, devoted most of her time to helping Gigi raise her children. Together they raised this family, digging their heels in deep so we all could have roots and stability.

My mother shared with me what she knew and had been told herself. The story I was told struck me sadly, as I listened intently with a child's ear.

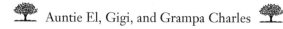 Auntie El, Gigi, and Grampa Charles

Eleanor May was older than her sister, Virginia Elizabeth, by only two years, but she was more mature in her protective and maternal caring. I had only known them both as Auntie El and Gigi.

Gigi, better known as Ginny then, was seventeen when she met Charles. Ginny with her dark hair, energetic personality and dark brown eyes, and he with his quick wit and intense charm, quickly made a striking pair. Eleanor was cautious of the man from the start, as any doting sister would be, but Ginny married him less than a year later in spite of her sister's skepticism.

The marriage was a rough one from the beginning with little money and a baby on the way in the first year. They always seemed to manage with a little help from family, but after fifteen years and six children, it became a stage for emotional trials. The ongoing bills and cramped space of a small cape started to take its toll on both of them.

Charles was a contractor and his many small jobs around town as a handyman kept them above water. Ginny picked up a shift or two at the small diner in town while Ellie sat with the children. This was not the life Charles had planned as it wore him down as a man to see his wife working only to come home to screaming kids and an empty refrigerator most evenings. When Ginny worked she was allowed to take home leftover rolls and side dishes from the kitchen, which helped them through some weeks, but handouts were a knock to Charles' ego and they pulled his spirit down.

These memories and stories flood my mind as the music from the radio plays softly and the wind whistles through my car window.

 Ginny

Virginia was slender, with wavy dark hair pulled back on her head by a folded scarf that tied behind her neck. Her brown eyes and dark features complimented her milky soft skin while her lipstick, striking and alluring, shimmered in cranberry, spicing up her dull pink uniform.

She slipped on a white apron that tied around her waist. It hung the full length of her lap, ruffling out around the scalloped edge. Her small, plastic nametag read *GINNY* in black capital letters. The sun started setting earlier every day, and with it, the night got cooler. She grabbed her white button-down sweater, threw it over the short, white-cuffed sleeves as she waited for Eleanor, her sister, to come sit with the children. Charles was working late again.

Ellie pulled her car up to the front of the house and left it running. She was taller than Ginny by a few inches and her heels added to that distinction, while her tightly pulled bun showed off the length of her neck and hid the length of hair. Plainer looking than Ginny, she was unaware of her attractiveness, but still she carried herself with a confidence that most wished they had.

She lived with their mother only a block away, not too far to walk after Charles got home. It was a beautiful night and she didn't mind the short walk through the wooded path between neighborhoods.

Ginny took Ellie's car to the diner, the solution to Charles having the truck on those long working nights.

Ginny met her at the sidewalk, buttoning up her sweater as she went.

"Darn," Ginny said as she fumbled with her purse.

"What is it? Am I late?" Ellie asked, concerned for the time.

"No, I'm missing a button."

"Come back in. I'll fix it for you," Ellie offered.

"I can't. If I'm late one more time Gus will give my shifts away."

"Well, go then. I got the kids."

"Thank you, El. I don't know what I'd do without you." She hugged her lightly and then rushed off.

Ginny arrived just in time, punching the clock in at exactly 6:01. The diner was busy as usual and the smell of mixed foods and the sound of clanging silverware and dishes all brought the reality of their hardship in one overwhelming assault on her senses. She pulled her sweater off and rolled it in a ball, tucking it under the counter with her purse.

"Nice to see you on time today, Ginny," Gus hollered from behind her in the kitchen. "Take the counter tonight. Nancy is sick again."

Nancy is always sick. She took a pad and pencil from the stack at the register. *Or, at least hardly comes to work lately. The only reason Gus keeps her on the schedule is because she's young and pretty and she brings in the men.*

It was a passing thought, but Ginny didn't care; the counter was the busiest and Nancy's absence meant more tips for her. Not that Ginny was hard on the eyes, but fifteen years of a rough marriage and six kids left her feeling less than herself and more tired every day.

The evening progressed as usual and Ginny watched the clock relentlessly. The turnover at the counter was speedy and smooth. The constant wiping of the counter, taking orders and pouring coffee left all the faces a blur.

The bell above the door chimed as it opened and closed, creating a symphony all night. With every ring, Ginny looked up hoping Charles would stop in for coffee before he went home to relieve Eleanor.

As the clock ticked on, the stools remained empty longer, showing them for the red checker-like dots that they were. Ginny was tired and there was no sign of Charles. The diner wouldn't close until ten o'clock with an hour of cleaning and stocking, and it was only eight-thirty.

Two familiar-faced gentlemen entered and sat at the end of the counter.

"Where's Nancy tonight?" one asked, surprised to see Ginny in front of him.

"Sick."

"Oh, well, Ginny," the other said, with a glance at her name tag, "It's her loss and your gain to get our company tonight." Their laughs were deep, hearty, and playful.

"It must be my lucky night, boys. What can I get you?" She smiled her best smile.

"Coffee and pie, please."

"Comin' right up," Ginny said, tucking the small pad and pencil into her apron pocket.

One gentleman's voice was so deep that his whisper reached the length of the counter to the coffee station. "Sick? The only thing sick about Nancy is that married boyfriend of hers."

"Shh," the other quickly responded.

"That's what I heard. Married with six kids, I think. Lives right here in town. He came to fix her sink or something like that." His words softened as Ginny stood in front of them.

With a pot of coffee in her hand, her pale face and watery eyes made them gasp.

"Are you okay?" She barely heard them ask.

Ginny placed the coffee pot down so fast that it almost fell off the counter. She covered her mouth with one hand and ran off.

"What did I say?" one asked the other.

"I told you to be quiet," the other answered with annoyance

A few minutes later Ginny came out of the restroom, snatched her purse and sweater from under the counter, and rushed out the door. She heard Gus yelling to her, but she couldn't stop herself. Her legs couldn't move fast enough to get away.

She hardly caught her breath as the thoughts flooded her mind of Charles's elusive behavior lately, his lack of interest in her, and his avoidance of the diner when she worked. And beyond that was the knowing that more times than not, Nancy had been *sick* when Ginny worked a late shift.

Ginny pulled in front of the house. Shutting the engine off, she sobbed uncontrollably.

Eleanor came out to check on her early arrival home. "What happened?" Ginny couldn't answer through the tears.

"Did Gus fire you? That big bully! I'll give him a piece my mind. Wait until Charles hears about this."

The sound of Charles' name sent out a wail so loud that Eleanor suggested it would be best if they went inside before the neighbors heard. Ginny shook her head. "I don't want the kids to see me like this."

"They're all in bed. Come in and I'll make us some tea."

Over tea and tears, Ginny filled Ellie in on what happened and what Charles had been up to. The devastated sobs that came from Ginny were more than Ellie could stand. All she could do was listen, hold her hand, and tell her that everything would be fine, whether she believed it or not.

The children were upstairs in the two small bedrooms. Lillian just three, Betsy eleven, and Ruth thirteen in one room, and Raymond five, Edwin ten, Teddy fifteen in the other. It was a school night so all were sent to bed early.

The two younger boys were still awake waiting to hear their father's truck. The familiar sound of the door shutting meant he was home and everything was fine. They wouldn't sleep until they saw him.

Charles, on the nights that he worked late, would always peek in their rooms when he got home. Wide-eyed boys greeted him and that made the day worth every minute, "Why aren't you asleep? All big boys need their sleep."

Through their smiles they'd say, "Just waiting for you, Daddy."

"Well, I'm home now, so go to sleep," he'd say, re-tucking them in and telling them goodnight.

But not that night.

That night was different.

On that night, that truck door slamming didn't mean seeing their father. That night, it was the sound of their lives changing forever.

Charles pulled up just before ten o'clock believing he had plenty of time before Ginny's shift was over. The truck door slammed with a metal toughness. Ellie's car in front of the house made him question what was happening. When he saw they were in the kitchen, Ginny, still in her uniform, Ellie reaching over the table handing her a tissue, he knew that Ginny knew. He walked the short distance to the kitchen, slowly, afraid to look Ellie in the eye. Ellie shifted her bottom jaw sideways, restraining herself, as she dunked her tea bag up and down. She didn't look up.

Charles felt if he could just get Ginny alone that he could explain it all away.

"Maybe you could leave us alone, El," Charles sheepishly whispered while leaning against the counter with his eyes locked on the black and white tiles beneath his feet.

"I don't think so," Ellie said as she stood up to face him.

Charles shifted back to a stand in anticipation of El's reaction, but Ginny grabbed Eleanor's arm, stopping her before the situation could get out of hand. "It's okay, El. I need to talk to Charles alone."

"Are you sure?"

"Yes, thank you."

"Only if you're sure."

"Yes, go home. I'll be fine," she said while pressing a tissue against each eye.

"Okay. I'll call you tomorrow." She leaned in and hugged her. "Pack those kids up and come to Momma's if it gets bad. Okay?"

Ginny nodded her head and started to cry again.

Ellie walked by Charles with a stiff posture and stared at him, waiting for him to look up as she resisted every urge to backhand him. He didn't dare lift his head until she had left.

Beneath her tears, Ginny had the same nagging feeling that flared up in her most doubtful moments. Ginny's heavy heart began to wonder. *Oh my God, where did I go wrong? Why is he doing this? What am I going to do?*

Through her toughest questions, her mind hitched on the moment Charles asked her to marry him. She was a senior in high school and had plans to start art school after graduation. She was once going to do something with her life. She once had dreams of her own and she had bypassed it all to be with him. Could that be the decision that she would regret after all these years? She thought of her children upstairs and how much she loved them. How hard it had been over the years, but how she always believed that as long as Charles and she were together, it could be done and it would all be worth the struggle.

Now she could only think of the moment she decided to put all of her faith in him. Now all she could think was how her life would be different if she hadn't. It was all too overwhelming for her to take in, and it weakened her to think her life, her children's lives, would never be what she planned. She sensed Charles' distance from across the kitchen, but still remembered being young and in love. She harbored that special feeling from years ago, from a time when it was all so new.

 Ginny and Charles: The Beginning

Ginny, at seventeen, was a good student and artistically talented. The walk home from school that day was particularly nice, and the snow had almost melted away as the sun warmed the air helping all anticipate spring. Her best friend Trudy walked the mile with her until they had separated a few blocks back. She rushed to the mailbox like she had every day for the last two weeks, shuffling through envelopes hoping to see her name. Today, one envelope was handwritten to Virginia E. Winters with a return address from Greenwich Art Academy. She ran inside to the kitchen hoping her mother or Eleanor would be there to open it with her.

As she opened the front door, she knew the house was empty for it had that particular silent sadness that Ginny felt whenever she was alone. It filled the air and got heavier over the years since her father had passed away. It was a feeling she could never shake and she tried to avoid it whenever possible. Without her father around, she felt an underlying fear of insecurity that kept her in the past. His death triggered a struggle within her to find the footing she needed. This perpetuated her uncertainty about everything, especially her future.

On that day, she was so excited to check the mail that she had forgotten that both her mother and Eleanor were working the afternoon shift at the diner. She threw the pile of mail on the counter, took a deep breath to settle her nerves and grasped the unopened letter to her chest. Entering her bedroom, her books landed heavy on her bed and the envelope was placed gently on her dresser. Ginny quickly walked back to the living room picked up the phone receiver, which sat on the sideboard table. Trudy answered on the second ring.

"It came. It finally came," Ginny announced.

"And?"

"I haven't opened it yet."

"Why not?"

"I'm scared, Trudy."

"What's there to be scared of? I thought this is what you wanted?"

"It is. I just—"

"What?"

Trudy was answered with silence.

"It's Charles, isn't it?

"Well, I just don't know how he will take it. If I leave in the fall."

"He should be happy for you."

"Yes, I know. But…"

"Oh my God. Are you in love with him?"

"I think so Trudy, but what does that mean? I don't even know if he feels the same."

"I'm coming over. Don't go anywhere." The phone clicked and within minutes they were sitting on Ginny's bed together staring at the unopened letter that lie between them.

"Do you want me to open it for you?" Trudy asked while reaching for the envelope.

"No!" Ginny snatched it before she could reach it.

"Okay, okay! Don't get upset. I just don't know what the big deal is. If you got in, it is good news, right?"

"Yes, I guess. I don't know. I am so confused right now. Do you think he will wait for me? If I got in that is. Do you think this will change everything?"

"You will never know until you open the envelope."

"I know but I can't. Not now."

Ginny jumped off the bed, opened her top dresser drawer, stuffed the letter under some personal clothing, and slammed the drawer shut. "Let's go down to the diner and get an ice cream soda. That always clears my head."

"Okay, but I don't know what you're doing, Ginny. This is all you have talked about for the last year."

Ginny had already left the room and Trudy found herself standing before the drawer that held the letter. She reached out, too curious to let it go.

Ginny poked her head back in the room. "Are you coming or not?" She saw Trudy's hesitated hand near the drawer handle. "Not now." She grabbed Trudy's other hand and dragged her out of the room.

Down the street, they walked while talking and giggling. Their wool coats swung open in the afternoon warmth, and their low-heeled pumps clicked on the sidewalk. They both found conversation easy, but today it was hard to stay away from the subject that was on their minds.

"You deserve this, Ginny. This scholarship? You deserve it."

Ginny's head tilted down and her eyes jerked away from Trudy's. Her smile faded. "I guess," she said softly. "But it is so far away. What about Charles? What about my mom and Eleanor? Can I actually leave them all?"

"Well, you know your mom and Eleanor will be fine and happy for you, and as far as Charles goes, what about him? You've only been dating a few months. You're going to throw it all away for him?"

"You don't understand. If you had a boyfriend, maybe you would, but it's different. He is different."

"So, I've never had a real relationship before? Is that it? I'm unqualified as a friend to say you deserve better?"

"I didn't mean that."

"Well then what do you mean, Ginny? I just don't get you."

"It's just…"

"It's just what? Why don't you talk to El if you don't trust me? She will tell you. I notice you didn't wait to get her opinion. We both know what she will say."

"It's just all so much. What if I can't do it? What if I'm not good enough? What if he doesn't wait for me? What if I never find anyone else?"

"He is an idiot if he doesn't. And you can do it. I have no doubt at all about that."

"Easy for you to say."

"Because it's true."

"I don't want to think about it anymore. Charles is picking me up tonight. I will open the letter with him. Don't mention the letter to El or my mom while we are here. Promise?"

"Okay, I promise," Trudy whispered as they came upon the diner window.

Ginny pulled open the heavy door and the bell rang above them.

Later that night, Charles was fifteen minutes late. Ginny paced in the kitchen as El finished the dishes.

"What is wrong with you Ginny? I have never seen you this nervous to see Charles before."

"Nothing," Ginny snapped. "Mind your own business."

"I would if you would stop seeing him."

"Why? What do you care?" Ginny pulled the curtain aside to check the street again. Charles' truck was coming around the corner.

"I care because you are my only sister and it's just the three of us now with Dad gone. He wouldn't approve."

Ginny turned toward Eleanor, giving her a quick hard look. With no response she left the kitchen, and Eleanor, to fetch her coat.

Eleanor walked to the kitchen doorway speaking louder while drying her hands on her apron.

"Someone has to say it, Ginny. You will go nowhere with him."

Ginny had disappeared to her bedroom to get the letter from her dresser drawer. She paused before stuffing it into her pocket. Passing through the living room she pretended not hear her sister say, "You will see when you leave next fall. He will be the first one to hit the road running to someone else. If Dad was here, that boy would not have the sense to show his face around here, and you know it."

Ginny rushed, trying to beat Eleanor's voice out the door, but the last words she heard were, "You're wasting your time."

Charles and Ginny drove in silence until he pulled into the wooded side-road that led to the lake. He parked just before the water's edge where the moon reflected off the water. Charles turned to her with his hazel eyes and blond hair. "You're awful quiet tonight. Everything alright?"

Ginny barely heard him as she searched his face for answers to the unknown, nervously crinkling the letter in her right jacket pocket.

He didn't wait for her to answer, "I have some good news," he said, touching her cheek with his hand.

"You do?"

"Yes, I got the job with that construction company." Their eyes met long enough to make Ginny melt ever so slightly.

"You did? That's fantastic!"

"Yeah, I start in two weeks. There is a whole new neighborhood going up in the next town. The foreman said he should have work for me for the next year at least." Charles leaned in to kiss her, but she shifted her gaze and glanced down before he could. "What? I thought you would be happy."

"I am, Charles. I just have some news of my own." She pulled the now-wrinkled envelope from her pocket and placed it on her lap.

"You got in." Charles swallowed slowly without looking directly at her.

"Actually, I don't know yet. The letter just came today. I wanted to open it with you."

"Okay, so open it." His tone was less than what Ginny expected.

The dome light in the truck was dim but she could see that his eyes were glossing over with tears.

Ginny felt for him for she knew him, knew his pain, and knew the sadness beneath his smile. Their long talks had reached the depth of his childhood and the abandonment of his father along with the neglect of a single mother who was distant and bitter. She knew Charles cared for her. She knew he tried to break free from the anger of feeling alone most of his life. She knew she filled a very large gap for him. She could see it in his eyes, hear it in his voice, the internal struggle between being excited for her and the once again chance of being left for something better.

Ginny's hands shook, partially from the chill of the night but mostly out of sheer wavering emotions for what this meant to her life. She never looked up, for if she had, she would have seen Charles staring out the driver's window without an ounce of attention to her.

Charles could hear the letter being torn open and the shuffling of paper. Suddenly, without thinking, he turned and grabbed her hands, crumpling the letter between them. Before Ginny could read a word, he pulled her chin up so her eyes met his and he blurted out, "Marry me!"

"What?"

"Marry me, Ginny. Stay here and marry me. With this new job, I can start putting money away. Maybe even build our own house in the next couple of years. It doesn't matter what is in that letter. I want you here with me, not miles away in some snooty art school. You belong here with me. I can take care of you."

He talked so fast that Ginny couldn't believe what she heard. Her eyes searched his face once more, this time for truth, for some kind of sign that told her what to say, but there was none. Her heart sank for him. Her thoughts raced with excitement, for every girl dreams of hearing these words, yet she still held the letter, unread, its contents becoming more insignificant by the second.

That acceptance letter still lived in her private dresser drawer with all of its creases, aged to a yellowish tint. It had been taken out and read more times then she could count since that night. She had memorized every word. This letter had been her reminder, in times of doubt, that someone else thought she had the potential to be someone other than a mother and housewife. There is no wonder that that letter, that day, came to mind as she sat waiting for her fate with Charles to be shown to her.

 Ginny and Charles: The Separation

The door, shutting behind Eleanor as she left the house, brought Ginny back to her reality fifteen years later—sitting in her waitress uniform and drying a tear-stained face. Charles' apologies came quickly along with the unsettling feeling of his emotional hold on her. She was inclined to believe him, and he knew it, but this time Ginny refused to listen, refused to give in to her internal fear of being alone and unloved. She mustered the strength and the words to tell him to leave, to never come back, to let her be. He argued and pleaded, knowing he was wrong. As she walked away, locking herself in the bedroom, his lack of control over her grew to an incessant rage, one that never left him, and left her, once again, with an uncertainty about her future, an uncertainty about the men that said they loved her and then left her to fend for herself.

Eleanor sat in the car for several minutes wondering if she should leave. She heard screaming, crying, and doors slamming as Charles apologized loudly.

The children watched from the bedroom windows as their Auntie El finally pulled away. Shortly after, they witnessed the same of their father as the muffled sobs from their mother penetrated her bedroom door.

The images of this story flicker through my mind as the sunlight crisscrosses my windshield. This drive home, with my boys safely in the back seat, is slow and haunting as sadness engulfs me. I remember my mother the day she spoke of her father leaving them that evening. Her voice was shaky and deep like she was far away, and it pained her to speak of it. I could almost see the sweet little faces of her and my aunts and uncles peering out the window as their childhood fell apart.

 Lizzi and Ruth

"I watched Auntie El leave that night from the boys' bedroom window," my mother told me. "We were all scared. We had never heard our parents fight like that before. We all stayed in one room, afraid to go downstairs. We listened as my mother cried and my father banged on the bedroom door begging for forgiveness. It seemed like hours. My mother was yelling at him to leave and I remember your Uncle Teddy standing helpless at the window as he watched our father pull away in his truck."

"It must have been awful," I said, feeling sorrier by the moment.

"It was. My father never spent another night in our house, and every time we saw him after that, Nancy was with him, which just made it worse. Teddy never understood any of it and neither did I. We didn't dare ask."

"How do you know what happened?" I asked.

"Auntie El finally told me one day. I was eighteen and pregnant with your brother by the time I heard the whole story. I suppose at that point she wanted me to know the details."

I was young myself when she shared this with me. The sadness on my mother's face was hard to bear. It was the first time I saw her as a little girl, as someone other than a mother, vulnerable. It was then I knew there was pain behind those eyes.

I felt bad for my mom and my aunts and uncles after hearing that story, but it did make the tension I had always felt between Auntie El and Grampa Charles very clear. Come to think of it, I don't ever remember Auntie El speaking to Grampa Charles at all, and the few times I ever saw them in the same room together, they never made eye contact.

A strange sense of disconnect washed over them and filtered down to us in acts of odd behavior. As I got older, the only way that I could make sense of it was by asking questions and listening to their stories.

Grampa Charles was not a very big part of our lives, and what I did know of him was not exactly sweet and cuddly. He was abrasive, harsh, and cranky. A scary person, he was, to a shy little girl like me. I never saw much affection between him and my mother, or any of the family members for that matter. Nancy, our step-grandmother, as we knew her, was very cold and unapproachable. No one would even say hello to her on the rare occasion they did visit. They would wait until she came in to summon Grampa to leave. Only then was anyone polite enough to say good-bye.

I got an odd feeling when they were around.

I must have been around six years old, but I remember one visit in particular.

 Remembering Grandpa Charles and Nancy

Grampa Charles was in the kitchen talking with my mother and Aunt Betsy while Nancy stayed outside.

I watched her from the living room window. I kneeled on the sofa, looking over the back of it, peeking through the curtain just enough so I could see her, but she couldn't see me, or so I thought. Her pale face was framed in by her hardened black shiny hair, which puffed up on top and winged out at her shoulders. She stood there in her pencil-skirt that stopped above the knee, a button-up blouse and high heels while she chain-smoked her cigarettes one by one.

I watched her puff away as she leaned against the car. Her left arm crossed her body just below her chest giving her right bent elbow a resting place. The cigarette was mechanically maneuvered back and forth with dramatic gestures of stiff, bony fingers meeting angry, puckered lips.

Her face was plastic looking. Her drawn-in eyebrows and unnatural large, thick eyelashes held her rigid expression. Long draws on the cigarette, as if it was her life source, made her seem even angrier. Longer streams of smoke would blow out her lips, shifting her face to the sky. When the cigarette was short, it was thrown to the ground and stomped in a twisting fashion showing her long legs and high heels.

I watched her curiously and intently until she looked up from squishing her third cigarette butt into our walkway. Her face tilted up, looking in my direction with crossed eyes and her tongue hanging out to one side. I closed the curtain quickly, realizing I was caught, and ran to my room where I stayed until they were getting ready to leave.

Nancy had summoned Grampa Charles to leave by beeping the horn and they all went to the front yard. My mother insisted I come out and say goodbye. When I did, Nancy winked at me with those dark long lashes of hers. I hid behind my mother's leg, unsure of her. *Was she playing or being mean?* I was curious about this mystery woman who was family, even though she scared me deeply.

For days after their visits, my mother was withdrawn and quiet, distracted constantly by long conversations with her sisters. Nancy was clearly the source of aggravation as her name was the one who was mentioned most. When this happened, I knew deep down to be an extra good girl so as not to cause more problems for my mother.

Even then, the tension seeped into our roots, shifting our foundation.

One day, not too long after, I was playing by myself, as I often did, when my mother caught me holding a piece of chalk like it was a cigarette. She was furious.

"What are you doing?" she screamed.

"I'm being like Nancy," I said, proud of my imitation of her.

"Well, knock it off. Never act like her. She's a horrible person."

From then on, I was nervous to mention her, never mind *like* her. Throughout my childhood, I felt confused about my Grampa and Nancy and the nerve they touched when anyone mentioned them.

These relationships became clearer only as I got older and found out the truth. The stories started to piece together a not-so-pretty picture of Grampa, Nancy, the divorce and my family's deep-seeded pains.

Being a sensitive child, many of the stories weighed heavily on me. I felt every intertwined emotion, burying them deep as they now lay twisted up in the roots of my past.

I travel home today from our short visit with Auntie El far from those times and memories, yet with every corner and turn of the wheel more memories bring me further away into the past.

CHAPTER 13:
JAGGED EDGES

Happier memories, washed away by the tide years ago, splash back down on the shore of today, waiting to be found, to be gathered up and taken home, and cherished forever.

I decide to take the long way home so I can drive by the sandy beaches. My mind continues to drift in and out of time. With Nancy gone ten years now of lung cancer, Grampa Charles of a heart attack three years after that, and my own father passing almost fifteen years ago, I wonder why it all still lingers so deeply in my heart. I don't believe I am the only one, because if I were, my family would not be where we are today.

I pull into a small pick-up/drop-off area along the beach entrance. I am tempted to feel the gritty sand between my toes and feel the wave's splash on my face. I watch as blankets are shaken so not to steal the sand from the shore and sun-struck faces march away from the breaking waves. The boys look up for a moment asking, "Why are we here?"

"No reason," I say, for the truth is my memories are surfacing quicker than the waves are hitting the shore.

I park the car for a moment and look at the long sandy strip, watching a string of buoys all in a row. I can't tell if they are reacting to the waves below or to the motions of one another. Two girls exit the beach, stepping from sand to pavement in laughter carrying handfuls of shells.

I spent a large part of my childhood on the beach. A pleasure I shared mostly with my Aunt Lillian. Together, we searched the sand for treasures that the ocean had given up. I think of her often these days in the separation of family. I miss our connection, our shared love for nature and our candid conversations.

Our motivation was to collect gifts the sea had tossed ashore, just waiting to be discovered. Funny, how the shells and sea glass have been long forgotten, but our time together lives with me forever. The walking, the talking, the silence, it all added up to moments along the shore, treasures we collected in our pockets, memories I hold in my heart.

Through the windshield of the car I watch the waves pull in and out. I imagine the many possessions the large ocean must hold. Keeping every special item captured and hidden from the view of today, like our days together that have been swept away, just buried beneath the waves of time.

As I watch the waves gently roll in, memories of my Aunt Lillian splash down on the breaking shoreline.

 Lizzi and Aunt Lillian

I was just a child but always found her intriguing, carefree, and inspiring. She was my mother's younger sister. She loved nature, art, and animals. I saw myself in her and wanted so badly to be the person she was.

As a child, whether it was walking on the beach or strolling through the woods, it was Aunt Lil who was right beside me, pointing out the birds and the trees, collecting pine cones, sea glass, and driftwood. Maybe it was the simplicity of nature that brought us together along with the naïve nature of where our shallow roots would bring us that allowed us to bond as the children we both were. For she was older than me by only ten years, no more than a teenager herself, but her maturity in my young eyes gave me the comfort of looking up to her all the same.

At the time we were so close I thought we would grow beside each other forever, but we were children, just children of the same family, small branches of the same tree. As life circled on and the years created space between us, the thickness of our connection separated us and we found ourselves on two opposite sides of the tree, destined to grow outward and away from one another.

I can only hope that nature can bring us together again someday, much like our walks I remember so well.

Aunt Lil was kind to me. As a mother figure, or a friend, she always filled an important role. Our talks were truthful and heartfelt. One memory falls into place as the sight of the ocean waves persuasively sways my thoughts to the past.

It was a beautiful spring day, probably a Saturday because I didn't have school. The beach air was crisp and the sand was cold. Being the end of one season and the beginning of another, the beach attracted few people and gave us the isolation in nature we enjoyed so much. A few echoing seagulls walked among us.

Aunt Lil was tall and thin with long light brown hair that reached the middle of her back. It was silky straight, tucked behind each ear. Her big brown eyes dominated her petite nose and bright smile. I wondered if I would ever be as attractive. Her short, cut-off jeans with a leather loop belt accented the length of her legs as her plain pink t-shirt fit her wiry body like a glove. She was only eighteen, but I looked at her with admiration. All seemed right when I was with her. We walked quietly absorbing the sun and each other's company.

We pocketed shells and sea glass, dipped our toes in and out of the cold water until they tingled in frosty splinters. The sun's heat could quickly be swept away by a cool breeze. Our silence was an invitation to deeper thoughts. With half the beach behind us, I felt a question emerge from somewhere, "Do you like Nancy, Aunt Lil?"

"Why do you ask, Lizzi?"

Her tone was not of surprise or annoyance, which made me feel comfortable in my curiosity. I was testing the grounds with her to see how forbidden the subject really was. It was one more piece of the puzzle.

I was careful with my wording for my mother's pain seemed so embedded I was not sure what Aunt Lil would share. I told her what I knew about Gigi and Grampa being married once and how he had left her for Nancy. That was all I knew at that point. The hard stories had not been shared yet. I never thought to ask about Jeanie. It wasn't until later that I realized the element she brought to the family. I was only eight—maybe eight-and-a-half by then—and I wanted details to make sense of it all. I knew if anyone would tell me the truth, it would be Aunt Lil.

"Yes, that's right, Lizzi. He did."

"Do you remember that?"

"No. I was too young. I just know my father wanted to be with Nancy more than us, I guess."

"So, do you like her?"

She hesitated a little while brushing off a green piece of sea glass with one hand as it lay in the palm of the other. She pulled her arm back and whipped the piece of glass as far as she could back into the ocean. "Too many jagged edges," she declared. "It wasn't smooth enough yet."

The silence between us was filled with distant breezes. The ocean quivered in anticipation for her answer. "Nancy is an evil, mean person, Lizzi. Never trust her."

Lil picked up a few shells, looked them over quickly, and stuffed them in her pocket.

"She does scare me a little," I admitted, with a flash remembrance of the face she made at me.

"She doesn't like us kids much!" Lil avoided eye contact as she peered up at the empty sky before us as if her words were written in the clouds.

"Why not?"

The same tension and strange feeling I always felt when Nancy was mentioned came through Aunt Lil's voice and over me while she spoke.

"She wants your grandfather all to herself, I think. And she hates the fact that he loved my mother once, and we are that reminder."

"Has she been mean to you?"

"Yes, Lizzi, she has. Awful and mean."

"She has?"

She continued with a story that would stick in the mind of any young girl.

 Little Lillian

"After your mother and father got together, your Aunt Betsy, your Uncle Ray and I—being the younger kids—were sent to live with my father and Nancy for the summer. Nancy was not happy about this and was quite mean to us when my father wasn't around."

Her story washed over time as we ignored the chill of the water. Continuously, the ocean reached out and grabbed our ankles with small drifts, only to inhale each wave with its own breath and release them to the cool air.

"I was right around your age, Lizzi. I will never forget it. Nancy really hated us. I know now that my father didn't really care that we were with him. He just wanted to hurt my mother, so he was happy to take us away from her. But Nancy? She was just evil."

Lillian was the youngest of six children from a divorced home, trying to find calm and safety wherever it was offered. Little Lil was her nickname, although she was growing out of it fast. The cuteness of being a young girl was disappearing in the wake of adult issues. Still, her innocence was bright and obvious. A rush to her father's car pulling up the drive gave her a burst of excitement, which she hadn't felt in weeks. Her friend's birthday party had finally arrived and it was something she had been looking forward to since school got out. The move to her father's house for the summer had left her confused. Time with her father was what she had wished for most, and yet her time with her step-mother thus far had been difficult.

"Can we go, Daddy? Can we go?"

"Is your bag packed? Your chores done? Have you been a good girl for Nancy today?" At this point, he was just teasing. He knew how much this party meant to her. It's all he and Nancy had heard about for days.

"Yup, all done." She tried to catch her breath between sentences. "Everyone will be there. I don't want to be late."

"In a minute, honey. Let me change and then I will bring you."

Little Lil was tall and lanky even at that age, and hung onto her father's arm while skipping beside him. She was giddy at the thought of an evening with friends and smiled at her father relentlessly. Her joyous welcoming was all too contagious. He found himself laughing with her as they entered the house.

The door swung open, breaking Lil's laugh in mid stride. Nancy stood just inside the doorway, arms crossed and glaring. The next thing Lil knew was the pain of her arm being squeezed and yanked to the side. The smell of Nancy's smoke-filled breath met her face.

"You're not going anywhere tonight, little girl."

The sting of Nancy's grip took over Lil's senses. Her small hands slipped loose from her father's arm. It happened all too fast for her to react. Confused and frightened, Little Lil saw the smile on her father's face drop from sight and felt Nancy's grip get tighter. Tears filled Lil's eyes.

Charles stood without saying a word as he watched his daughter plead in pain.

"Why? What did I do?"

"Oh, Charles, don't let her fool you." The harshness of her voice filled the air, "Wait until you see what she did to her room today. Defiant little brat." Her squeeze tightened until Lil winced in pain. "Stop being a baby. I'm not hurting you."

"Daddy, I don't know what she's talking about."

Nancy stared at Charles. "Go look at her room, Charles. It's a mess."

Lil heard the front door slam behind her father's back, locking the happiness of her evening out forever. "No, it's not!" She pleaded, crying for her father's attention, but he walked right passed her. "I haven't been in there all day."

Charles marched down the hall with a boiling scowl. Nancy twisted Lil's arm, pushed her to follow her father, poking and shoving her in the back as they went.

Rushing by both of them, Nancy flung open the door to Lilly's room. "Look what she did! I go to all this trouble to make her feel at home. I give her nice clothes and a nice room and this is how she treats them."

Lil sank into her own devastation, unable to believe what she saw. The room was a complete disaster. The blankets were off the bed and thrown around the room. Clothes were scattered everywhere, drawers pulled out and thrown on the bed and floor. Everything in the closet was off the hangers and there were scribbles in crayon all over one wall.

"I didn't do this. Daddy, I swear. Please believe me." Trying to get her father to look at her, Lil pulled at his arms and begged him to believe her, but his cold stare told her all she needed to know. He grabbed her by the shoulders, peeled her off him, threw her on the bed, and left her without a word. His little Lil lay on the bed sobbing deeper than she ever had before. Nancy left only for a few minutes, returning with a bucket of soapy water and a sponge.

"Stop feeling sorry for yourself and clean up this mess. If you know what's good for you, you will tread lightly around here from now on."

Nancy exited the room with one more slam of the door and a half smile, knowing that Charles would always choose her over his kids.

After Aunt Lil had finished telling me about Nancy, sadness had fallen over the entire beach. We walked in silence until I had the nerve to inquire further.

"Did you do all that?" I timidly asked.

"No! Of course not!" Aunt Lil proclaimed.

"Then, who did?"

"She did!"

"No?"

"Yep, and my father believed her, too. I had to stay home from the party, and I was grounded for a week. It took me all night to clean up that mess. She's crazy, Lizzi. I'm telling you, she is cruel."

I didn't know what to say to her. Our walk became solemn. My steps in the sand even seemed heavier and the quiet of the truth fell between us. We finally reached the end of the beach where the large rocks formed a jetty into the water. Suddenly Aunt Lil busted out, "I'll race you back." She started running before I knew what was happening.

"Wait for me!" I screamed, trailing behind her by only an arm's length.

We giggled and laughed, splashing our legs with salt and sand as we watched our footprints disappear behind us like the story had never been told.

In this moment, back in my car, I watch the shoreline empty of people. As this day begins to end, I wave good-bye to another memory. For the jagged edges of sadness have been washed over with time. As if tumbling around for years has dulled their imprint to a delicate keepsake, smoothing and soothing their once sharp impact. Those dangerous pieces of my life that cut so deep, now can clearly be held in the palm of my hand and can be examined without fear, as if they now lie lifeless, harmless, and precious for me to treasure with every flaw iridescently clear.

I watch a few more waves, one…two…three…four…five, splash down on the darkening sand, and think how we are all shells of the past, echoing the sounds of our distant memories.

CHAPTER 14:
A ROOT OF TRUTH

The seeds of laughter struggle to take root in the soils of pain.

A horn beeps loudly from somewhere behind me, snapping me out of my thoughts. Moving forward, the beach disappears quickly behind us, as the winding road folds me in and out of my memories. Home we go while emotions fill my body, and I am amazed how I am so deeply bonded to situations that occurred before me and were beyond my young understanding.

Thoughts of family linger. Aunt Lil's story brings me to thinking of Aunt Betsy and Uncle Ray, two other younger siblings of my mother's. There were times I sat among them, seeing them for themselves. Though I was too young to understand at the time, it filled me with excitement to be shown a glimpse of their past.

All were younger than I am today, and I, then, was younger than my children are at this moment. I only knew I was with them, part of them, accepted by them. They would speak to each other in ways only siblings can, knowing each other, laughing at things I did not understand, making me see they had a whole other life before me. I loved watching them interact with each other. I always wondered why that side wasn't shown more often. It was real. It showed their true personalities, a good side to them. There were private jokes and even the language was different. I enjoyed listening to every word and found comfort knowing they had good memories as well as bad.

🌳 Uncle Ray and Aunt Besty 🌳

One particular morning, when I was twelve, a head cold kept me home from school. I woke to the house feeling hollow and airy, barely a sound penetrated my bedroom walls. With a sleepy and foggy mind, I walked to the kitchen to find my mother with Aunt Betsy and Uncle Ray having coffee and tea. Closing in on the chatter became comforting for I found that being sick allowed me special insight into the adult's sharing time.

"Morning, honey. Feeling any better?" said my mother.

"A little, I guess."

"She doesn't look sick to me. Ruthie, are you sure she is sick?" Uncle Ray smirked and winked at me. "Are you faking to get out of school today, Lizzi?"

"No!" I smiled for the attention, knowing he was only fooling. I sat in the empty chair next to my mother as I rubbed my eyes awake. "Can I have some hot chocolate?"

The room felt as though a conversation had been broken in mid stride. All was silent as my mother poured boiling water over the chocolaty powder. I stirred slowly while adding some creamer. She sat back down, and with my silence, my presence was soon forgotten. I sat amongst them, head heavy from my cold, eyes tired and crusty, my body achy and warm with fever, covered in flannel pajamas and wool socks. The warm chocolate went down smoothly, and I couldn't think of a better place to be than listening to them speaking freely.

Their laughter and conversation were pleasant and easy, their voices more real somehow.

I watched my aunt and uncle as they sat next to one another. Their differences were clear to me. Her tightly curled hair was perfect on her head and a buttoned-up sweater laid smooth over a collared shirt that was cinched close to her neck with a string of pearls. He was easy and casual, from his long, sloppy, blonde hair that stuck out of a baseball cap, to a snake tattoo that kept trying to slither out of his green army jacket sleeve onto the back of his hand, right down to his baggy, holey jeans with torn hems that hid work boots, laced with different colored strings.

Feet on the chair, hugging my knees to my chest, the mug was warm between my hands. I listened carefully. The three of them appeared as the individuals they were. In all their differences, my mother clearly fell somewhere in the middle of the extremes. Her plain look, wearing less expensive clothing than Aunt Betsy and no jewelry matched the hominess of our surroundings. As her hair hung loosely curled to her shoulders, she showed no concern for the early gray streak that ran down one side of her face.

The mood was light and airy and I felt warm in the face of family, but like always, all conversations led back to the beginning. It was Aunt Betsy who seemed strained in the light-heartedness, cracking under the pressure of her own smile. She cleared her throat, suppressing the giggle that seems to choke her. She stopped the return passage of it dead in its tracks. "Have you heard from Dad lately?"

"Not in the last couple of weeks," Ray answered with little interest in their father. He cleared the laughter from his throat while looking down at his coffee mug.

"He stopped by last week when the kids were at school," my mother offered, sipping her tea without looking up.

"He did?" Betsy inquired. "Was *she* with him?"

I listened intently for their tone was too curious to ignore. I had heard stories over and over, from one or the other, but to hear them speak to each other about them in this private setting was rare. Suddenly there was a feeling of togetherness, an us-against-them stand, which is one step away from a divide-and-conquer scenario.

"Of course she was, but she stayed in the car."

"Why did they come by, Ruth?" Betsy asked.

Silence cleared the air before my mother continued. "He asked about everyone. Mom, you guys, Lil, Eddy. He looked old to me somehow, like I hadn't seen him in a while. I guess I haven't. I just hear from Teddy how he is doing."

"Don't you find it ironic that it's Teddy he stays in touch with after all that's happened?" Betsy found the door she was looking for to keep this topic rolling. I heard the sassy attitude coming out, the one that my mother referred to in her stories. "I mean, Teddy does everything in his power to avoid him for years, while we just wanted him to come around more, and now Dad goes to see him regularly. Maybe we should have run away or thrown rocks at Nancy like Teddy did when we were little. Maybe that would have gotten his attention."

The silence from Ray was loud. His boisterous laugh that filled the room a few minutes before now hid in its own echoes. He sat across from me, mug to his face, noticing my stare. He winked at me, rolling his eyes up like a child would as if the conversation had turned too adult even for him.

I had always loved Uncle Ray. He was the funny one, the jokester of the family. He knew how to sidestep the holes in moments of tension with his humor.

Most of my memories of Uncle Ray came from when I was very young. Many days I would accompany my mother to meet her younger siblings after school.

Lil and Ray were in high school. We had been going over there ever since I could remember. My mother made us snacks, helped them with their homework, and started dinner on the days Gigi worked. Jeanie, my older half-sister, had her own homework, so I played with my brother, Chris, and my cousin Jacob, until they were done. Jake was uncle Teddy's only son, and more of a brother to us as he was with us more days than not.

All of us together—that's how I remembered it. The older kids were fun. They would do things I would never think of. Ray was the oldest of us and always made us laugh. He would be the one playing with his food, throwing grapes in the air and catching them in his mouth. He'd talk through his bologna face that consisted of several holes bitten out of lunch meat to make eyes, nose, and a mouth.

"Hello, I'm Mr. Bologna Head," he'd say with a deep voice while sticking his nose through the center hole and trying to make the mouth move with his lips. It was always the same jokes, but sometimes we would get so silly and laugh so hard, milk would come out our noses. Yes, those were the things I remembered: bologna faces and milk coming out our noses. But it was Ray that would always get us going.

There was something special about him. He never made me feel like a little kid. He always included me in on the fun. When we teamed up for kickball games, he picked me first, saying, "Lizzi's with me. Come on, we will kick their butts today."

He jumped off the bus and picked me up like he truly missed me. He was the one who taught me how to ride my two-wheeler, pushing me from behind and never letting go until I was ready.

His practical jokes landed him in some hot water with the teachers and other adults several times. But he didn't care. It was all worth it to him.

Once we had to pick him up at school in the middle of the day because he put a frog in the teacher's desk. He got in the car and nudged me with his elbow, whispering, "I did it just so I could spend the day with you, Lizzi."

"It's not funny, Ray. You are in big trouble today, mister," my mother yelled from the front seat. I covered my giggle with my hand so she wouldn't see.

He spent the next couple of days with us. I didn't know it then, but now I know he had been suspended. He never seemed to care.

To this day, Aunt Lil hates snakes, rodents, worms, salamanders, and toads because these were Uncles Ray's weapons of choice. Aunt Lil and my sister, Jeanie, were his favorite victims because they would scream at any yucky, squirmy, slimy thing he could find.

"Watch this," he'd say, grinning his way past me. "You stay right here."

I sat on the step as he ran into the bushes. He had taken a dead snake the cat had caught, tied it to a string, and hung it over a high branch. I saw Aunt Lil and Jeanie come out the back porch. They walked past me in their chatty state as Ray started to call their names. They went closer to investigate and the snake was lowered over their heads, getting caught in their hair. It was quite funny as they screamed and ran, but Jeanie started to cry and my mother got mad. Then the screaming really started. Ray just rolled his eyes, the same way as he did across the table from me, and said, "Gee, it's just a snake."

I giggled more times than I could remember when I was with him. Then one day, he was gone. I overheard lots of phone conversations and concern for him, but never a clear word to us kids of his whereabouts. I remember words like "Army" and "enlisting" coupled with anxious phrases like "what was he thinking" and "we will never see him again." I didn't understand and it all felt muddled up with the subject of him. He was gone a long time, it seemed, and when he returned, I barely recognized him. He was a man and spoke very adult-like. And I was no longer his little girl. He was no longer the prankster I had known. He had grown and changed, even his sense of humor had become something I didn't completely understand, but I knew he was still in there somewhere because his eyes said so. Words became his weapon of choice because the adults always laughed more when he was around.

Sitting across from an older Uncle Ray that morning, I saw a glimmer of the person I knew years before. I could almost see the smirk behind his eyes that was thinking up his next trick. His smile connected us to the past for only a second, then he disappeared again into the conversation.

"How is Eddy doing, Ruthie? I haven't spoken to him in a while," he asked with true concern and a slight attempt to change the subject.

"Ok, I guess," my mother answered with the same heavy-hearted tone that came with the subject of my Uncle Eddy. "He was staying with Teddy again for a while, but moved out last week. You know Eddy. He can't seem to stay in one place for very long."

"Is he staying out of trouble?" my aunt snidely inquired.

"Well, he's been sober for six months now, if that's what you mean. And has been holding down a steady job, too. I hope he sticks with it this time," my mother offered in defense of him.

"Well, hopefully he can finally get his life together. It's time he grew up a little, don't you think, Ruth?"

"We all have our struggles, Betsy. His are just different then ours. He will figure it out. He needs support from all of us right now. Maybe you could call him. Give him some encouragement for a change."

"Oh *you* and *mom*, always in his corner, defending his every action. It's always *Poor Eddy. Everyone needs to help Eddy.* It's getting a little old if you ask me. It's about time he takes responsibility for his own decisions."

"Why are you so hard on him, Betsy? None of us had it easy growing up. His experiences were just as difficult for him."

"I am sorry, Ruth, but I don't see it that way," my aunt sharply sent her words back at my mother. "At least he has always had our mother. He always got to stay with her. He had her all to himself that one summer. It wasn't like that for us, right, Ray? Living under the thumb of people who didn't want you, who found any reason to ridicule you and make you feel worthless at every turn. He got to stay in his own home. What I would have done to have had that choice."

Ray did not answer. He sat quietly refusing to give that time in his life the power she insisted it still had.

"It wasn't all that easy for him either, Betsy. Yes, he got to stay at home, but he was all alone most of the time. It was clear that Dad didn't want him. Mom worked all the time. I did what I could, but I had Jeanie to take care of and a baby of my own on the way. And Teddy, well, he lived there but was barely around. Auntie El could only do so much for a confused, depressed teenage boy. He went from having his whole family there to having no one."

"I still say it was the worst for us. Nancy was horrible, and she had Dad wrapped around her finger. It's sickening when I think of it now. You remember don't you, Ray? How horrible it was?" she continued, hoping he would defend her words.

"Who forgets living with the Wicked Witch of the West?" He answered her this time only to lighten the heated conversation.

I laughed out loud, which annoyed my mother, so I hid my smile behind my empty mug. I did not want to be asked to leave.

"Ruth," Betsy continued, annoyed that Ray was not playing along, "you weren't there. Nancy really was crazy. I still can't believe some of the shit she use to pull."

The conversation continued with the daggers of Aunt Betsy's words and the deflections of Uncle Ray's lighthearted attitude.

"Remember when she told Dad she was missing money from her purse, and later that night pulled a five-dollar bill from my jeans in the laundry? God, she was awful, wasn't she?"

Uncle Ray responded with a little chuckle, humoring the absurdity. "She sure was! Remember when she came home from the store with a broken tail-light on the car, and she told Dad I must have run into it with my bike? I told him it never happened, but she insisted I was lying. Dad believed her that time, too."

"Dad always believed her. That was the worst part," Betsy said.

"No, the worst part was working all summer to pay off fixing it."

"Dad was so mad at you."

My mother had, of course, heard all these stories many times before but felt the need to validate their existence once again by adding, "What was wrong with her?"

"Remember, Ray? Remember the time Dad found a pack of Nancy's cigarettes in Lil's dresser?" Betsy talked faster now that she had their full attention. "He thought she had been smoking. Lil was only seven years old for God's sake. I still remember the smirk on Nancy's face when he screamed at Lil. Nancy loved every minute of it."

"She was good, I'll give her that," Ray added. "She really had him fooled."

The stories skipped along and, with them, any happiness, past or present, was quickly engulfed by the anger and frustration of an earlier time as if all their pleasant interactions were no match for the roots that held them down.

Is this true for everyone?

I wish I knew, for within these memories and stories grew the subtle, unspoken understanding that happiness and laughter were not tolerated without acknowledging the pain and sacrifices that came before us.

CHAPTER 15: UPROOTED

The strongest of trees are still at the mercy of the passing storms,
and the weakness of the ground in which they grow.

I have driven these roads many times before, coming and going from various appointments, errands, and trips. My children most often are with me, but today I feel a comfort for their presence and almost wish it could go on forever, for this short journey is one that our destinations end together, safely in our home. As a mother, this is my greatest wish that in the end home is with family and family is always their home. As I continue down this trail of memories I find my mother, Ruth, for she has also tried to hold everyone together, even in the most difficult of circumstances. Now, with a bright light being shown on the past, I find her childhood stories to be a beacon of truth to the shaky ground we all were raised on.

 Ruth

My mother, Ruth, is a kind woman, quiet, easy-going, and soft-spoken. I have always considered us close, so this situation, this family problem, has been a tough division. She has always been honest with me when my questions about family were tough, though I believe there was little way around the truth when it was laid out for me every day.

Her strength always showed through, as she is the center of the family. She has always been the one others turned to, yet in some ways the one most felt they needed to control. She always accepted her role within the family, taking on the attitudes and problems many depended on her to fix. She stuck with her husband through many years of neglect and alcoholism, and she still managed to raise the two families she was mothering, her brothers and sisters and us, her own children. My mother has seen much in her lifetime. It was no wonder the gray streaks have completely taken over.

She cared for her siblings at the young age of thirteen, sending her straight from child to adult sooner than anyone intended. Who could have blamed her for seeking comfort in the arms of a man who was old enough to take care of her? And now this family mess, I believe, has been harder on her than she will ever admit, for she is not the one who seeks comfort or asks for help, but the one who accepts the needs of others as her own burden.

I was a sensitive and curious child, and my mother's stories of being a young girl thrust into a life she never imagined weighed on me with heavy emotion. I feel for the person she is, and the life that unfolded for her as the one person, even to this day, everyone counts on. One afternoon she shared a mixture of laughter and fear as she recalled specific events that identified the breakdown of her childhood.

It was shortly after that day of Aunt Betsy and Uncle Ray visiting that she opened up about the years that followed her father leaving. She was only thirteen years old when her life was turned upside down as her parents, Gigi and Grampa Charles, separated and Nancy suddenly became family. The night that her parents fought was just the beginning of a new way for Ruth to live and an abrupt ending to her childhood in many ways.

Being the oldest girl, she was left to care for the younger children and had to help out around the house, more often than not. It was a lot of responsibility for a shy teenager. I could hear it in her voice that she was still questioning if she had done a good enough job. "I only wanted everything to be normal," she said, and her words stick with me to this day as she spoke of those trying years.

A year had passed since her father, my grandfather, had left the family. Her mother, my Gigi, had finally found some relief from the tears that haunted her. For Ruth the days were long, rolling into one another with the texture and consistency of thick fog, endless and uncontrollable. Ruth struggled to stay awake in school and dreaded the bell that signaled it was time to go home, for there, her real life continued, never seeming to change, not even with the fallen night skies, rising stars, or a full night's sleep. Morning would come with an endless loop of watchful pain and inner disdain for her surroundings. She was filled with emotions that she never allowed herself to acknowledge, never mind feel. Memories of an easier time, and visions for her teenage years, were ripped from the book of life that had been written for her. Those pages were torn out and burned before her to an unrecognizable crisp. Tears put out the flames and yet the ugly charcoaled scraps of what were supposed to be laid thin and flaky, blowing away slowly with every whisper of questioning. Soon all that would be left would be the darkened ash of past dreams, staring up at the sky unable to move or grow.

Spring had come with the muck that stuck to her soles with every step she took, and whispers of prayers faded to the sound of confusion, the echoing of children in the halls, and the dinginess of winter's debris. Life had become a chore that lay over her like a wet blanket, torn, heavy, and useless for its original purpose. But she carried it around, held it in, and picked herself up every day, for her struggles were from the wounds of all whom she loved and cared about. At almost fourteen, she felt her efforts weren't enough, but she also feared for the results of her absence. And with all that was true in her life, it was all to be kept quiet for she knew her job was to protect, not letting a soul know of her real-life struggles. Drawn inward, her quietness made her invisible to ensure others, in authority or judgment, would not intrude on her family or ask questions.

Teddy, her older brother by three years, was a stocky young boy with dark brown hair and bright blue eyes. His anger masked his sadness while a stiff jaw, absent smile, and narrowing eyes hid his handsome innocence. His outward appearance was tough and each harsh step was a pounding force. Teddy was hard to contain. He hardly sat still. Most days he could be seen with a stick in hand dragging it along a bordering picket fence or using it to swat a passing tree. A pocketful of rocks bulged out his jeans, ready to be fired at the tin cans lined up on their stone wall or at an unsuspecting squirrel that crossed his path. He was a boy of few words, but he made his presence known. Ruth described him as difficult since their father had left, but she also knew the real side of him that was torn up by their family events.

 Charles and Nancy Visit

Teddy had grown to hate their stepmother, Nancy. As Charles tried to keep a stern hand over his children, Teddy willingly defied him every chance he got. Charles rejected any responsibility for the mess and anguish his actions had caused the family, holding little tolerance for any outward displays from his children. Anxieties ran high for everyone at any sign of Charles and Nancy's appearances. Surprise visits were the norm, and this day was no different.

The sun set quickly that Friday evening as the older kids in the neighborhood finished one last game of stickball in the street. Ruth could hear the rumblings of play from inside where she set the table. She stepped out to the front door for only a moment to check on the younger children playing quietly in the yard and called the others in for supper. Her father's red pickup truck was sitting at the corner, hovering over the scene in his calculating way. An instant knot grabbed Ruth's stomach as she called Betsy over to keep an eye on Ray and Lil. Ruth rushed inside to warn her mother. Her mother, Ginny, was putting on her uniform for her Friday night shift at the diner.

Ginny took a deep breath while fumbling with her earring. Her shaky hands were apparent as her daughter Ruth stood at the door, "Did you hear me? Dad and Nancy are here. What should I do?"

"Nothing, dear. Go say hi to your father and then get the little ones cleaned up for supper. Your Auntie El will be here any minute."

"But Mom?"

"Just do it, Ruthie. I will deal with your father." Her voice shook and her eyes glossed over as she stared in the mirror. She knew he was trying to rattle her and make her late for work. She lifted her head, took a deep breath, smoothed out her uniform, checked her hair one more time, and headed out for the expected confrontation Charles had in store for her. Knowing Ruth had spotted him, Charles pulled into the driveway quickly with a sharp turn and abrupt stop, not wanting to give Ginny any time to prepare for his arrival.

The game had broken up and there was no sign of Teddy or Eddy in the crowds walking back to their homes. Lil and Ray ran to him immediately as he exited the truck. Nancy stayed put in the passenger seat emotionless, looking straight ahead. She flicked ashes from her cigarette out the opened window.

Charles picked up Lil and set her on his hip. He ruffled Ray's hair, "How was school today, kiddo?"

"Good, Daddy. When are you coming home?"

"I don't know, honey. You go play with your sister. I need to talk to your mother for a minute."

Charles gently placed Lil down next to the dolls and trucks and the two got back to their play. He entered the house in the opposite demeanor, slamming the screen door behind him. Betsy and Ruth sat quietly on the sofa trying to stay out of the way, hoping their Aunt Eleanor would soon show.

"Hi, girls, where are your brothers?"

Ruth and Betsy refused to answer him. Teddy had been difficult lately, but now that Eddie had joined in on the defiance, Charles found himself angrier than ever. Ginny entered the living room with little acknowledgement for his presence as he scanned her from head-to-toe. She was attractive and he felt a twinge for what he was missing. "Where are the boys, Ginny? Can't you keep track of your own kids? What's wrong with you? You're an idiot if you can't control them."

"Oh, they're probably over at Mom and Ellie's house, Charles. Stop making such a big deal about it."

Charles stood in the doorway to the kitchen refusing to move as Ginny tried to pass by him. She squeezed through with some effort, not allowing him to intimidate her. His stare at her was broken by Betsy's voice.

"They're hiding from you, Dad."

Ruth elbowed her deep in the arm.

"Ow! That hurt."

Charles turned to her with tension building deep in his face.

Ginny brought his attention back to her. "They just want their father, Charles."

"Well, maybe that's what they need, Ginny. Maybe they need to live with Nancy and me. They need some discipline, and if you can't provide that, then we will."

Ginny's silence filled Charles with satisfaction, allowing him to relax for only a moment. Through a cracked voice, Ginny spoke up. "You need to leave, Charles."

"I will take these kids, Ginny. Don't push me. What kind of a mother doesn't know where her kids are? And look at this place. It's a pig sty." He grabbed a pile of papers that were on the chair next to him and threw them all over the floor.

"How about you girls? You want to live with your dad, don't you?"

Betsy couldn't help but react. "I'm not living with that witch out there. We don't have to live with them, do we, Mom?"

"Quiet, Betsy," Ruth's elbow jerked sideways again.

"What? I want to know."

"Quiet," Ruth whispered.

Charles walked over to stand over Betsy and Ruth, bigger than life, ready to engage in any argument that came, even if it was with his daughters. "Oh, your mother is just a slob. She isn't fit to be a mother."

"Don't talk about her like that! And besides, what are you doing here, anyway? You don't live here anymore, remember?"

"Betsy, Stop!" Ruth tried to cover her mouth with her hand, but Betsy pulled away, removing herself from the couch by way of climbing over the arm.

"This is still my house, young lady. I can come here whenever I want to, and don't you forget it." He turned to Ginny standing behind him.

Betsy stood with one hand on her hip and the other pointing out at Nancy still sitting in his truck, "Well SHE is not welcome here. You should just leave."

"Betsy, stop it," Ginny demanded, scolding her.

"Why do you side with him? He is so mean. He doesn't love us anymore."

"Betsy, go to your room," Ginny demanded.

Betsy stomped her foot and began to cry.

"Leave now, Charles, before…"

"Before what, Ginny?" A sense of victory came over Charles' voice as he stepped toward her. Before Ginny could answer, a bloodcurdling scream came from outside, cutting through the room. "Stop it! Stop it, you brats!"

"You're denting the truck."

A rush out the door revealed Lil and Ray still playing in the yard, and Nancy standing outside the truck with her head down, digging something out of her hair. Ducking, she screamed, "Stop, stop!"

Her perfectly coifed hair-do was a hair-sprayed knot with ends sticking up in all directions. Ruth and Betsy tried not to laugh.

"Charles! Charles! Make them stop!" Nancy pleaded.

The sound of rocks hitting the roof, windshield, and hood of the truck became apparent as Teddy and Eddie's voices came from a tree above the driveway. "Take that, you bitch!"

"You boys get out of that tree right now!" Charles yelled while running over to help Nancy as she began to cry.

"You see, Lizzi?" I remember my mother's smile, as she continued the story, "After the boys started pelting the truck with stones, Nancy stepped out to scold them and they started pegging her with them too. The stones got stuck in her hair."

"Nancy picked at her head rapidly with both hands. One hand still held her cigarette between two fingers. With that hand, she tried to pluck the stones out with her thumb and ring finger. The ashes fell into her well-treated hair, igniting a smoldering fire beneath her bouffant. She began to scream and dance around, bobbing her neck up and down like a chicken while beating herself relentlessly in the head to put it out."

My mother began to giggle, as she seemed to remember ever-vivid detail.

"My father started smacking her in the head, too. Smoke puffed out in small clouds around her. Her tears began melting her face. Streaks of makeup smudged her cheeks while one eyelash hung limply like a spider. I had never seen my father so mad before. Teddy and Eddy knew they couldn't come down. They knew if they did there was going to be hell to pay. Betsy and I were laughing uncontrollably so my mother sent us inside. It was the first time we had laughed in weeks and it felt so good we couldn't stop. I could tell your Gigi was on the edge of laughing herself as she scooted us inside with Lil and Ray saying, "Stop that, it's not funny. Your brothers are in big trouble. Take Ray and Lil upstairs." We got to our room and rolled on the beds in uncontrollable laughter. The image of Nancy dancing around, screaming with an eyelash gluing one eye shut, her hair sticking out, smoke billowing from her perfect do, black dripping down her face, and my father smacking her in the head made tears roll down our faces."

With that description, we both started to laugh—her for the memory, me for seeing my mother laughing that way.

Between breaths of laughter, I had to ask. "Whatever happened to Uncle Teddy and Eddy? Did they get in trouble?"

"Not really. Auntie El showed up and Nancy was so mortified that my father took her home. It was quite a while before he came back to the house, and even after that, they never parked in the driveway again. Only on the street where there were no trees."

"Uncle Teddy and Eddy stayed in that tree until it got dark. They were afraid our father would come back. They finally got cold and hungry and came inside. Secretly, I think Auntie El rewarded them with cookies that night."

"No one ever talked about it again, but every time I saw my father's truck with those little dents in the hood, I couldn't help but smile."

It was a short-lived laughter as the story went on. The smile subsided on her face, and I, too, could not ever look at Grampa Charles the same again.

"Unfortunately, the next time I saw my father it was anything but funny. A deeper shift was about to take place for us and I realize now there was nothing we could do to stop it. My father had his own demons to fight and wasn't going to leave us alone. I can remember it all like it was yesterday. A night that I wish had never happened."

 Grampa Charles and Uncle Teddy

Young Ruth moved about the kitchen clearing dishes from the table and placing them in the sink. She yelled for Betsy. "It's your turn to do dishes tonight, Betsy!"

"I'm doing my homework."

"Well I have homework, too, and Mom won't be home until late tonight."

"Not my problem," Betsy said with a slam of the bedroom door.

Ruth knew right then it wasn't worth the fight. It was easier to do them herself. Auntie El would be checking in on them later, but for now, Ruth needed to keep the peace.

Suddenly, the front door flew open with a startling crash. Ruth rushed to the living room. There stood her father, Charles, riffling through a pile of mail. "Dad? What are you doing?"

"Where is your mother?"

"She's not here."

"She's not at the diner either!" He continued in a rage from one surface to the other, digging through piles of papers and letters and throwing them to the floor.

"What are you looking for?"

"Where is she? Who is she with?"

"What do you mean?" Ruth pulled the curtain back from the front window to see Nancy and the glow of her cigarette within the silhouette of the truck. "What are you doing here? I think you should leave."

"Where is your mother?" he screamed, while heading down the hall to Ginny's bedroom.

Ruth followed him with a panicked feeling. "She is out with her friend Marilyn. Why? What do you care anyway?"

Ruth turned to see Betsy, Ray, and Lil on the stairs listening to everything. Eddy and Teddy stood just outside their bedroom door staring down at her. "Go back to your rooms," Ruth whispered sternly.

Charles continued his rant. "Is she on a date? Is that where she is? Don't lie to me Ruthie. You don't want to do that."

Ruth was visibly shaken watching her father toss her mother's bedroom and pulling out drawers, throwing her clothes all over the room.

"What are you doing? I told you where she is! Leave, please, just leave us alone." Ruth begged but he didn't hear her—or stop. Trying to stop him, she grabbed at his arm as he moved quickly around the room. He reacted by harshly pushing her aside. Ruth landed on the bed with her father pointing his finger in her face. He screamed, "Stay out of my way. You'll say anything to protect her. Just remember, this is my house and no other man would ever be allowed here. You hear me?"

Charles reached down to grab Ruth's arm when Lil, now standing just outside the bedroom, started to cry. Charles pulled back just enough for Ruth to get by him. She scooted Lil up the stairs with Ray, Betsy, and Eddy. She left them all in the girls' room and told them to stay there until she came and got them. Ruth crossed the hall to look for Teddy, but the boys' room was empty.

"Dammit, Teddy. This is a hell of a time to take off," she whispered to herself.

Silence took over the downstairs and she thought for a moment that her father had finally left. Out of breath and scared to look at the mess, Ruth rushed to her mother's room, but Teddy was already there, blocking the doorway. Ruth froze in place as Teddy held his baseball bat behind his back.

"Leave now!" Teddy screamed. "And don't come back."

"Oh, look who's Mr. Tough Guy now. Why don't you just run away like you usually do? Or hide in a tree?" Charles was mean and threatening as he stepped closer to Teddy. "You have some rocks you want to throw at me, little boy?"

Teddy didn't budge. He just slid the bat to one side of him, letting his father know he had it. It dangled there in a swinging motion longer than Ruth could stand as her heart jumped into her throat and tears filled her eyes.

She gulped back the fear. "Teddy, why don't you go to Auntie El's house and cool down?"

"No!" Teddy snapped back, as one tear finally rolled down Ruth's cheek. "If he wants to leave us, then he should just leave us alone. Stop bringing that bitch around and stop harassing our mother."

Ruth only heard the anger in Teddy's voice and saw the questioning in her father's face from where she stood. Teddy's grip tightened on the bat handle, turning his knuckles white as Charles looked him up and down.

Charles finally broke the silence, "Fine, but you tell your mother I am not going to be paying her a dime if she is going to be whoring around town."

He slowly walked toward them. Teddy refused to step out of his way. Charles jerked forward as he passed by him, making Teddy flinch. A mean smirk came over Charles' face. "I didn't think so," he mumbled while passing by Ruth. Teddy stood, tense with his teeth clenched, until he heard the front door slam shut.

"It was tough, Lizzi. I don't know what came over my father, he was crazed. I was so scared. Teddy and I stood in silence as we heard the truck pull away, and without a word or a look my way, Teddy turned and walked up the stairs to his room. We never talked about it again. There was something missing from him after that. I never saw him as a playful young boy again. Reality hit us hard that evening. Something words can't explain. I calmed down the younger ones and put them to bed. I straightened up my mother's room the best I could and hoped she wouldn't be too upset. I was so afraid he'd come back, so afraid he was going to hurt us after that. I had never been afraid of someone before. My father changed everything for me, I cried for hours."

"How horrible, Mom. What did Gigi say?"

"She only knew that he came by to cause trouble as usual, so she didn't think much about it. We never discussed the details and I never told her about your Uncle Teddy. It was just so strange. I had a hard time making sense of it myself and didn't see the need to upset her. Besides the next time I saw my father, he acted like it never happened, like it was all a dream. But everything was different after that night. We were not the same family anymore. We felt scattered as individuals, growing our own ways with only the idea of family to cling to. It wasn't until your father and I were together that I felt really loved and safe with anyone again."

My mother's gaze was of a damaged young soul that day, one I had never seen before, but it fit, somehow, like a piece of the puzzle that put a face on the pain, giving me the imagery necessary to see how my family has tried to overcompensate for the loss of their childhood.

As this drive home continues, and the stories and memories flood my mind, Auntie El's words soothe me. "Care for them and they will come back." I hear Gigi coaxing me to fix this, fulfilling her wish to see us whole again.

I am too easily carried back to that place where they lived, breathed, and suffered as confused children. I know their lives were uprooted, ripped from the foundation, left raw and abandoned to the elements that life had in store. To this day a hole remains in the heart of our family waiting for us all to fall in.

CHAPTER 16:
GROUND CHANGER

*The ground shimmers and shifts beneath us, vibrating memories
up from the past. Creating the hills and valleys of today.*

All journeys start from somewhere. Where may not be of any meaning to some, but to others to know where they come from is essential to finding their destination.

As roads of yesterday intertwine with and lead to roads of today, it is difficult to discern or recognize all our true beginnings. Roots twist and turn reaching far down for stability and nutrients, thinning as they go. From where I stand today, views of my horizons or previously traveled roads also seem to narrow to thinner paths. My true destinations are yet to be seen, *but where did my path truly begin? Is it from my memories, the memories and experiences of those who raised me, or is the ground we build our futures on just a perception of what is told to us?* For me today, I can only go back as far and clearly as I can remember. I see my future as my own, starting with the path of today, and that the past that was told to be mine was truly their path at the time. As my life was born of theirs, I always accepted the responsibility of the ground before me. Today I will remember and honor the stories knowing my connection to them while releasing it all to the past. For the critical choices that were made then were not intended to cause the suffering that is occurring now.

The closer I get to home, the further back my mind goes, narrowing my actual experiences but still solidifying the distance we have all traveled. I know little of the time before my own, a time that even Aunt Lil was too young to know completely, but old enough to feel the consequences. Our history, which is still too shaky to even question for many, forked a very limited path to today.

These are the times that still hold the hollowness for me for they have never been discussed in detail, only factually told in bits and pieces. Ingrained intuitively, I imagine a scene here and there, but not enough to jump into the turmoil that shifted our foundation, that created mine. These places are still filled with hesitation. I hesitate to feel the truth, to know the truth in terms of fact is one thing, but to truly feel it is certainly a ground changer.

I find the emotions are the glue that hold it all together, connecting the moments and making them real. I reach back with my thinning knowledge to gather the moments which are full of emotion, ones that bonded and dismembered this family.

I have run for years from the truth of it all, never knowing if I could truly know. Like running through the woods, running frantically from something I know not of, with a voice from overhead saying, *Don't look back. Just run. Don't look back.* I ran and ran believing that voice, that inner voice that came from so many that I care for, the ones who said it was too painful to do so, until looking back is all there is left. Now I realize to face what is behind me is the only way to really move forward without fear of it catching up to me. For better or worse, I need to see it for what it was, for what it is, and that's all I can do.

Don't run anymore, don't run, just stop! is what I hear now. *It is not yours to own, to live through its filter any longer. Let it stand beside you, be a part of you, but it no longer holds the power it did in the past.*

So, in the best light possible, I piece together the solidness of the rocky terrain behind me, knowing that the truth stands on its own, gathering the future through the vibrations of its aftershocks to someday fade out and settle to a landscape still of its history. As I turn around to ask it, *What do you want?* It replies to say, *Nothing, I just am. I am not for you to feel or to know intimately, only to be your view from where you are, or from where you are going, I am from which you came, not good or bad, just a piece of the ground once traveled and created—if you wish to look.*

This is my truth, my view, my knowledge that comes to me in this ending daylight of going home, to be given the breath of today.

My eyes tear and fog my sight as the sun goes down around me. The car tires rhythmically tap the smooth pavement running beneath us, and the faint shear outline of the moon follows us home. This late afternoon, early evening light hits me as my day is ending and my thoughts glide to memories I cannot control as the words of my mother echo from a distant uneasy place.

"I loved your father, you know." She would say in a defensive way as if I had asked, usually during some random event like washing dishes together or to break the overwhelming silence between us on drives to Gigi's. Many times, she proclaimed her love for him. The topic would stem from some random conversation of the confusion or dysfunction within the family. She was apologizing while clarifying the details of our existence.

I never meant to make her feel insecure about it, and I often felt my presence was enough to do so. Any questions were more a normal curiosity about how abnormal our situation was. The distance between us would intensify, initiating the undertow of family issues. This dragged my mind to more questions, which brought up the family issues.

The dishes clanged, the water sloshed, and the spigot ran over the glasses or the tires crunched over the stone drive, dipping into potholes without hesitation. Either way, my mother never looked my way during these moments of confession. I know she loved him very much, and him her for that matter, for them to be together as long as they were, for them to endure the perception of their relationship and accept the situation as it was.

I would dry each dish as she washed and handed them to me and then wait patiently for her to finish the next glass. One that had been thoroughly rinsed yet was lost in her thought being tumbled over and over through the running water. As if her extra efforts of rinsing could wash away any quilt or shame that was left and send whatever pain that still lingered down the drain with the passing water.

Sometimes, I would watch the trees flash by the moving car window wishing I could stay with them deep in the forest, touch them, listen to them, instead, one hand stayed on the car door handle resisting the consequence of hitting the pavement and rolling to a less complicated place. She once told me he offered to run away with her, live somewhere where no one would know, where they could raise us kids without the confusion. My mother proclaimed this was not an option.

The conversation, that time, was brought on by another family squabble or mishap amongst my aunts and uncles that left her distant and in thought for days. This was just the common background of static that ran through the family and rose to a deafening screech too often to ever get any peace, all stemming back to the relationships that made up our family. These shadows that blurred our family lines are kept in their comfortable place of the past, yet I feel to shine a light on what I know, dragging it to the forefront may lighten its existence, and fade the emotions of its memory.

And for my Gigi, I always saw her as kind, gentle, with an innocence that I could see in her face but could never explain. A trusting softness layered beneath wounded insecurities seemed to move her through the family and disconnect her from her true feelings. As her granddaughter, I watched her with a sympathetic eye and a collective understanding for her matriarchic position, as she was left to feel the burdens and the pain of a love that changed her family. So, with a deep compassion I will fill my hollow space with the emotions of that time. I don't know if I could ever completely know the pain or emotions that hold this story, this family together and apart, but this is the string of unchangeable events that got us here.

 Gigi and Rusty

It was late 1950s. Money was limited and the small house was all they had holding them together. Ginny's separation and struggles with Charles had claimed a part of her, a part of her soul that left an emptiness she couldn't fill with items of this world, no matter how hard she tried. The fragmented cluster, which they called family, was stuck together through their emotional loyalty. Auntie El was at the helm trying to steer all of them through the murky waters.

The truth was the night that my grandfather had barged into their house, the night everything changed for my mother and Uncle Teddy, my Gigi was dating someone, someone who would change the foundation of their future, like it or not.

Russell Stern, better known as Rusty to his friends, was a man a few years shy of Ginny, and he gave her an emotional comfort she longed to have. He was a worldly man, a navy man, a drinking man, a married man with all the confidence that Ginny lacked. He carried himself with an air of arrogance that was glazed over by his deep hazel eyes and charming smile. All of this was anchored to his own deep-seated pain as he moved through life without purpose or concern. He was about to leave a deep wake within this family that still washes over us today.

Rusty was not a bad man as I saw it, only a man with an inner sadness that he tried to mask, and in his efforts, proceeded to disperse his self-destruction like the cologne of alcohol that too often infiltrated his being. This sadness grew from his own damaged foundation that only a troubled boy could hold onto. Sent to an orphanage by his own mother at a young age, he was left to become a man on his own. This piece of neglect burrowed deep into the corners of who he was, hiding away from everyone that knew him. Eventually, those hidden corners shaped the man he became and the people he touched.

Meeting Ginny was a comforting reprieve from himself and he was drawn to her simplistic style and meekness. The merging of her naïve nature with his swaggering persuasiveness was smooth and effortless. They were a coming together of passing ships: her aching in silence over Charles' betrayal, and him selfishly committed otherwise. Soon their colliding would change the course of both their destinations. He never meant to stay or to get attached to this family, never mind settle down.

Rusty came and went for two years, in and out of their lives like the submarines that brought him there. It was early 1960s, and Ginny, a divorced mother of six, found herself pregnant and longing for the stability that she felt only he could bring her. He was deeply self-centered, never feeling an obligation to another. One more hitch in the road along an already rocky life, he welcomed the distance that the sea and deployment brought him. Ginny so hoped the baby they shared would give him a new sense of life, but that was something neither time, nor a child, was about to change.

Teddy, a young man of nineteen, drove the quiet, small-town roads in the family station wagon to pick up his mother from the hospital, left to be the man she depended on once again. As Ginny held her new baby girl in her arms, Rusty was absent, deployed once again. Teddy, unable to make sense of his feelings for the circumstance before him, could not find it within himself to either accept or welcome the child that was complicating his life further. Like one more wedge between the life he once knew, and the outside world that neither welcomed him nor rejected him, he stood in the balance of a life resistant to normalcy. His love for his mother and dislike for her choices fought within him and stirred up resentment that his young mind could only internalize.

Ginny longed for more. She held strong for what might come to be, settling for her unfulfilled personal relationships, she never allowed anything to change her love for her children. However, soon the reality of a child out of wedlock for a divorcee would play a heavy burden on her children as rumors and opinions flew and townspeople talked. Charles and Nancy jumped on the bandwagon to degrade her as a mother and a woman. Auntie El tried her best to pick up the pieces, but there was little she could do to ease the dramatics as the whole family seemed to be capsizing right before her eyes.

Teddy, already fitted with a rugged exterior and an edge from the life that had come his way, continued to watch the dissolution of his family, the exhibitions of his father's infidelity, the cruelty of his stepmother, and the mocking of his mother and younger sibling, none of which he could control and none of which settled lightly in his personality. He, today in the throes of being cut off from his own grandchildren, clearly rode that angst straight into his adult life.

When Rusty first came into their lives, most of the children welcomed a man, a father figure, into the house, but Teddy was pushed aside. He was left as neither the little boy in need of care, nor as the man he felt he had been forced to become. Where did this leave a boy, a young man on the cliff of adulthood, as he was left to watch the demeaning of the mother he loved and feel the shame of what was to come?

Permanently estranged from his own family, Rusty welcomed the feeling of home whenever it suited him. He held his responsibility to Ginny, providing for their child and staying in their lives whenever he could, but the deep attachment that Ginny once longed for had finally hidden itself within the busy times of trying to make ends meet once again. Rusty's distance from his true self could not be bridged by Ginny's affections or the child that carried his name. Ginny accepted what little he could give, with only his presence and financial support to comfort her. His emotional distance greatened, and within a short two years, their relationship had become one of convenience and friendship. He was physically in her life with no intimacy, she had their beautiful little girl and the judgment of the times gave her lighthearted personality little concern. Her other children at their young ages felt the brunt of society. How cruel children and others could be. Little did Ginny know that the resentment her own children held was transforming all their relationships, especially toward their own half-sister, for they could not bring themselves to feel ill-will toward their own mother, and the man who had injected his way into the family dynamics was not going away, but his staying would be for a reason no one could have predicted, imagined, or in some cases considered acceptable.

Rusty came and went with the tides. His obligation to their daughter, now two, was met as he saw it, and his wife was a distant connection on paper alone. There was still a lonely insecure superiority that he carried through his days, as he was part of the family with no specific responsibility other than his sporadic presence. His drinking and arrogance, with a tendency for the complicated, soon found him woven deeper into this family than he had ever dreamed.

Ruth, a young eighteen, cared for her two-year-old half-sister. She was innocent in the ways of the world, but mature in her nurturing. She had raised her brothers and sisters for the last five years of her young life. Her days were spent at school, her evenings cooking and cleaning. Rusty often knew the pain she felt, the neglect that lingered, and he connected it to the part of him he had buried, but had never forgotten. Many nights she cared for him, always accepting him, never judging him. This grew feelings of warmth that were stronger than his will or logic could fight. She had grown before his eyes to a beautiful young woman.

He saw her differently than anyone had before. Nearly twenty years her senior with his strong presence, he had a neediness that Ruth couldn't decipher. She saw a vulnerable side harnessed by his insecurity that seemed to fade in the light of her eyes.

She only knew that she felt alive and noticed when he was around, and the need to feel attractive in the narrow surroundings that were her life became her focus. Easy prey for his ego some said. A shameful mistake many agreed, but still the same, to this day she says she loved him, and my father her.

Eleanor was deeply dispirited over their relationship, feeling she had failed her sister and the family as the courts intervened. With a dying mother and the constant pull of her heart, she did her best to pick up the pieces as they fell. My parents' relationship stemmed into an exploration of Ginny's competency, and the children's welfare, all coming apart at the hands of Charles and Nancy. Any questionable circumstances soon turned even more complicated with my mother's pregnancy at the age of eighteen.

Charles and Nancy rushed to the courts, for Ruth was now legally an adult, but they found their revenge and took Betsy, Ray, and Lil from Ginny as quickly as snide remarks swirled around their small town. The three children were ordered to live with Charles and Nancy, immediately, and soon found themselves caught up in the windstorm of their sister's relationship. Ginny responded indifferently about the affair, surrendering to her daughter's happiness. Judged by many, she floundered only in her own guilt of what was. I asked her one day, how she felt about them being together, and her only response to me, as her eyes fell away from mine was, "I wanted my daughter to be happy."

I knew then, even at my young age, that it pained her, but her love for her daughter overrode any other instinct. Some saw it as her weakness, this lack of conviction to protest her young daughter's lover. Some have questions how it could have happened in the first place. Others can only remember the pain that saturated the whole family. Yet, I cannot vote, for without these events, I would not be here. For Rusty, my father, a man I never knew entirely, a man that stayed married to my mother for over fifteen years, a man that is also my sister Jeanne's father, did what he did, loved whom he loved, and suffered in his own life in ways others may never know or want to admit.

I believe, or rather choose to believe, that he did love my mother, that she was the match to his insecurity, regardless of his age, the match to his immaturity, regardless of hers. She was a savior, a mother figure of nurture and caring that he was in need of. And for Ruth, maybe he was a father figure, at least a caring person. Together they tried to make it work. Together they got through the next fifteen years only to realize that inner demons stay when life is dragged along, time changes little when perceptions are held and difficult beginnings are your foundation.

This is my story, my family. And for Jeanne, my half-sister, my mother's half-sister, Gigi's and my father's daughter was a savior for me, while for others she is a target for their pain. Still my mother raised her as her own, never treating her differently, never making it an issue. Neither did Gigi. It was others who held onto the pain, creating a permanent shadow that remains their dark comfortable place, a hole unable to heal.

More than the stories were the underlying tensions that seeped up with every interaction. The past seemed to plague my family, their presence and their beings. I felt every dripping ounce of it, from moments of silence that hung in the air just waiting for a chance to explode with anger and defensiveness to moments of detached laughter that were rooted to who we were and where we came from. All of this gathered in my foundation, paving the road to where I am today. Now I am motivated to rebuild my surroundings, creating new views for the future, for my children and myself.

Yet here it still lies, affecting all that I have grown to be. The truth is I can only change what is before me. I will put my best foot forward into the light, allowing my past to be the road that got me here, not the path I need to follow. I will turn to this family hole and face it before anyone else falls in.

I can create a strong presence for my children, leaving the darkness in the past, hoping that the home I head to is a history that snugs deep down into the foothills of calm for them, filling their foundation with security, memories, and a place from where their roads will branch, because my roots are theirs, and I wish for it all to be surfaced, named, and placed where it belongs so it cannot sneak up on them, chase them down, or disrupt the lives they will build.

I must begin by healing myself.

CHAPTER 17:
LEANING TOWARD THE LIGHT

As we lean in toward the light, we bathe in possibilities for the future.

I turn directly into the sun's glare. These windy roads are familiar with many stone walls and patches of tree. I know home is near when the air gets salty again. Deeper thoughts are fading to the roads behind me and my past has brought me to where I am today. Everything settles in the glow of the twilight as my family history reminds me of the distance we all have traveled, only to find ourselves separate from one another.

I feel the scattering of the family like a puzzle that has been tossed into the air, landing sporadically, waiting to be reassembled again. Maybe we are all scattered pieces of a bigger picture waiting to be placed correctly, positioned just so, so that our edges meet up with one another's once again. Today, the pieces that fall around me add up to my childhood and the life I knew. I can only follow the light home and hope by leaning into my memories I will be guided on where to turn next.

The family struggled through with the support of Auntie El and each other. In their world of abandonment and dysfunction, my mother continued to help raise her sibling the best she could—as a young mother and wife herself. Grampa Charles and Nancy continued to make trouble for them, holding on tight to the family they destroyed. Through manipulations and control, Grampa Charles created a stagnant situation for the children to grow in. While his distance allowed them to get lost in their feelings, his anger was swift and calculating, keeping everyone on edge, and lost they were, just trying to lean into any warmth that came their way.

My father played a critical role in their fracturing, yet at times provided the stability needed. He played a lover's role, a father's role, and ironically a saving role as he fought through the courts to help Gigi get the younger children back home. With his age and financial support, as well as a word of apology and responsibility for his contribution to the family's upheaval, the courts were reassured enough to return the children home. Although this did very little for his character redemption, he did the best he could.

Am I the reminder of these painful roots? Is it my father's part in our history that keeps me separate in their eyes? He did create turmoil, so are they using him against me as their father used him against them? Where does it end? Is this the thorn that lies embedded in the side of the family tree? The one that carries the bitterness and pain into the present?

How dare I make a stand of my own thoughts? They have allowed me my presence, for years, without blame, so it seemed, but now as I lean in toward my own life do I remind them of the past?

There was good. I know there was. *Can't they see that? Or is it easier to keep the pain alive?* My relationships with them, our friendships, and who I have been to them...*is that not worth something? Am I not worth seeing as something good coming from the whole situation?*

Is this truth? Can't it be that beauty can grow in the soils of pain? Why can't they see that to reap the rewards of pain, we must let it go and welcome what has come from it?

As all the branches of a tree grow differently, uniquely with their own characters to survive, they grow outwardly away from one another. This *is* what we all are: tree branches growing toward the light, trying to survive with nothing but family and nature to guide us. By way of corners, or twisting and bending, we have all found our way. This is what makes a family, a tree, beautiful, keeping it full and balanced. It is just too bad that no matter how tall, how beautiful, or how unique each branch or tree is, it is still connected and dependent on the root system to nourish it and keep it healthy. Every member of my family is a branch of our tree yearning for the sun while reaching up from the depths of their damaged roots for support.

We cannot change our connection or our memories before we branch off. I am just hoping the strength and beauty of the growth above the ground can overcome the sadness and frustrations that affected it while it was growing, because these roots are not only theirs, they are mine. My wish for them, this tree, this family, is for the sun to shine as we lean in, ever so slightly.

All these memories have transported me home. Each memory being a second in a lifetime, each memory a rooted seed, growing within me, feeding the person I have become. Even with the known sadness, I like to remember the best of times when we were younger. Always having someone to turn to and looking forward to weekends at Gigi's. There are days I wish I could pluck out of the past and experience all over again.

I believe our strengths did come from each other, having each other, knowing each other, and being with each other. These are the bonds I wish my children knew of. It is sad that over the years, it became claustrophobic and restricting to be a family, as we were unable to grow side by side. As stunted as we may be, as a family, we continued to reach for our own light, and my heart knows it came from the original intention of happiness and comfort.

As I pull into my driveway, the emotions fade away like the dust kicked up behind me. The car halts and I pause with a sigh. Howls and barks serenade our return proving to be the welcome I need to remind me that I have branched out fully to a life of my own.

CHAPTER 18:
SWING AND SWAY

From sunlight to moon glare, life is a balance of contrasts, creating patterns of growth.

I sit, once again, on my porch swing, rocking back and forth, enjoying this calm evening. I gaze at the moon shadows as they cast off the trees, showing that even the darkness has layers and depths beyond the obvious. Shy and subtle, they are the faint distinctions, hidden amongst the landscape, creating the mood of the night.

The trees stand steady with no breeze to entice them, and I feel their relief of the sun gone by. I recognize a day of discoveries, memories, and emotional heights, and I, too, am relishing this moment of rest. These moments of recovery are the ones that allow us to heal and grow. Like the light against the darkness, the day compared to night, or the coolness after a warm day, nature soothes the intensity of one with the relief of the other. I recognize and am grateful for this balance life provides. From moon glare to sunlight, and all that happens in between, these are the changes that are welcome and necessary for growth.

In moments of darkness, I try to remember the light, while in the light I cannot imagine how dark it can be, but each blend into and complement the other, as if it were not for one, the other would be tedious. So back and forth we go, day after day, night after night, swinging and swaying. Day and night the world turns, shifts, and grows with this special balance nature provides.

Tonight, I accept the darkness and relax in its beauty knowing this moment is the calm needed to contrast an emotionally infused day.

The night sky is clear, reflecting a sliver of light from the crescent moon. The surrounding stars, plentiful and bright, share in the waning darkness. I search the shimmering sky for familiar markers like the North Star, Big Dipper, or Seven Sisters. Clusters and dustings, single and bright they shine in patterns giving the night its sparkle and the darkness its lure. I stare at them for long minutes, contemplating their existence and the space that echoes between us.

In this moment, I see the night sky as a reflection of the past with glimmers of memories caught up in the weave of time. I feel blessed for the distance before me as this gift of perspective brings clarity to hidden truths, recognition of patterns, and acknowledgements of purpose.

I stare intently, wide-eyed and open-minded at the stars that hover above, lacing the sky, flashing like memories in my mind, some dimly lit fading to the backdrop of a lifetime, while others shine brightly, prominent and bold in the forefront of my thoughts drawing attention away from others.

I sway gently, squinting in the night-light trying to gain insight and focus on those memories that are further away, fading to time and losing their sparkle.

My focus brings clarity as patterns are revealed. Maybe it is not one that needs to be seen, but rather the creation of the many together that makes this view unique and exciting. I will take this into consideration while reflecting on my colorful past and know that the most beautiful scene before me shines in shades of black and white.

Every night is as unique as each given moment, and here it is for me to see so I will capture, in my mind's eye, the beauty before me, in case it is gone after the shadow of tomorrow's light, knowing a day will make all the difference in time, light, view, and perspective.

With the morning, like any tomorrow, as the sun begins to shine it will change what I see, and once again as the sky opens up, wiping the view of the past away, it will leave me with my memories and wide-open spaces to create new ones. *Oh, how things are perceived differently in the light.*

But for now, I will honor the night and be grateful to the darkness for it allows all the rest to shine brightly against its backdrop, bringing on this mystery of space, magical thoughts, and a deepness, which extends our world upwards into the past. It is the intangible beauty holding the night steady and true, waiting to give the daylight and the future its welcome.

I swing and stare into the tranquil night and welcome the crickets, night frogs, and fireflies that are awakened by the silence and darkness. In their serenades of chirping, croaking, and flashes of light, I am soothed by their hypnotic harmonies, taming tones, and silencing tunes. Their awakenings signify the slumber of a day while joyfully accepting there is life beyond it.

The North Star stares back bright and permanent. I imagine it is Gigi's shining light taking its place in the fold of the past reminding me to move forward in the midst of all that is, for I know from where she is, all is clear to her now, and her deepest sorrow will never be known. So, in the light that shines before us, may we all be guided forward so we can see our way back to a time of trust and togetherness.

As the sky opens up to my thoughts and prayers, and my day is closing, a falling star graces my view in a streak of light, withering, melting and fizzling out across the sky. Into the dark, dense scenery it disappears, and even though I am sad for its demise, I close my eyes, swing lightly, and wish this wish on the fallen one.

May I be guided forward in the light of tomorrow and blessed with happiness, love and family.

I slowly swing, trying to break the grip of the past and relinquish my experiences to the patterns of my own background. Like the night sky and the ground below, they have created the world I know, but with balance and change, distance and time, I can gain perspective and clarity to their purpose so I may grow.

As this night rolls into another day, I will abandon my sad thoughts and find a new outlook in the sunlight, find a way to balance my experiences, change my view and give myself the strength to hold us up and see the beauty within the darkness.

I sway, in one last prayer, thanking the stars and the evening sky for the reminder of beautiful things that are always present even though it is only in the right light that we can see them sparkle and shine.

May we recognize and honor every glimmer of light that layers the shadowy nights, for every tomorrow will cast sunlight across the sky, clearing the slate for a new day and bright future, and by the grace of God, the night will turn again, with one more memory added to the fold. May every twinkle of light remind us of the past while offering us a glimpse of tomorrow's dawning light.

CHAPTER 19:
A BREAKTHROUGH

*If not today, then tomorrow, they will call again, and again, until
I answer, surrender, or rise to the challenge before me.*

The pillow shades my eyes from the loud morning light forcing its way
through my window. I hide under my blankets wishing the stars back in all
their silence, but the sun and the birds are relentless as they draw me into their
world. My thoughts are immediate, reflecting not on where my children are
or whether Jeremy has left for work, but on the uncovered truth of the past
that lies deep in my backyard, in my life, in the form of a hole. I reflect on this
discovery and how this issue has risen from beneath the covered landscape and
awaits my company and solution.

There is a sense of energy that comes with a problem to be solved, a control over decisions to be made. I know what I have unburied and must face in
the hours to come. It is the unfinished business, the unfinished project that
hangs in the balance of being a colossal mess or a beautiful masterpiece. One
false move, one poor brush stroke, one wrong word, or wrong step, in this
case, may render it unfixable.

With this type of control and/or consequences comes the responsibility
of action, so I lie here wondering if I am worthy of such a chore, wondering if
I am capable of finding a suitable answer or if I have the inner strength to create goodness from such chaos. But the sun calls and the birds cannot be ig-

nored, for if not today, then tomorrow, they will call again, and again, until I answer, surrender, or rise to the challenge before me.

This catapults me from my comfortable bed leaving messy covers, tossed pillows, and a black Labrador sound asleep behind me. Excitement tingles my sleepy body as I turn my thoughts into action. With a hands-on approach, I will work it out, plunging mind, body, and soul into the issue.

Downstairs in a flash, bed head and all, I find coffee made, kids still asleep, and Jeremy gone for the day. Coffee in hand, bare feet, and two dogs by my side—the dynamic duo, Penny and Buddy—I find myself standing above the hole. Its appearance turns my stomach, for the deep rigidness blemishes my surroundings, and I know there is more here to be recognized and revealed.

The fresh morning sun casts a fresher look across the opening, illuminating a cave within. The sun shines and the birds dart across the sky, flying wildly as ever, showing the world did not end because of its unearthing. Equally surprising, at closer look, in the newness of the day and after a restful night's sleep, its intimidation has lost its impact.

I breathe deeply, taking in the openness of the dewy morning air. I feel the realness of the opportunity before me to restructure a piece of my past and future.

I know I will need physical, tangible tools at hand and in place along with an open mind for a successful outcome.

I see with compassion for the first time the cruelty that was buried here. It was covered over with beautiful, shallow appearances. This I now know and, therefore, cannot blame it for its growth. Below it corroded, with only the permission of neglect, to finally affect all my surroundings. I too have turned my back on many truths for far too long. Merciless, it pushed forward and down until someone noticed. So, I too, must push back to prove growth is possible in this forgotten space.

I head back inside to plan my strategy, to gather my wits and items for protection. I am capable with the right tools to create what I want, what I envision. Tools of life, physical or otherwise, are important in such an endeavor. I plan on using all that is accessible to me to see this through. A mission is what I am on so early in this day and my beliefs will be put to the test.

I dress for the heat of the day and the hard work ahead of me. I throw on an old pair of khaki shorts, and a t-shirt, then pull my hair into a ponytail and through a ball cap. Next, I gather my tools to help and protect me when the going gets tough. Sunglasses will keep me focused when the glare tries to gloss over the truth. Items from my shopping trip come out ready to play as I pull off tags and stickers, feeling the anticipation of dirtying them up.

My walking stick has made the cut for necessary support and strength. A shovel will pierce the ground that hides the reality of it all and dig out any misconceptions. Gloves slide over my fingers to protect, grip, and hold on to what is solid. Boots are pulled on to dig my heels in deep during questionable times that try to pull me under. They will help me to stand tall and keep my balance while I am deep in the center of it. They will give me traction to gain ground in any slippery situation. And, last but not least, a rake to smooth over any rigidness in the end. Feeling persistent and strong, gloved up, boots on, and tools in hand, I march out with my convictions intact.

I must be a sight, for the dogs are startled at my appearance. They bark and approach slowly, sniffing the air to access the intruder who has entered their territory. Then, there's a silliness of tail wagging and jumping as they are relieved it is just me. I think for a moment that maybe the hole won't recognize me either. Holding onto that illusion, I believe I just might be a match for this challenge. I will take all the help I can get.

I believe Gigi is laughing at me as I walk to the hole with my tools awkwardly weighing me down. She snickers at my over-dramatic approach. I can hear her jolly giggle shaking her words as she says, *"You silly girl, what have you gotten yourself into?"*

Her laugh is what I miss the most, the lively twinkle that came to her eyes. I am suddenly transported back to a time she used those exact same words. I find myself six years old in her bedroom curious and alone.

 Gigi and Lizzi

A box full of clothes held the door to her closet shut. I tugged on it with little strength, sliding it ever so slightly. The door popped open on its own, welcoming the movement. Swinging heavily until it hit the box again, it opened just enough for me to squeeze into the dark space. Scarfs, belts, purses and hats draped the inside of the door on various hooks. Reaching up on my tippy toes, a thin string clicked when pulled once, draping a hazy dim light over a crowd of garments. Dust lingered in the stream of light that bent around stacks of small boxes on the top shelf. The air was old with forgotten time. A faded smell crinkled my nose like I had found the essence of Gigi's house. Colors dull and vibrant, some covered in plastic, others left to the elements, were hung and jammed together so tightly they refused to allow me between them.

Below was a mound of treasure piled high of shoes, boots, and more purses. I dropped to my knees to get a better look. A strange brass figure stood in the corner. A lady smooth like liquid, topless, with only a beaded necklace and fringe skirt stared back at me. As a lamp, she proudly stood with both hands above her head holding a torch empty of a bulb and bare of its shade. She was cold to the touch. Unable to move, she peered intently at me while I rifled through pieces of Gigi's past. Tall, laced black boots, sandals with broken straps, green and clunky, blue and satiny, brown flat and tasseled all worn and deflated of the feet that once filled them were tossed aside one after the other until I found one dusty shoebox beneath them all.

The top came off easily. Within its flimsy cardboard walls, straps of gold crisscrossed and sparkled, attaching themselves to thick, solid, tall soles of the same color. Their shimmer ignited my excitement. I took them out where they shined like new in the pure light of the bedroom. Undisturbed for years, they accepted their mission. I left them on the bed where they waited for me to complete my ensemble.

Scarfs and more scarfs hung lifeless within reach, as did the fur wrap that felt oddly plush in my small hands. The lining was soft like silk, but between the two surfaces, a dry and stiff interior was telling of its age. It covered my shoulders and then some, hanging so loose that each end touched the floor. Two scarves slid off their hooks easily. One was red and blue covered in white daisies, another flashed purple and black in plush velvet, but both wrapped around my neck softly. A blue-beaded bag was flung over one shoulder. A bright yellow sunbonnet, a little out of reach, was well worth the effort and placed on my head. I stood in front of the dresser to see how I looked. A silver bowl full of Gigi's more personal items called to me. The large colorful plastic bracelets slid on big, knocking each other up my arms. The perfume went on heavy until my eyes watered, and a pair of thick, white-rimmed sunglasses was ready for the wearing. They slid down my nose with every shift of my head, but with my chin held high to keep them on, they instantly transformed me to the starlet I knew I was. Climbing onto the bed, my little feet slipped through the buckled gold ankle strap of the shoes. As I stood carefully, the closed toes, each decorated with a small bow, kept me from sliding right through them. I stood wobbly on the softness of the mattress, but the height brought me into full view of the mirror. I moved side to side to see all angles and to make my pink sundress sway beneath my glamorous look. I waved at myself like a queen to her disciples. I posed and smiled like a model before her photographers imagining the flashes bursting before me.

Gigi stood just outside the door smiling at the actress loaded up with the gaudiest garments she had seen in a long time. With a tease and a smile, she said, "What have you gotten yourself into this time, little girl?"

I laughed, happy to have an audience and proud to display my fabulous look. Gigi laughed at me. I danced with the scarf in each hand, waving it at her in sophisticated play.

"Is the young starlet ready for lunch, madam?"

One last finale was in order, for an actress always exits well. I tried a full twirl, barely being able to lift the gold heels from the bed. I made it halfway around when the weight of the fur and the height of the heels were too much for a fully graceful finish. I fell backwards quickly toward the floor. Gigi was there just in time to catch me, pulling us both back to the bed for a soft, harmless ending. I don't know who started first, but after the fear subsided within us, we laughed harder than I had ever before.

Today, she looks down on me and just shakes her head as I walk loaded up with garments of a different kind headed toward another close call if I am not careful. I look toward the sky to smile back at her. The neighborhood hawk circles above. Marching on, my pursuit ends with the screech of the hawk and me staring down at what has halted my life. Today is my time to rethink the grounds of the past, to find out how deep and far back we must go to start growing again.

The shovel pierces the ground easily, breaking through with the first blow. Dirt falls without resistance and sprinkling echoes can be heard from beneath the surface. I feel strong as I power down on the shovel handle, digging in with every jab. I feel the excitement of uncovering the truth and exposing it to the light once and for all, taking its power. I feel it give in easily, almost as though it is relieved to finally relinquish its grip on the façade. More strength rips through me, and I crush the edges bit by bit. Suddenly, like one big open wound, all of its flaws glare up at me…big, weak, and lifeless.

The sunlight pours through the large gash in the ground. The dark hollow home of the past is exposed once and for all, with no place else to hide. I stand in awe of the size to which a small issue has grown. Sweat beads up on my face. The sun beats down but flashes of fear beg for answers.

What have I done? Can I ever replace what is missing here? What does belong here if not what I thought it to be? Can I create and rebuild life from this mess? What will ever grow in this deadened area?

In my haze of slight panic, I realize this is nature at its core. Nature being all that is, it is its own truth, and will create its own answers. This hole, this whole issue, no longer stands alone in the light of day. I now accompany it and vow to stand with it, and in it, until it is healed. I will face the problem, knowing I own it, and all its depth and hollowness. I am here to do the work that needs to be done.

I study what is before me with the sun's rays casting down, showing a dark hollow hole lined with lifeless, stubborn stones, and weak, rotting wood. In raw form, it consists of the driest soil, hardened and ridged, while roots lie cracked, broken, and weak, abandoned by their strength.

To the far edge at the bottom of this space, a single root hole remains. It travels deeper beneath the surface than I can see. This is the path where life connected to the earth, but now only represents questioning darkness. Though much smaller in diameter than its host, it has not collapsed on itself yet. I feel it looking for something to fill it as small pebbles roll to its call.

This was once the rooting system that grounded, fed, and supported a life above it. How sad a sight, knowing this lifeline to its blossoms and buds were buried and forgotten about. A sadness burns within me—I sigh for what it once was.

I feel a need to be closer to it, so I lower myself to its side. I sit with my legs daggling in. We are one, my hole and I, as I kick the walls with my heels. These edges are stable and support me while containing the nothingness they own. The bottom stares back daring me to enter the emptiness, but without these edges, *what is there to be empty of?* Space resides here, empty of nothing but what we think it should be.

In this space before me, this emptiness of ground, hope calls, echoing my need for help. I realize here lies the hope I was looking for.

After all, space is the ultimate never-ending-of-hope for what can be. This space is my big question mark for possibilities. In its last stage of ruins, attention has been called, now a last hope it is, my hope for growth to come again.

With the ground opened up, so has an opportunity. Here, this space, *my space*, awaits the growth of something new.

Patches of green grass have fallen to the will of gravity. Small they may be but together they gathered in great strength. These small clumps that once covered over so elegantly are, now, just pieces scattering the bottom of what they protected. In disarray, they have surrendered unaware of where they went wrong. They are small mounds of life, with roots intact, which have been engulfed in the truth of what wasn't there to support them. They are so tiny, in contrast, to the massiveness that they covered. With all their might, they tried to protect the devastation beneath them while propelling upward toward the sky. They were expected to be strong. In the end, they could not withstand the pressure of the life that surrounded them.

These small chunks of today now lie deep in the truth of the past, and although I am sad to see these healthy pieces in this way, it brings me peace to know that there is healthy ground beginning to fill this hollow place. I begin to see how the truth of today can fill in the holes of yesterday's pain.

The green grass against the lifeless dirt at the bottom of the hole seems bright and hopeful. I see them as the tiniest parts in life that can breathe truth into the ugliness. Realizing that the truth is not always beautiful, with work, it truly can be the beauty in the world.

Creating beauty with truth may not be the easiest path one can take, but false beauty is temporary at best. A beautiful life cannot hold on and grow without the support of the truth beneath it. The beauty that once lived here now lies at the bottom of the hole, awaiting its own fate of being buried and used for the rebuilding of what it should be, will be.

I look down on it, and I am tempted to call Auntie El. She would appreciate the opportunity before me and certainly have the touch needed to make this a beautiful place again. But I must find my own way this time. It is my foundation at stake and my footing that needs traction. This is one journey downward that she cannot lead me through.

As I sit here in my rambling thoughts, the warmth of the midmorning sun melts me backwards onto the grass behind me. I lie down, staring up at the sky knowing Gigi is watching. I smile back at her again. I close my eyes and place one hand on the black Labrador snoozing beside me. Her fur is hot to the touch.

I whisper *thank you* to Gigi and to the universe for all the space, hope, and opportunities that are placed around me. I drift off to a light sleep in the heat of the sun.

CHAPTER 20:
ROCK BOTTOM

The ground may be shaky and weak but it is fear that collapses our foundations.

I must have dozed off just long enough for Day-Z to wake up and find me at the edge of my mission. I open my eyes to a wrinkled hound face drooped over mine. She has already slobbered my sunglasses and began to lightly nibble my nose. This was a sign of affection for the otherwise intimidating creature. She stands over me as our noses touch, her tail wags, rocking her whole body side to side, and drool limply hangs from her jowl.

"Yuck, Day-Z."

As this gives her proof that she has found me, she leans in lower until the whole side of her head is mushed against my face, drool and all, and then she drops her weight so her neck rubs on my head. This, too, is an affectionate ownership interaction for her, a bloodhound trait I have come to know. You have not been properly hugged by a dog until you've been rolled by a 120-pound bloodhound.

This certainly is a wake-me-up. I push her off me, patting her face vigorously with one long floppy ear in each hand. "Silly girl, get off."

Proud of her find and satisfied with the attention, she swaggers off to sleep in the shade.

I, on the other hand, find myself still connected to the hole.

My legs folded in, proving I have not left its side during my moment of reprieve. My sunglasses are removed to wipe the slobber from them. The sun's glare is striking and sharp. I sit in silence awaiting the universe's wrath for puncturing and revealing the past to the world. I imagine in this moment, it sucking me in, rolling me down its dark tunnel, never to be seen again.

The heat is building up, and I wonder if it is from a power source of strength within me, or if the sun is the messenger, scorning and scorching me for my attempts to unbury past agonies.

Leaning back my elbows are locked to brace me, I look in the face of my attacker. *Why not? Bring it on.* I might as well face all the heat at once. I stare in the face of the blaze, squinting at its haze when a passing cool wind whispers in my ear, "All is well."

The sun warms me, warns me, trying to weaken my focus. I close my eyes once more, feeling the breeze praise and caress me for my courage.

Nature chimes in with the chirping birds, and the whispers of silence that occupy the air between me and the screeching hawk somewhere in the distance. I wish to melt into the plush tightly knitted blades of grass as they mesh together like a family waiting to catch me when I fall.

I sit up straight again listening to the sounds of nature and the sunlight bathing me in warmth. I know my work has just begun, so I breathe deeply and smile, for I know in this moment that there is life here, to be found, to be lived.

I am completely motivated now, wanting to connect with the past and face my fears with the intention of releasing the façade and allowing beauty to come forward. To do this, I must excavate the damage and start new. The wound has suffered; the pain cannot be ignored any longer. Sympathy and acceptance start in the rawness of the soil. Standing in its core is where the healing begins, by facing buried truths, owning the limitations of its walls, knowing its substance, and kicking the stubborn stones that have lain heavily for so many years. These stones are solid characteristics, some holding qualities of strength and resilience, others of regret and disappointment. They scatter my past disregarded and neglected and now they are being called upon to secure my intentions. Long ago buried, they need to be brought into the light once again. Necessary and waiting, they are of learned resistance, but will be handy in rebuilding my landscape. Ones of strength will stand well as foundation, filling in the gaps, as others, of beauty and elegance will come out to shine in the sun as stone gardens or walls to beautify my future, creating boundaries in my physical world. Others will need to be soothed, those whose qualities are no longer needed, ones of past mistakes that need to be deflated of their pessimism and slumbered to their place in the past. I will sort through them carefully and study them, but first I must lift them, hold them, and dust them off to see their true shape and character. I will reacquaint myself with these characters like old, lost friends.

I scoot myself to the edge, planning my descent into this intimidating place, ready to rescue every last hopeful image. I stare deep into the depth of the past knowing this is the heart of the future. All rolled into one hole, the past devastations lie before me. Its presence is here for me to heal and its future is in my hands.

My over dramatic mind takes over as I shove off with a push of my arms and the swing of my legs. With the pull of gravity, I plunge myself down into the depth of my fear, not knowing where I will land. From my perception, death feels like a possibility. I feel gravity pulling me down and the wings of courage guiding me as I fall into the center of this lifeless place. It feels more like a leap into oblivion than a jump into a hole as the mind has a knack for magnifying that which we are afraid of.

During this flight of faith, I remember a time when fear was not part of an adventure, when the rope swing at the quarry was fun and invigorating, and the dangers never occurred to me when I was weightless, fearless, and boundless to thoughts of the past, present, or future. Those were the days. But today I feel heavy with time behind me, and the weight of the future before me. *Oh, to be young again.* I surrender to the weight of all I know and think about for the fear is in my mind of the work to be done, not the depth or size of this simple hole.

"Catch me! Gigi, catch me like you did that day, cushion my fall, keep me safe as I jump to test the boundaries and obstacles life has placed before me. Be there to laugh this off with me and tell me again it is my wild spirit you love so much."

I shut my eyes and hold my breath. My boots are like cement that grab my body and pull me in. There is no turning back now as I feel the sting of the ground smashing against my feet. This leap of courage meets the bottom much sooner than my expectations. Embarrassed by my dramatics, I land only a few feet from where my toes dangled.

Crunchy, uneven ground of scattered stones and the sound of the earth crackling beneath me radiate shock waves through my body. I know I have reached my destination. I can feel the substance of its core as the grittiness vibrates through my teeth and my stomach fills with knots.

I land on an uneven bottom as my descent has turned out to be the shallows of my imagined fear. Before I know it, my legs twist to the pressure of hitting the ground. I can taste the earthiness and my balance is tested.

Heaviness weighs on me, but the walls hold me steady. I reach out in desperation. Ironically, these perceived dungeon walls are the ones supporting me now, catching my fall.

Leaning against my surroundings, I can feel its solidness. I realize it may be rocky down here, but steady ground has prevailed so here I am at the bottom, where looking upward is the only thing left to do.

I inhale the stale, dense air, opening my eyes to a confining space. Familiarity welcomes my presence with a pounding heart, but there is light, natural sunlight showing details my darkness has never let me see before. I see the dirt for the simple substance it is, similar to the dried-up memories of past painful experiences. At my feet, the root hole stares up at me docile and unapologetic for its existence or unknown destination.

I stand up straight finding the depth and size of what I feared is really an illusion. No longer a child in the large sea of adult issues, I can stand tall in this problem. With a brief arch to my feet, I can see the tall blades of grass up close in all their greenness and thick gatherings.

I reach above, feeling for my walking stick. My chunky gloved fingers tap around until they meet up with my new friend. I pull it close. Into the hole my stick comes. Down the root hole it slides. Deeper it goes being swallowed up by the tunnel left behind. I catch it just before it is out of site.

Obviously, strength is not the only quality needed to keep me from the harm of a place like this for the length and solidity of the branch would not have stopped it from disappearing.

Improvising, I throw in a few old roots and debris hoping to fill it a little, yet they disappear quickly, only radiating more emptiness through me. I change strategies and dig out the first stone I see. I pull it out and roll it over the mouth of the tunnel that is fearfully hungry for more than I can give it right now.

The stone moves easily covering the root hole. Like a puzzle, it fits, finally finding a place where its stubbornness is effective. The rock blocks the entrance where so many trickles of rain have washed away good soil. If only it had found its place earlier maybe some damage could have been prevented. I stomp on it fiercely to test it under pressure. Only a slight adjustment locks it in place, and I feel the gathering of energy that has already begun, stopping the downward momentum. Now an upward momentum can surely begin.

I brush off my gloves proud for the strength and quick wit it took to handle this unexpected snag, and I look above me into the light that shines strong and bright.

I know as I stand here, this hole has truly engulfed me, yet I have survived. Now that I have willingly come in, I must prove that escape is possible. I must loosen its grip so I may work freely. For healing to begin, it cannot contain or control me anymore.

CHAPTER 21:
EXPOSURE

The truth is held within these walls that surround me, for I am what they hold.

My first attempt to climb out of my makeshift grave proves to be a sign of over-confidence. It literally knocks me back a few steps. I fall back into the hole, taking the hint that it will not give me up so easily. It gladly reminds me that my distance to my goal is further away still.

I reach for the surface with little success. Grabbing onto apparently solid ground again reveals false security. Only loose, rooted grass-crumbles pull away from the world above. My return backwards reminds me of my place and the depth of which I am in.

I look to the sides that held me up during my entrance. I grab my walking stick for strength and dig my free hand and feet into the walls. Surprisingly, the walls prove to be friendly. I begin climbing as if a set of perfectly formed stairs has appeared amongst their rigidness. My long staff holds up to my expectations, supporting me until I am above ground again.

With little effort, I find myself in the true world once more, breathing lightly in the fresh, welcoming air. I feel confident that I can remove myself easily as I work on this project alone, so I do.

I climb out and jump back in, again and again, to let it know it can't hold me any longer and to rid myself of the fear that it may take me down and never let me go.

Once more I enter, treating it as an extension of my landscape. It is no longer the forbidden place of festering animosity; it is the gaping wound ready to be healed.

My boots have packed down all the loose dirt, branding the bottom with my unique footprints. I have secured this piece of my life as sturdy, the route out is familiar, and although I am at the bottom, it holds me strong. My trusty walking stick leans comfortably next to me, ready for extra support at any moment.

My familiarity of this place is a little unsettling, frightening really, for I am comfortable here. A shiver of eeriness crawls up my spine. I wonder if I have lowered myself to its level for healing or if my inner trickster has found a way to bring me home to where I belong.

This can be a slippery slope, as one can be comfortable in the messy confusions of life. This is what I fear, for a comfortable dysfunction is my familiarity. In the same breath, *who better to defeat a problem than one who has a deeper understanding of their surroundings?* This gives me an edge. The question that crosses my mind now is: *How does one stay a part of the condition, the hole, while trying to fix it without contributing to the problem itself?*

Getting lost in my surroundings, finding comfortableness where I do not belong, finding myself in too deep, has been my pattern. Wandering off track where I appeared to be welcome to only find the path has disappeared before and behind me. A walk in the woods as a child proved to me my naive trusting nature. The trees welcomed me, my path seemed clear, and time went by without a whisper. It wasn't until the snow started to fall covering all that was familiar that I knew I was too far from home. My path back home was engulfed in my surroundings and what started as a good intended walk with nature turned quickly to panic and confusion. Although I was welcome, I knew deep down that I did not belong. With fear and determination, I climbed to the highest stone peek I could find where distances beyond the trees could be seen. The church steeple stood behind many bare branches in a white tip and gold cross. Sometimes, a sign from above is just what we need. It was a further walk home by the street from there, but it gave me a clear direction to a safe place.

To have direction gives comfort as we explore the unknown. Today I question my actions, looking for certainty where there is none. *If I dig in this area, where will it take me? Is this truly the bottom of this matter? Will I take away support from the surface in my attempts to start new? Will my actions affect any goodness that is still present? How far should I dig? Will I know where to stop? Will I compromise my destination with every move?* But sometimes answers only come with time and action. Today I will move forward, although the outcome cannot be told or seen.

I start to dig slowly and gently, at a kind and respectful pace. I wish not to offend. I scratch lightly, finding the soil to be dry and flaky, falling easily to the floor.

This must be removed. I must reveal the life within these walls. I must find it.

I begin to dig, but the walls refuse to reveal the life behind the scars. Their stubbornness is frustrating. The lack of cooperation on their behalf triggers my aggression, and I find my pace picks up. My annoyance rears contempt for the whole situation.

Suddenly family and conversations that have gone nowhere attack my thoughts and attach to my actions. I think of times when my words, my efforts, have fallen on deaf ears. I find myself now speaking to the walls.

Why don't you see that I am trying to help, trying to find the connection to the life that was once here? Why are you making this so difficult and not recognizing that my actions are not to hurt or toss aside what is here, but to keep us present, connecting our worlds once again?

The walls only stare at me in silence.

I find my movements uncontrollable and my thoughts in a whirlwind. I must dig deeper, work harder so they will see. I must remove all the deadness that is around me until I reach fresh ground that is capable of life running through it.

I must know for sure that the soil is rich and flourishing before I place total confidence in its ability to support future growth. I will dig until it returns the respect and kindness I have shown, and then they will see. They will see that life is more powerful than the lifeless corroded bickering that has created these dungeon walls. *I will show them!*

Please Gigi, let this all stop here. Let us all find fertile ground once again. These are your roots, too, your seeds, and buds trying to survive, trying to grow. Please, I only want our roots back.

I panic, digging faster, determined to prove life and goodness exist down here. I scratch frantically, searching, not realizing my movements have brought me full circle to the same thickheaded clump of soil that I started with.

Frustration fully sets in for the walls have landed around my feet, and yet, dry lifeless dirt is all I find. I move quickly, now checking all areas, clawing at all the walls around me. As I dig out the walls, they close in on me, narrowing my thoughts to their demise. Full-fledged anger takes over. I know I must completely acknowledge the walls that have held back the growth all these years. I must feel firsthand what this problem consists of.

Where are you, Gigi? Where are you? Where have you been during all this destruction? Can you not see we need you? All of us need you to find our way home? You are the steeple within the treetops and we cannot find our rock formation to climb. Have you abandoned me in my anger? Is this not the reaction you were hoping for? Is this not your problem anymore? What else am I to do? How could you have left us? Left us with this hole? Left us to start again without you? How does a tree survive without its roots? Is there an answer here, or am I truly just weaving thoughts together, mucking up my own head with false beliefs?

I have never been angry with her before. I have never talked to her like that.

I am sorry, Gigi, I am sorry, but where does this stop?

For the first time, I hear her silence and feel alone.

My emotions are getting the best of me and I want to scrape and claw, exposing it all to the light, all the rawness, the tenderness, and goodness that hides beneath the surface. The gloves come off. I want to bare it all and feel the essence of what I'm dealing with. No more barriers between the issue and myself. No more softening the blow. I want to face the depleting source. I want my fingertips to dig in deep, unearthing every detail.

I gouge at the walls with a strength that I have never felt before. My fear is set aside. As the walls give into the lashing of my anger, they fall lifeless to my feet. I see at this moment, this dull substance, this focus of my attack, has no real control in its natural state. It is nothing but the ground and soil, which I have allowed to hold and grow my beliefs, and yet its harmless form has been given so much power over the years.

My anger turns to sadness as I realize the power I have given it, that the space it took up only magnified its lifelessness. The ease with which it is being removed only makes the space wasted on its presence more heartbreaking. It has grown thick to cover the goodness, but it is willing to fall away. I realize that energy is all that was required for it to step aside. I find myself hating it.

I beat at the wall with a closed fist, feeling my strength lessening. My heart pounds faster and the task seems endless, as more and more rigid dirt appears beneath another layer.

Where does it stop? Gigi, where? When will these walls come down and show us the life within them? Why did it have to go so deep? Where can I begin again? Is there just one root left for me to hold onto?

Still no answer.

Her silence scares me.

I find no life before me.

With one last burst of energy, I grab at the gritty wall and retrieve a fistful of dusty soil. It stares back at me in a solid clump, claiming a piece of my sanity. I gasp and a tear breaks free. *How could something this small be the death of me? How could this break my spirit?*

"IT CAN'T!"

I scream from deep down, from somewhere within, from the quiet girl that never said a word and it roars out with my tears. I refuse to accept defeat this time. I will speak up until someone listens, anyone.

It will not get the best of me, Gigi. I will power through. I have set forth to create goodness where pain had been placed, and I will for you, for me, for the family, and show them that the walls that have been built up over the years are only housing the pain, holding it in, not allowing it to mix with the sunlight, or with the healthy soil beneath us. I will show them how these walls can be broken down, changed so they can be seen for the useless protectors they truly are.

I squeeze my fist tightly, pulverizing the clump into the little pieces of which it was made.

My hands are filthy with this problem. As I rub it deep into my skin, I can feel the gritty, sharp texture in every smudge. I roll it over my fingertips and smash it between my palms feeling it fall away, forever.

Tears blur my focus. I can feel the soil coating my hands as it seeps into my core. Feeling the truth of its destruction, my eyes fill until steady drops fall to the ground mixing with my stagnant surroundings. The dry dirt soaks up my tears like a welcoming relief to a meaningless thirst.

Yes, meaningless. Meaningless pain has created all this anguish. How does that happen? And my tears are their reward.

I finally see this whole problem for its true smallness. It has grown in the soils of insecurity and taken over so much of my life, and to think I had to stand here right in the center of it, holding it in my hand to truly see it.

I reach out again, trusting that my efforts will yield results. I scrape some more. I dig deeper, knowing life exists and is calling out to me.

Finally, within my darkened walls, a root reveals itself. With hope, I grab at it quickly before it can disappear. I test its strength with one quick tug, but hasty expectations bring me crashing down. It breaks from someplace deeper, sending me backwards in one swift snap. My head hits hard as I land against the wall and ground behind me.

Dirt flies in my face, laughing at my attempts. Spitting at me, it shows itself for what it is, cruel false hope.

Who am I to challenge nature at its core?

The disruption has caused an avalanche and more and more dirt falls. I feel it covering my face as my head spins in dizziness.

This is it, my courage has weakened and my beliefs tested, and now they will be buried with me, forever.

CHAPTER 22:
LOSING GROUND

Deep in this hole I dig for life. I find my own beating heart, excited for what I will discover.

I look up to the world above, which seems further away than before. A narrow tunnel of light stretches in, reaching out before me. The real world seems miles away from where I have landed, and a foggy haze surrounds my mind. I see my four-legged friends—all of them—looking in on me as they gather around the opening. They must have felt the vibration of the ground under their feet as my hard work came tumbling down on me. *Have they come to rescue me or gawk at the inevitable?*

They pace and bark at me, knowing they are too far away to help. I see them moving and hear their barks travel down echoing into words. My dizziness confuses me. I blink my eyes to clear the uncertainty from my thoughts.

They are lying at the edge, now, looking in at me. Around the hole, they form a circle above me with their paws slightly hanging over the edge. Their noses are dropped down between their paws. I see their barking motion, but the sound travels to me in an assessment of my situation.

My doubtful mind plays out my thoughts through their observation.

"What is she doing?" Penny, *my chocolate lab, questions with little sympathy for my position.*

"I don't know, but look at her now," Buddy, my yellow friend, replies in his studious voice, appalled at what he sees.

"She must have been crazy to dig that up," Mysti, my midnight lady, adds in her ladylike tone, embarrassed for my decisions.

"Yah, what did she think was gonna happen?" Day-Z, my instinctual hound, answers in a matter-of-fact, could-have-told-her-so attitude.

"What good did she think would come of this?" Buddy completes his thought on the subject with a shake of his head.

"She shoulda left well enough alone. It wasn't that bad," Day-Z announces.

"Why did she think she could make it better? Why?" Penny again questions in complete confusion for the whole debacle.

Mysti, still baffled by my motives, adds, "Why would she bother? It wasn't hurting anyone, anymore."

"I never noticed it, myself. What is the big deal?" Penny now laughs at the absurdity of something so little being important and serious. "Life is too fun to worry about such issues." She pokes at Buddy, wanting him to run off and play with her.

But he is too serious to let it go. "She could have just covered it over, and left it alone, and nobody would have known. Now look at her. Unbelievable! Buried alive in her own mess. She thought she was so smart to dig all that up; to try to better her surroundings. Who does she think she is to want better than what has been given to her?"

"Uh! What's one to do these days?" Mysti gives up with sad disappointment.

"Well, there is nothing anyone can do now. What is done, is done." Day-Z walks away with a sad face and a drop of her head.

My own fears bounce around me, and I find myself spinning in my own dirty, emotional grave. I shake my head and blink my eyes to clear the uncertainty, but a shooting pain keeps me immobile. The light-headedness slowly fades as the sprinkles of falling dirt become further apart. As I regain my focus, the dogs are nowhere in sight.

I know none of that is true. This is all worth it. There is life down here, too. Life can be better, and I will survive whatever it throws at me.

The dirt that sticks to my face is light and fluffy, different than what I have been digging through. It feels wet on my face, not just from the moisture of my tears, but the dampness of healthy soil.

I lift my hands easily. I can feel the coarse texture of my grimy hands clumsily removing and adding more dirt at the same time. Nature has fought back in retaliation for my persistence of revealing life behind these walls. Its anger has frightened me, but only for a moment. I rise and the dirt falls away easily, letting me go. Healthy soil lands around my feet.

Pulling my feet from the dirt that has deepened to my ankles, I feel the heaviness release itself to the floor. I stomp on it with all my strength, pressing it into the bottom creating new height beneath me. All the dead soil pulled from the first layer of the walls now mixes with healthy soil and I can feel the energy building with the ground.

I pack it down tight. With new ground, I stand a little taller, a little closer to the world above.

Amazed and a little giddy, I look to the walls that have finally released their defenses. And there it is. There in the soil is a sign of life. A small root reaches out to me like a lifeline from the depth of nowhere. It says, *We exist.* There is goodness and life in here, left over from the past, trying to grow with you. We will grow if you give us good ground, solid paths, and nourishment.

I see now that within the darkness life can survive.

This empowers me to move on. I know there is more work to be done, more life to find and to acknowledge. Within the pain that is part of life, grows goodness. Here goodness and life wait to be acknowledged so it can grow. This is nature's way.

Buried pain, a buried past, it all adds up to a weak foundation and growth that has faded into the shadows. But time reveals all, emptying us all of what does not grow. We will need to start again from the rawness of life itself. From where it began and died. I must continue to dig until I uncover more healthy ground.

Excited, I give great attention to digging until life shows itself fully, until it reveals all that has been buried. I feel the heat of the sun burning down on me as I struggle to remove all that is negative. Filtering the good from the bad, I chop away at my surroundings, watching all that I thought to be secure crumble to the floor. Finding solid stones, I toss them to the surface where they can bathe in the sunlight. They are solid, strong characteristics of nature that have been buried and forgotten, like little pieces of my own personality that have been abandoned within. Strength, courage, and clarity being just a few, I find more and more truths behind my beliefs in this eye-opening and invigorating excavation of pain and life.

More live roots show themselves raw and vulnerable like nerves that have been stripped of their protection and exposed to the elements. I feel for them and know their pain. I understand the sting of a slight touch when sensitivities are high. I try to be gentle.

Just as I am feeling my success, the ground loosens beneath me. I start to sink back down. The dirt below seems to be melting away. I see the root hole has spoken up once again, not willing to lie quietly. It is sucking all my hard work and goodness into its core. From around the rock I have placed over it, it has found gaps and is breathing in my progress. The soil, my foundation, is still being pulled to the oblivion of emptiness. *What could it want?*

Two steps forward, one step back, my pattern repeats itself. In this case, two feet up, to be sucked back down, and I have to ask: *How much can I give it? When will it be satisfied? What can I do to fill a void I have never seen? If it gets hold of me this time, will it ever let me go? Will this rocky darkness of the past be my home forever?*

My darkest places are hungry for me and all the goodness I have found. This root hole is no different. It cannot stand for the good to be exposed. It will not let me be, even if it means destroying itself in the meantime. It lies in wait for all it can gather, reminding me of its comforts, taunting me to come back to the emptiness, warning me of the life beyond it.

Is this really my foundation? Based on darkness and emptiness? Never meant to be trusted? Never meant to be sturdy? Is this the way it has always been? Or am I just seeing it differently now or more clearly as it sucks everything out from under me, once again, leaving me nothing to stand on?

I watch it, helpless, as what is below me, pulls in my surroundings, never seeming to be full.

My efforts are being mocked. How do I fight the forces of nature, of human nature? Maybe I should get out and leave the repetitive destructive behavior; and allow it all to cave in on itself once and for all.

CHAPTER 23:
CLOUDS OF LAUGHTER

Silence is heard with the rumbling clouds as teardrops release from deep down within.

Here I am, deep in the hole, trying to create a steady foundation to correct the pains of the past. I have found the flaw amongst the landscape. I opened old wounds so they can heal. I dove in to get my hands dirty and let it know I am committed. I have removed false appearances that hid the truth of growth and goodness. No matter, I still find myself sinking deeper, even after heights have been reached and goodness found.

Now, here I stand deeper than before. I have been lowered to its level once again. I am exhausted by my efforts and my exit has been compromised by my own actions as the way out is now without structure.

A solid, heavy stone covers the hollow entrance to the root hole, which extends to unknown voids, yet still from around the edges of solidness, weakness prevails. *Down, down, down.* It is all disappearing through the small cracks between the rock and emptiness. I can only watch as it inhales all the goodness I thought I had found. This is proof once again that truth may only be one's perception.

The stone is too large to be sucked in, but all around it, weakness has affected its purpose. Obviously, intentions aren't enough.

I pull the heavy stone from the mouth of the opening. I examine the root hole once again. Watching it pull in all that it can reach. Like a magnet, everything runs to its side and disappears into obscurity. *And I wonder what it could be hungry for? What will be enough destruction to give it its fill? Where does the upward spiral truly begin?*

So, I feed the hole with all that I can give it, cursing its existence I push healthy soil and rooted grass chunks into its needy mouth hoping to see some progress, hoping it will accept all that I have to give. Surrendering to the process and to its existence, I pray for a sign of peace, or at least a truce.

More and more it takes until I realize that my soul is what it really wants forever. I panic for I hear its call. Hope dwindles. Choking in the stale air around me, I wonder if it has already taken me down and I just don't know it yet.

The walls that allowed for my easy exit were diminished to the rubble that now disappear before me. Air is hard to come by. On my knees, hands in the dirt, I wonder what it is going to take to correct something that has taken a lifetime to create. I desperately want it to see, that breathing in goodness and letting it nourish you is easier than sucking the life out of all that is around, but it does not seem to care. This smaller hole, long and deep, is not exhaling or filling up.

The surface seems out of my reach now, and I am stuck here between empty space and hollow ground. I am in the middle of nowhere.

What have I gotten myself into? Where is everyone? Does anyone even know I am here in the depths of this problem? What will they say when they find me? Will they even miss me enough to look for me? How can they not see what is here? What I am dealing with? Gigi, where are you when I need your guidance the most?! Will I ever find my way out alone?

I cannot feel her presence, and I know no one will hear me, no matter how loud I scream. I'm too far away from their world and what they choose to see.

I am deep in the creation of goodness, but I have become mucky, sweaty, and tired. I sit back in my mess, lost on what to do next. Leaning against the wall, I have a resting thought. Maybe I will just melt into the filth, letting us become one, once and for all. Then maybe it will be satisfied.

I find it eerily comfortable as I watch the sun through the opening in the ground disappear behind a wave of clouds.

The coolness feels good at first. It clears the questions and relaxes me. I close my eyes in confusion and exhaustion. Tears well up and roll downward like the soil around me. More tears crawl to the surface from deep inside my core, from a place I forgot existed; a sad place within me that also needs to be filled. Like the core of this hole that no one knew existed, these mournful places need to be filled before life can begin, or they will continue to suck the life from all that is good.

Now I see, in this moment of dark stillness, the sadness was always there dragging my happiness into its depths, eating it up one mouthful at a time. Like gravity, it pulls at the wholeness, threatening my foundation.

All I can see now is hope being dragged down, and I am in too deep to see what is above anymore. The essence of doubt is thick and the air is stifling. All around me, what began as a quest for a better foundation has landed me smack in the middle of a long-buried problem. I'd say I want to crawl into a hole, but that deed is done. I have to smile at the irony, in spite of myself.

I can feel the clouds rumbling overhead, and with worry, I realize I never thought to check the weather. It's just like me in my passionate narrowed pursuit to have forgotten a major detail.

I hear thunder in the background, and a few drops land on my face, melting the dirt to muddy streams. The tiny rivers on my face blend so well that the tears and raindrops become one. The sky opens up, scolding me. *In my haste of confronting nature has it now turned on me, too, trying to wash me away forever?*

I can feel every drop pebbling my face in little pinpricks of sensation. The coolness is refreshing and the dancing raindrops play all around me like a well-scored masterpiece. I can taste the saltiness of my tears as they run over my lips. The mud is washed away from my face, and my clothes are drenched in nature's cleansing wrath.

My clothes feel heavy from the rain, but I feel the strength of my muscles to withstand the pressure of it all.

As my tears are washed away, so is the last of the dry dirt surrounding me. The rain has replenished the ground with moisture. What I thought was an attack, was a gift of nourishment. In my fear, help has come.

I feel a giggle erupt from deep inside, from the same place the tears flowed. It was also hiding from the truth. With my face toward the sky and the water pouring down, laughter bursts out like the rain from the clouds, just too full, with no place else to go.

I close my eyes, and I enjoy every moment of this dark cloud as it cleanses both of us. Nature has showered down upon us as we soak up every ounce. It came to let me know a cloud does not always darken our lives, or block the sun, but that it can give nourishment and hope when needed. Nature finds a way.

As the cloud dumps on the hole and I, a personal cloud has been lifted with faith for the future. My strength has been renewed with the essence of the soil, washing away the chains of insecurity and depression. With the rain, I feel a release from being bogged down by my surroundings. What once grabbed my ankles and made my every step feel like I was pulling through the mud has been miraculously washed away.

I breathe deep and the tiredness rolls off me with every drop of water. The goodness soaks in as a light protective shield keeps everything negative from sticking. This energy infuses with my sweat and tears as my body overcomes the dread that was once buried but never gone.

Yes, the beautiful grass grew over much sadness, smiles were worn and the rains never washed them away, but pain still waited and corroded below. Now I see this pain for its weakness, for its sadness and how it weakened my world. Accepting it for its restless past, it can now be a calm starting place for future growth.

In this rainy silence, I feel the goodness flowing through the ground, straight from the past and into the future. It will flourish with time, a little help from nature, and a few adjustments to my collective beliefs.

I feel Gigi's presence again, her softness, her understanding. I can feel her longing for my happiness. She is here with me. She always has been. I am sorry I ever doubted her. I should have known she wouldn't leave me.

Thank you, Gigi, for your silence. For letting me hear my own voice and feel the rains wash away the fears that held me back.

CHAPTER 24:
A CLEAN SLATE

In the muddy ground, a clear thought shines through.

The rain has subsided, proving to be a passing shower. As the sun holds its position behind the content clouds, the humidity gathers and the soil releases a steamy essence. I stare at my walls, knowing they housed much pain, but I see them now bright with rawness and light. They may have once had the ability to hold emptiness, but will now soon embrace growth, and beauty will prevail.

I cannot believe the energy and power I have given such an issue. It clearly only needed acknowledgment.

The root hole still lies open-mouthed beside me, but no longer gathers energy. It now peers up at me, unresponsive and meaningless, not hungry and bitter. I cannot believe I have lived and breathed through its filter of unsatisfied emptiness. My need to fill it is urgent, but rather than fearfully and frantically stuffing it, I give to it with kind, gentle motion, tucking it in, putting it to bed forever.

I generously place anything that I can find into the quiet opening, conceding to all the holes in my life while letting them know I am all-in until it rises to meet me. Dirt piles in, pebbles gather, and a few stones of the right size land within sight. They clack together like a cue ball hitting its mark, and dirt falls around them coating and cushioning each as they sacrifice themselves for the growth of this hole.

As the dirt rises to the occasion, I pack it down with my bare hands feeling the moist, gritty texture under my nails. I feel the wetness squish up around my fingers and time slows to a dream's pace.

I look to my once dry soil, now transformed to a muddy mixture, and start to play with this moldable, controllable, and tangible substance. I scoop and knead. I find myself splashing lightly in the muddy mess and molding the ground as it sticks to the palm of my hand. It rises and falls to the motion of my playful pat. A childish grin widens as I play with the muddy surface. It feels spongy and rubbery as I smooth over the ground. I wipe it clean and glossy. It appears to me as a clean slate, ready for input.

I drag my finger over the surface, gouging a line through the middle then covering it over, patting it smooth once again. With one swipe, the imperfection is cleared and time has forgotten its presence. I wish life's mistakes were so easily corrected.

The surface waits impatiently for more. My fingers run deep in the glossy tablet. I see without effort, designs appear in the mud. I forget time and age while hearts are drawn with love written through them. I sit happily as the water still heavily soaks my clothes. Without worry or discomfort, I continue to write simplistic words from my childhood. I rewrite words that only the heart knows and remembers from a simpler and happier time. These words consist of dreams, wishes, and favorite images. They have the essence of hope and fantasy. While images of unicorns, pegasuses and shooting stars dance in remembrance of magical moments, this muddy surface becomes a playful connection to the past.

"Love forever" written in code, initials with the "&" sign between them are splashed over quickly. They are replaced with a saying I remember writing over and over a lifetime ago: "Shoot for the stars." I leave these words scribed in the mud. A swirly design decorates them in.

I remember clearly the times I had doodled this phrase on notebooks and book covers as a teenager. Each letter was designed with its own character; colors and glitter were added, stars were drawn in all colors with curved lines leading up to them. I had loved that saying and never knew why, and after all these years, it had been buried in my memory with all its sparkle, color, and ambition intact.

The sound of the hawk calls from above breaking through my playful thoughts. I look up from my hole noticing the sun is struggling to beat through the passing clouds. The rain has left a fresh clean smell and a crisp cool feel in the air. Down here, even the mustiness seems new. The soil glistens with a sheen of life and hope, for it is the first time these walls have been caressed by rainwater in a long time. They seem to smile from deep down, sighing in relief for being rescued from their own deep dark secret of existing.

Soaking in every drop of moisture and sunlight like they are answered prayers, these walls shimmer with gentle appreciation. A breeze reaches down and gets caught up within this space, blowing like a whirlwind, touching every inch, circulating around me and through me. I breathe in, experiencing every moment of relief.

As I look up to the sky, I see the hawk circle again. Her screech is distant and echoes like a call from the past, asking to be noticed and to see what she sees through her eyes from above. Perspective belongs to the hawk. She has the sight to see the bigger picture. Her eyes can see the tiniest of movement, the smallest of potential for survival. She flies and maneuvers, watching for her chance to grab a piece of the future.

I hear her now loud and clear. She screams at me to see what is hiding in the bushes, under rocks, and around the corners waiting to be discovered, hoping I, too, will see the future and grab it. I look down in thought, for only a moment, and the message is clearly written in the mud. From deep down in the ditch of my fear and frustration the answer is spelled out in my own handwriting: "Shoot for the stars."

In the muddy ground, surrounded by a misty fog, I get a glimpse of what can be. I look back up to see the hawk gracefully ascend. I see that the connection to the earth and the sky is a shorter distance than I ever knew. I feel a smile and a squint tightening my face as a ray of sunshine splits a cloud to shine in on me.

The hawk circles twice, three times. She knows the rules of nature and will gather her energy to survive another day. She knows her limitations; she knows if she tries and fails, she will rise again to fly amongst the clouds and search again. She will soar with freedom, knowing nothing else but the will to live and the ambition to keep moving forward. Life for her is the hunt, the capture and the freedom that comes with it. The rawness and simplicity of what she knows is amazing, yet her little body holds the strength, independence and the fight to survive.

With admiration, I watch her loop back once more and as she flies off, her scream echoes to the far distance, warning all she is on the prowl. She commands respect.

As the muddy words begin to dry before me, solidifying my awareness, the sun wins its struggle over the clouds. I feel a connection to the simplistic nature of respect and perspective clearing the slate of the past and offering me a fresh new start to shoot for the stars.

CHAPTER 25:
A PLACE TO GROW

Within my heart there is always room to grow

The sun shares the sky with scattered clouds, but they are white, wispy, and unthreatening. I follow the call of the elusive hawk and climb my way out, leaving my words behind and below. I am grateful to breathe fresh air while sitting at the edge of my hole once again.

The dogs have found their way back to me after retreating to the deck's overhang during the passing rain. Mysti lies next to me, soaking up the sun. Her black fur shines in the heat, her paw moves slightly as she dreams of chasing that one squirrel that always gets away. Buddy pokes slowly through the yard, but keeps me in sight. Penny blends into the background with her chocolate coat and chews on what seems to be a delicious stick. Day-Z lies motionless on her side, molding into the rock that is shadowed by a large tree, the highest point in the yard and fitting for a queen's throne. Her floppy ears limply cover her eyes giving her a perfect outdoor napping experience.

This moment of peacefulness has placed me above this issue as my words stand prominent at the bottom of the hole. I will leave them as a permanent imprint of positive power. Looking down, a sudden new perspective has shrunken this whole problem before me to its rightful smallness. The fear of what it was gave it size, like a mere shadow being cast on the tiniest of objects. The darkness was cast long and thick, growing and waiting for the light to come around. Now my long-buried fears and false beliefs have been shined upon bringing truth to what is before me. An inner knowing has dissipated the encounter to what is, rather than what it seemed to be, as all challenges have the ability to shadow over us and overwhelm. When in reality, its shadow is much bigger than its reality. I look around finding the world quiet, too quiet, like there is something missing from this picture. The field beyond my house is silent, but sways gently like the ocean waving me toward Mr. Hansen's house.

Oh yes! Mr. Hansen! He has gone to Florida. I must check his house and feed the stray cat. That I will do, as I am reminded life outside of me goes on and I have responsibilities. But first, I need a plan for what is before me, a plan for this piece of me that has been opened and left vulnerable to the elements.

I soak up this moment, knowing it is time for change.

A piece is missing right before me and the possibilities to fulfill it are endless. I know the strides I have made, but what belongs here still escapes me. I know this space needs nutrients for strength and a great foundation, *but where does that come from? Where shall I look?*

Although compared to the world and the experience of it, this gap in my foundation seems small enough to handle now. The big question still is, *What will replace it? What belongs here?* Whatever it is, I must start with solid ground.

I must pack it full of strong natural ingredients so it will not cave again to the pressures of the past or future. I imagine roots weaving like veins into the ground and bringing life to every inch. I want to give this space a second chance to bask in the sun, to come out from the shadows of others and grow to its fullest potential.

I envision vividly green and inviting grass as I stare into the hole, noticing life around me. I see for the first time how perfect this spot is for growth. The distance from other objects is great enough to get perspective, but close enough to enjoy the company of others. This is a perfect place to start over; a perfect place for something, *someone*, to grab onto the ground, root themselves to the earth and grow forward and upward to new heights. This is a perfect place for a seedling to be replanted, or a soul to connect with nature. This is the perfect place to grow in the space of unlimited skies. A tree once grew here and will again, given the right care, time, and attention.

Of course, this can be risky for new beginnings are not always easy. They can come with fears: transitional fears, fear of growth, and fear of choices. But here, we will grow.

CHAPTER 26:
BEYOND THE CANOPY

We are all nature, destined to shine in the sunlight and grow beyond the canopy of our limitations.

I lay back again, the grass cushioning my body as the sun beats down. Sleepiness washes over me as the sun's haze tires my eyes. The trees sway gently above. Their shimmering leaves sparkle, bending my mind to thoughts of their existence. They watch over me, studying my presence in their own thoughtful way. Oh, what they must see in all their silence.

I know that nature talks to us, but most of us don't listen.

Auntie El talks to her flowers. "I find them to be very conversational and good listeners. Their smiling faces always agree," she said one day as she gently placed them in a vase, one by one. "None of them are judgmental, and they are full of life with sturdy stems always reaching for the sky. I could not have better friends to care for."

I look up to the trees and wonder if, as God looks down on his garden of life, *does He see us all growing beautifully like individual flowers? Are we all just one big garden being tended to?* We all look to the sun, look beyond ourselves for nourishment and survival. *What is the difference between a tree, an animal, or a person?*

We grow grounding ourselves to the nature and nurture around us. When we are young, we are shadowed by those who are bigger and stronger for protection and safety from the elements of the world around us. We accept these boundaries until it is time to break free and reach beyond the collective group.

We all strive for our moments in the sun, wait our turn to shoot beyond our collective canopies to experience the world. The questions are: *Will our elders block our growth or give us room to grow? Are some of us destined to hang low, stay below, and live within the boundaries others have set? When does shelter and protection become limitations? How are any of us so different?*

Trees are born without a choice of surroundings, standing without legs in limited views. They grow year after year, season after season, maturing and changing, moving only as the breeze and time allows, while grasping for secure ground. I feel this connection to the trees, deep in the roots of my soul, for what surrounds us, changes us, and we have learned to move as others and nature saw fit. With all the twists and turns, the world grew up around us, some in beauty, some not. Our essence is the same. With strength and a passive nature, our existence has been preserved as we have absorbed life through a listener's ear. I have been internally affected by every word, every story, as the trees have been formed by every storm, neither of us knowing the true changes we would endure.

I struggle within to emerge from the life that was set for me. I wish to grow, to stretch my branches, to be my own, fill my own space. Too often those around me have crowded my attempts, and my strongest branches have fallen again and again. With no room to grow and a limited view, I have diminished my size, surrendering to those above and beside me.

My mind has held so many limited thoughts that they are difficult to dismiss.

The view and growth is for others, stop trying. Silence is your purpose. Shade those that are smaller, house those that are in need, be colorful for the view from above, for then they will not see their own smallness. You are the tree in the forest and without the dutiful trees the forest will cease to be.

I stare up at my friendly trees as they stare down on me. I wonder where they have sacrificed. *What would they wish for if they could?*

Would they wish for legs? Use them to draw up from the ground and travel to a brighter destination? Would they go where their branches could reach far? Where their view is open and clear? Leaving behind all they have known, removing themselves from what gave them nourishment and protection? Would one chance never re-

turning again? Would it seek to be larger, stronger, and more beautiful than the world around it?

As I lay here reflecting on my existence, the leaves shake and shimmer as if they hear me and agree. I realize we all have our own growth to master, our own destiny to climb, our own sites to see. The trees, my family, would all be where they are today with, or without, me beneath them. They were not particularly protecting me as much as surviving themselves, weathering the storms, growing from the light they were given, nothing more. Shading may not have been so much intended as protection or a limited belief system but certainly had the effects of both, and with their absence I have now found a new view and a new strength. I know I can withstand the weather, handle the changing seasons, and that my branches have farther to reach. I am destined to see new horizons. I am worthy of this and more.

Here, I melt into the warmth of the sun as images of a growing tree spring before me. I see it growing in spite of its beliefs, like a lonely child waiting for encouragement. I have a sudden urge to rescue that child, that seedling, to give it the legs it needs. To liberate it from limitations, to free it from fears of wide-open spaces, to release it from the ground that holds it down before it finds comfort in the shadows of where it was born.

The trees above me pause a moment in supportive anticipation, for just beyond my childhood home is where I will search. The trees are thick and the shadows cast a cool and damp feeling. Fallen branches will crunch beneath my feet in leaves piled thick, old and decaying. The neglected landscape cries out to me from a distance. It has been a long time since I have visited, only a passing glance and remembrance during daily commutes, yet in the recesses of my mind it remains as it was when I was a child. Today it is lost and forgotten by most, although like many places, it did not start out as it has become.

It was once a field of open space where kids played, a place where the sun got hot and the grass grew high, where we ran, played for hours, or sat deep in the high grass, cut off from the world; where worries were unknown.

We would braid the grass to make crowns or pick buttercups to spin under our chins. This was the place I would spend time sitting alone on the farthest bordering stone wall admiring the beauty of nature. Time and growth have changed all that.

Time has closed in on me. Age has created barriers and fears, condensing my world to tangible moments. But not then. Then, there were moments of thought, freedom, and nature at its purest.

My house was just beyond the next connecting stone wall. I could run through the tall grass at full speed skimming their tips with my fingers. Butterflies flew gracefully. Birds chirped and soared above. Time belonged to me, and space was a beautiful gift. The ground below me was solid and secure. A cruel world didn't exist out there, only nature, only beauty, only peaceful thoughts.

This field beyond my childhood home was a place where my memories began, a time of daydreaming that kept all hopeful images alive. Innocence prevailed, and the future was unknown. This is the essence of what belongs in this space before me: innocence, happiness, and growth.

Sadly, with time forgotten, the wind brought seeds and growth came again and again with no guidance. The beautiful field, once open and bright, now stands tall, thick, crowded, and heavy. There are many struggling to reach for the light, gathered together too closely to grow beyond one another. Maybe, just maybe with a little light and a little understanding, one may come out of the forest to grow and be seen as the individual it truly is.

This is where my lonely soul lives, with the seedling, waiting to be recognized and rescued. Yes, within this space, this place of my past, I will find a life worthy of replanting so it can stretch its branches and grow to its potential.

In that old field a seedling waits, so legs I will give it, and planting I will do, giving both of us our chance in the sun. This tree and I, how free we will be, to begin a new life where the sky is the limit, where the sun beats down, where we will learn to withstand the elements of nature on our own, where our beauty can be revealed from all angles, where our individuality will be embraced and we will not just be seen as part of the whole. We will start over in a place where our roots will not diminish from an oversaturated ground and where our branches can reach far and wide without intruding on others.

A tree, roots and all, will be brought out of the forest to shine in the spotlight of a sunny day. And we will thrive.

Excited for my plan and the future of this space, I look to the trees above me once more and I think of Auntie El and her flowers. I can't wait to tell her that trees are good listeners too. But I am sure she already knows.

CHAPTER 27:
SIGNS OF LIFE

Beyond our walls lies a view of the past and our connection to one another.

My idea is strong; however, my execution plan is weak. With that in mind, I stroll back to the house to check on my other responsibilities. I peel my ball cap out of my hair and throw it on the counter. The house is quiet. The dogs follow me in and I find the boys separately entertaining themselves with movies and games. Jonathan glances up at me with a quick double take, "What happened to you?"

I had forgotten that my appearance would show my dirty work from earlier, and I had to laugh a little while responding, "Oh, just digging out that hole."

His focus resumes on the screen. "You mean, you are making it bigger? Is that really going to do any good?" he asks, almost annoyed to see me so disheveled.

"I hope so. I don't want it damaging anything else."

"Well, you look horrible."

"Thanks!" A little proud that my hard work is showing, I head for the closest mirror to see for myself. I find muddy smudges and crusty damp hair flattened to my face.

"That wasn't a compliment, Mom," he yells from his room.

"Yeah, I know, but life can get messy, honey. Remember that."

A wet towel removes most of the dirt, but I give up after a few minutes.

"I want you both outside in ten minutes!" I yell, heading down the stairs.

"Okay," I hear in a synchronized muffled response. I ignore the attitude while simultaneously thinking that I can't wait for lacrosse camp to start tomorrow.

The clock reads 11:36 A.M., but I feel like it is being shy and lazy. My time in the hole fooled my senses in ways I can't explain, exhausting my mind and body.

I grab a tall glass for water. Ice cubes hit the bottom of the glass, cold and crisp. Under the spigot water rushes over them, as they begin to melt almost immediately. In cool crackles and snaps, it all fills to the rim and settles into a refreshing moment as I look out the kitchen window. Beyond the pool fence where towels and bathing suits hang in the sun, is the view of the field, my guardians in green, and then Mr. Hansen's house. From this viewpoint, only a hint of my problem exists. The handle of the shovel sticks out of the ground, right in my line of sight. I see how easily one could accept the view without dealing with the messy details.

Mr. Hansen's place gives off a sense of loneliness, even from here. I decide now is a good time to check on his house and that it will be a great distraction from my own thoughts. It will also set my mind at ease knowing that the stray cat is fed.

"Jonathan! Justin! I'm headed to Mr. Hansen's house for a few minutes. I'll be right back." My voice carries up the stairs, but gets no response. "Did you hear me?"

"Yes!"

"I want you out at the pool by the time I get back—both of you. Leave the dogs inside, okay?"

"Okay!"

I head out the door as my foot holds back the dogs. They are confused as to why they can't come. I don't want them to follow me, and they surely would, given the chance.

"No. You guys stay. I will be right back." I shut the door tight, with four droopy faces peering back at me from behind the divided glass panels.

I stop at my hole for one quick look, grabbing my walking stick for the short hike. I feel good about the progress I have made. I leave the hole behind, confident it will be there when I return.

I find the rocks on the stone wall solid, but shaky. I step up and over, while balancing with my stick. I find the walk to be quiet and not long enough with an uninterrupted breeze making its way through.

Mr. Hansen's garden is full and green behind the fence and is still shimmering from the morning shower. The back porch is full of old pots and gardening tools. A bench set to the left of the door holds several stacked pots in all different sizes, some cracked and broken, others plastic and full. A half bag of potting soil, along with several tools, lay about waiting their turn to be useful.

Five steps lead to the porch. One railing on the left guides me as I climb up. My stick clunks down on the other side echoing under each creaking plank. The wood is weathered beyond repair with speckles of blue paint still hanging on from years ago. A rubber mat that once said *Welcome* stares up at me, worn and thin, with only the "W" and the "e" barely legible. Three empty silver tin-dishes are scattered beside it letting me know the cat has been around.

I lift the corner of the mat, and find a single brass key that has darkened to a copper color from age and rubbed smooth from use. The key unlocks the door easily, but the door needs a little nudge of my shoulder to open. The house is dark, even in the midday light. A switch by the door flips without a response, so I try to find a table lamp to turn on. Before I do, a rug trips me. The back of a small sofa catches me, but I start to feel unwelcome in this empty home.

My eyes finally settle in the darkness. A floor lamp stands tall and thin turning on with one pull of a hanging chain beneath its shade. It only sheds enough light for me to see the problem. Long heavy burgundy drapes cover a large picture window at the front of the house. They do a good job holding in the darkness and shunning the sunlight while giving this home a cozy and private feel. I cautiously approach them, trying not to be judgmental of their position. I gently pull them to each side letting in the light that beckons at the window. I crease each one neatly the whole length down, relaxing their stiffness.

The room wakes up friendly and accepting to my presence. I find telltale signs of Mr. Hansen and his life outside of his garden and array of hats.

I am not a nosy person by any means, but I am curious about the lives of others. It is refreshing to see that Mr. Hansen is clearly who he appears to be as his life is displayed before me.

A worn leather recliner sits by the back door facing me, directed toward a simple table that holds a small box television set. Between them, an oval braided rug in deep blue, red, and black covers part of the hardwood floor. A rectangular coffee table sits centered on top of it. A small, round doily laces the table top while water rings randomly pattern its surface and the matching end table by the recliner. A remote keeps the end table company. A loveseat sits quietly, in a loud red paisley print. Not a cushion out of place nor wrinkled from use, it is softened by a multicolored crocheted blanket neatly placed over its back. The floor lamp glows by its side. Behind them a staircase leads to the upstairs, where I am sure the bedrooms reside.

If I were to sit on the loveseat, I would see directly into the kitchen over a butcher-block counter. Once in the kitchen, pots and pans hang from an iron rack to the left of the stove. A black iron skillet, a coffee pot, and a few tin canisters are the only obvious staples of daily use. Straight ahead to the opposite wall of the loveseat at the far end of the kitchen, mud-boots rest below a wall rack lined with hooks that are home to numerous ball caps. To the right of the hats and boots, a farm-style door, cut through the middle, leads to the garage. It is decorated with two heavy metal deadbolts and a wrought iron pull handle for each section. Mid room, a small farm table is cluttered with unopened mail and magazines, explaining the folded T.V. tray leaning by the entrance to the kitchen.

Wallpaper spreads from the picture window all the way through the kitchen stopping at the garage door. A yellowing floral pattern, not matching Mr. Hansen's rough persona, indicates years of appreciation.

A sofa table lines the long wall, connecting the living area and kitchen, moving one past the butcher-block counter through an open archway. Framed pictures sit comfortably on the table and hang randomly along the full length of the wall. Proudly displayed in the most noticeable spot in the house, Mr. Hansen would have to pass them several times a day. Some black and white, some color, they span the years and generations. I curiously study each one.

Pictures of his daughter and grandchild, I presume, occupy the edge nearest the window and living area. A small school picture of a young girl smiling with a missing tooth is dwarfed by others behind it, but stands out with her bright pink shirt and matching bows in each pigtail. Several others of that little girl growing up rest closely in various heights. One with the same girl, grown into a young woman, in a graduation cap and gown with her mother, father, and grandfather, Mr. Hansen, seems to be the most recent. From there, time drifts backward to the far end of the table nearest the kitchen ending with a color enhanced wedding photo of a young Mr. Hansen standing by his bride. Many others of his wife and daughter collage the wall and table. The young bride from the wedding photo ages through her daughter's school years and wedding, and then simply disappears somewhere when the granddaughter is around fourteen. It is interesting to see the joyful smiles and poses of the past, collectively spelling out a life of happiness. There are never photos of the heartaches.

After following time backwards down this strip of memories, I am drawn back to one photo that has been placed prominently midway down the table. It is clearly a pivotal moment in his history as all others seem to fan out from there, as if family has grown up around it. It is cozy and secure surrounded by the rest of his life and hovered over by family portraits. A black-and-white photo resides in an old mahogany frame that is beautiful, ornate, and striking. Setting it apart from all the others, it is the tallest and oldest, clearly his fondest memory of all, for it is upfront and in direct view of the reclining chair.

I pick it up slowly to not disrupt the placement of the others. It is heavy in my hands as I am warmed by what I see. Fading and cracked like the photos I have of Gigi and Auntie El together as children, its haunting image stares back at me. I scan the photo as if it were going to come alive. The young woman's brown eyes stare back at me with happiness behind them. I see a very young Mr. Hansen sitting by her. Her long dark brown hair falls behind her shoulder as her knees are folded to her chest, her arms hugging them loosely. Him with his arm around her slightly pulling her close, they both smile deeply into the camera. Then I realize where they are sitting. A tree large and wide dominates the background. Above their heads, a raw hand-carved heart surrounds a loving message deep in the oak's massive trunk. It reads:

"Hank & Elsie, forever"

Branches hover around them, and the grounding roots bulge beneath their legs. I can see the love between them in this picture. Tears well as this moment in history changes the significance of the simple hunk of wood to which Mr. Hansen had a connection.

I gently place the picture back to its resting place, hoping I didn't intrude on his past. From all that I see, he surely seems to have had a very happy and fulfilling life. I hope this is the case, and I suddenly feel I have overstayed my welcome.

I enter the kitchen area in hopes of finding cat food, and I do, by the far edge of the counter. It is coupled with a note:

Lizzi,

> *Thanks for feeding Brutus. Fill the dishes on the porch, and he should be good for a couple of days.*
> *P.S. How's that hole coming? Remember, the keys to the truck are under the front seat. Help yourself if you need it. Thanks again!*

H.

After the cat dishes are washed out and filled again, I shut the drapes placing them back in charge. I shut off the light and leave this simple world to its own ease. A little jealous of the quiet it instills, I find it comforting to know it's here waiting for him when he gets back.

The door closes with the same resistance as opening, but I manage and place the key back in its hiding place. As I turn to my left to grab my walking stick leaning by the door, I notice a rocking chair at the far corner of the porch. It is so distinct and unique I don't know how I missed it coming in. It is of natural wood, big and bulky as if a giant had hand-whittled it for his daughter's dollhouse. Too inviting to ignore, I approach it with great admiration for its structure and solidarity. I feel the smoothness of the arms and rock it back and forth with one hand. The movement glides quietness through me. The well-worn grooves in the deck support the half-moon legs that cradle the bulky frame and invite me to join the motion.

I feel a little intrusive as this must be a very personal spot for Mr. Hansen, but my curiosity wins. I sit comfortably in its deep seat that reaches up to meet my knees. My feet barely hit the porch floorboards. Its rounded back could relax the stiffest of muscles, and I fall backwards into its grip like a sleeping baby molding into his mother's arms.

My toes instantly tip me backwards and forwards, slipping me into a peaceful moment. I close my eyes to smell the freshness of the tall grassed field, imagining Mr. Hansen relaxing here after a long day of gardening, iced tea in hand. After a few minutes of soothing rocks back and forth, I open my eyes to a view of deeper understanding.

The garden is slightly to my left, set catty-cornered so the view of two sides brings on lots of greenness with flashes of color popping out from the tomatoes and yellow squash. The field that separates our houses spreads out before me to the right. The stone wall lines the swaying grass giving clear boundaries. Just beyond the wall, the distance giving it smallness, I see my shovel protruding from the ground where the old oak stood.

I think: *"Hank & Elsie, forever"*

They could see the oak from here. This is where he sits and remembers. This is his view of the past, his view of where life grew from, a view of where his life began. I feel sadness for the day he must have watched that oak being ripped from the earth as it was destroyed and carried away in pieces with no respect for its place in his life.

I see my house differently from here. How far away it can be, yet how intrusive it must have been. Maybe I can change that, ease his loss somehow. *How nice would that be?*

This view of Mr. Hansen and his past has touched a deeper part of me. I see that the view of one person's life is only that, a single view, but *what if we could all see the view as others see it? Would that not change how we all see everything?* Maybe seeing his life from his point of view today will help me see my life differently, too.

CHAPTER 28:
INTERTWINED

The boundaries we set are the seams that tie us together.

Funny how life connects people through the unexpected twists and turns of growing, finding, and caring. Through roots, yards, families, memories, or even photos from one's life, we may take a turn or forever be intertwined with another, maybe as a crossroad that changes the direction of our lives, or as a parallel route running close enough, long enough, for us to feel the same winds on our backs and smell the same flowers by our side. It is the paths that intertwine, the roots which twist around one another to become one, that create a whole new direction of growth.

This reminds me of a place I once knew, an acre of land where the fruit trees were planted and grew for generations. The land was farmed as the family grew, picked, canned, and baked pears and apples. An older gentleman, who was raised on this same farm, finally decided to sell this rooted part of his childhood. He told me that his grandmother would spend hours preparing the fruit for pies, jams, and jellies after he, as a child, picked the ripest of the pears and apples.

"People came from all over just for our fruit preserves and pies. They were the best for miles around," he told me one day. "It was a natural phenomenon. We had a secret, my grandma and me. At the back of the lot where the apple and pear tree rows split, there were two trees that produced the sweetest of fruit. You see, one pear tree and one apple tree had grown in too close to each other. Normally, too close to survive, but somehow they managed, and soon it was apparent that the roots had overgrown and crossed into one another. The fruit that came from those trees made the best pies that my grandmother ever made. They were not really pears and not really apples," he said. "Their roots had combined to help each other survive and altered their path of growth, by producing the sweetest fruit we ever grew. Our special stash we called it. And we never told anyone. When people asked what the secret was, my gram would just say that the sweetest things came from the unexpected. It never happened like that again. Those two trees were meant for one another, I guess. They lived for years, and one season, neither one grew a single piece of fruit. Just like that, they died off together."

This story comes to mind from long ago as I feel my life crossing with Mr. Hansen. We all run parallel with some, crossing our lives with others, but it is when someone's history or view affects something deeper in you, shifting your thoughts, and leading you to a kinder, better place, that is your roots digging in deep, searching for the core of who you should be. I feel the urge to connect with others, find what they are supposed to teach me. I want to learn and grow from them and maybe they will, too.

I feel strength in this truth as I cross back over the stone wall. The same stone wall that before today, I have only seen as a boundary. Now it seems more like a stepping-stone to a connection that was always meant to be. It flows now like a vein through our yards, our lives, connecting us, rather than acting as an obstacle to separate us. I step quickly and easily, this time, barely noticing where his yard has ended and mine has begun.

The birds have quieted, resting in the heat of the day, and playful splashes come from the pool.

The boys call me, begging me to come join them.

I hesitate for work still waits, and my dirtiness is starting to dry my face, but I am inspired by the photos of Mr. Hansen's family and think I want my boys to remember me, not just in photos, but in memories of times spent together.

I open the gate to the pool area and sit under the umbrella to remove my boots. I watch my boys swim and play as if I am not there, and I feel grateful for their happiness, wishing to be a part of it. Their silliness is contagious as I feel a spark light within me.

I jump up yelling, "Look out! Here I come!"

Two surprised boys watch as their mother, the un-fun type, jumps high and cannon balls between them, creating a splash so high I don't know if I should be embarrassed or proud. As I come up for air, I hear laughter. This time, I was not just listening to their happiness, I was causing it.

"That was awesome!" Jonathan yells out.

"You still have your clothes on!" Justin reminds me through his wide grin as water still waves high over his face.

"Oh, really?" I swim toward him in a friendly chase.

He tries to swim away, but I catch him by the foot pulling him under. I hear giggles bubble up from the water. His brother rescues him from my grip by jumping on my back and dunking me. We laugh and play and splash like the teenagers they are, and the rest of the day is light and happy, fulfilling a long-missed oneness with them.

Dinner is almost ready. The house is quiet and Jeremy comes home from work later than usual. The dogs are the first to greet him. The boys pound down the stairs finding the commotion as a sign that there is food to be eaten. The sun still holds strong in the sky.

"How was your day?" I ask, after he finishes filtering through the mail and leaving it on the counter.

"Good and yours?"

"Good."

Jonathan and Justin are searching the refrigerator for drinks as I take the pasta off the stove. Jeremy walks over and leans in for a kiss while loosening his tie.

"I am going to change. Is dinner almost ready?"

"In a few."

"What have you boys been up to all day? Anything good?" He asked, while grabbing Justin by the arm and punching him lightly.

"Not really," he answers swinging back but Jeremy moves too quick for him to make contact.

"Oh, tough guy!"

Justin laughs and swings quicker this time making contact harder than Jeremy expects.

"Enough," I hear myself saying. "Help me set the table and we can eat."

The boys do just that with little complaining while Jeremy heads upstairs.

"I will be right down. I am starving."

Jeremy returns relaxed and comfortable.

"Why aren't we eating on the patio?"

I take this as a request, not a question, and we all move our plates to the table by the pool. It is a beautiful night and the water sparkles with an echo of activity from the day. A good call on his behalf, but I don't find myself saying so as a simple breeze passes through.

The boys recount my award-winning cannon ball to Jeremy. He laughs with them as we enjoy the moment of family and food.

My shovel still stands beside the hole and is visible from the table.

"I can see you are working that hole," Jeremy says between sips of wine. "I thought you were going to call someone."

"I decided to check it out myself first."

"I don't know why you bother. There are people who know how to fix those things."

"Not this time. This time, I want to do it. I have a plan."

"Oh yeah? Should I ask?"

"Only if you really want to know," I say in jest, leaning back and wondering where this conversation will land.

"Not really," he says with a smile.

"I didn't think so."

He knows my projects are more in depth than he prefers. We have both learned over the years that what he doesn't know about he will not be tempted to control.

"You make too much work for yourself," he says with one last comment.

I know if I responded that he would eventually talk me out of my mission. This is something he wouldn't understand, and I would never be able to explain so I offer another serving to the boys to break the thought. They accept willingly. The conversation changes to sports, which always leaves me more listening than talking. I watch them thoughtfully as all three of my boys interact. I find myself grateful while pondering our connections.

They are my life, this space we share, our roles as mother, father, spouses, and sons separate us like stone walls separating yards and yet it is just a small step over that boundary to reconnect and become one again, if only for a day, blending our worlds together with good memories.

We so often overlook that which supports and connects us in this life, from the ground beneath the stone wall to the roles we play in our families, we all share certain commonalities that are placed before us. The truth is we are all one, walking the same earth, sharing the same feelings and needs to be wanted, loved and happy. Deep down, we are all connected, rooted to the same world no matter what is placed on the surface or labels we are given to tell us otherwise. I am thankful for this reminder and the connections I have made today.

My day ends with a secure sense of family, no matter the distance between some of us or the unknown factors that lie ahead, whether it is the family before me or others that remain estranged, I know we are all here to learn and grow from each other. The night is welcomed as coolness sweeps over in a deep blue evening light. A few clouds roll over surrounding the moon like an eye peering down at me. A new memory shines brightly in honor of this today.

Sports camp starts tomorrow and I feel our separation already, wishing all could be like this afternoon deep in the roots of fun and happiness, intertwined and connected with love and family. I know our lives are one, I know our days are different, but hopefully, over the years to come, our connections will be apparent and strong, and our roles in life will only be the ornate distinctions decorating and framing the bigger picture, not the separating factors to life's experiences.

CHAPTER 29:
NEW BEGINNINGS

The beginning is here; the end is ever changing.

Time washes over the night in simple dreams, but all of that is forgotten as the morning rushes in. My boys wake me with frantic energy, worried that we will be late for lacrosse camp. In a flash, my beautiful night has been interrupted with morning craziness. No time for casual coffee or a walk in my yard.

The kitchen is alive with the toaster popping, dishes clanging, and cereal being dumped and crunched. The refrigerator opens and closes too quickly to know who's getting what. The dogs are under our feet waiting for the slightest scrap to fall as Day-Z checks the counter with both paws.

"Day-Z, get down!" is the most common phrase during the morning rush. I pack lunches, snacks, and water in one medium-sized cooler as Jeremy tries to kiss me goodbye.

"Call me later," he says ignoring my agitated look.

My coffee will have to wait. I change my clothes and load the SUV as sports gear clangs together. A quick check of the coolers completes our summer initiation, and I know my leisurely mornings will be few and far between.

The morning drop-off is always a fiasco with duffle bags, gear, and coolers being unloaded. You can see the freedom on the drivers' faces as the cars dart off, empty of children.

The air smells crisp with the scent of freshly cut grass as the boys rush off. They run to catch up with friends as the cooler swings between them and gear is flung over opposite shoulders. I roll down my window to yell goodbye, but a slight wave of the hand is the only gesture I get in return.

Is yesterday so far away already?

I'm sure it is not at the forefront of their thoughts today, but I feel closer to them, still, and it helps as they go off on their own to hope yesterday will stick in their memories.

"Remember, Dad will pick you up," I scream in their direction.

All of a sudden, my day is free and the quiet is paired with a coffee from the local drive-thru. The emptiness of the car clears my mind, but I know something waits to intrude on this moment. I push out any scrambling thoughts by turning on the radio and slipping carefully into the music.

I round the corner of my street, passing by Mr. Hansen's mailbox. The house is too far from the road to be seen. I think of his note from yesterday and the offer of his truck. Maybe I will search for my seedling today. My mind drifts from the song. I try to refocus on my peaceful moment. The lyrics play softly and true as I push away thoughts of what the day will bring.

Enjoying my coffee on the porch and calling Auntie El will reset my day to the beginning. It is only eight-thirty. The sun still hides behind the tall greens and the dew has settled to a dull shine.

The dogs are happy I have returned so quickly, for many days they are left until at least noon when we leave so early. They run through my legs at the slight crack of the door opening, knocking into me and almost spilling my coffee. After one loop around the yard, they return to sit by my side on the porch.

Auntie El answers on the second ring with readiness in her voice, but to be polite, I say, "I didn't wake you, did I?"

"Oh no, dear, you have to be up before the crickets sleep to wake me."

I laugh a little at her quirkiness and ask, "What do you do so early in the morning?"

"Whatever comes to mind. Usually crossword puzzles or some reading. This morning I made more of those cookies your boys love so much."

"I wish I could wake so easily and get so much done," I comment, admiring her energy.

"Someday when the kids are grown and you have time to sleep, you won't be able to. Life is funny that way."

"How cruel," I say and we both have a good laugh.

"I saw the newspaper. Beautiful!" she says with a slight shyness in her tone.

At first, I am thrown off by her words, and then a wave of embarrassment and sadness sweeps over me. With the morning craziness and my own deep thoughts over the last few days, I had forgotten.

How could I forget? It is July first.

It has been three years to the day that Gigi passed away. I had called in the memorial a few weeks ago. Every year, I feel the sadness of her passing all over again. I remember the morning I said goodbye to her, how Aunt Lil and I spent all night in the hospital with her, how the doctors said it was just a matter of time. Everything still feels so fresh and, since she is still a big part of my life in spirit and memory, the anniversary of her death always feels like she is being ripped from my life again, like a harsh reminder that she is not really here.

How could I forget?

"I miss her, Auntie El. I really miss her."

"Me, too, Lizzi. Me, too! We can only honor her memory now in our own lives by growing and seeing the good in life. That's all she would want."

My breath is jagged as I think of Gigi and Auntie El together and how it must have been even harder for Auntie El to lose her only sister, but I manage to say what I am thinking.

"Thank you, Auntie El."

"For what, honey?"

"For being there, for understanding. For being you. For never leaving me alone."

She could hear the tears in my voice and paused to let my words sink in.

"Oh, honey, don't be sad. You will never be alone. We are all connected whether we like it or not. That is why it is so hard. Everyone feels crowded and lost at the same time, like not seeing the trees in the forest because we are too close to the truth to accept it. Time will bring everything back around to us. In spirit or in life, it is just the nature of things."

"I guess you are right. I am so tangled up in the feeling of everything that I can't find the end or the beginning anymore."

"The beginning is here, and the ending is where this beginning takes you.

Your Gigi knew that and wanted you all to have your own beginnings in hopes that your endings would all connect somehow. Sometimes we all have to jump from the nest if we want to fly back to it someday."

"You are special, Auntie, you truly are!"

"I am always here for you, Lizzi. Don't you forget that."

We end our conversation with plans for visiting later in the week, and with no one around, I begin sobbing uncontrollably for the loss of Gigi and for the connection I know will always be there. With my face in my hands, I cry until my tears finally wash away the fear of the unknown and I find the courage to jump into a new beginning.

> *In Loving Memory of our Gigi*
> *You will be a forever fixture in our memories,*
> *our sky, our hearts, and our prayers.*
> *Thank you for all your creativity,*
> *love, smiles, and laughter.*
> *You are sadly missed and happily remembered.*

CHAPTER 30:
SHIFTING GEARS

Life gathers in the thick of the woods, waiting a chance to grow.

A breeze comes by and dries my tears like the hand of Gigi wiping them away. I instantly know what I need to do in honor of new beginnings and healing the past. In Gigi's memory, I will plant a tree in this hole of mine. The empty space of hardship and devastation will be filled with life once again, filled with roots and growth, and be given a chance to feel whole again. By planting substance and solid ground in its place, my inner emptiness will begin to heal.

The old field of my childhood years is where I will search. A landscape of my past, now an overgrown forest, holds a piece of my future. There I will find a small tree, a lost seedling in need of light and attention, waiting to be rescued from a world of neglect.

Mr. Hansen's truck will be perfect for the job. As the day unfolds, I will march my way to his house and take him up on his offer. Healing starts today and growth will follow.

Lunch rolls around with the normal morning chores behind me. The dogs have found solitude in the coolness of the air conditioning, but I am restless to see my project through. I leave them behind, resting on the floor, grab my walking stick by the door, and find myself over the connecting wall, heading to Mr. Hansen's before I know it.

Mr. Hansen's house seems closer than ever. I bypass the house itself, vowing to check it later. The garage door slides open without hesitation. I find a rugged 1960-something pickup truck in a dull green color. It is slightly rusty, and rests peacefully amongst fellow antique tools hanging on the walls. It appears quiet, yet strong, different from the image of Mr. Hansen driving around town, for then it always seems frail and clunky struggles its way down the road.

Funny, how fitting he looks in it. *But me?* Oddly, I am excited to find out.

I throw my walking stick in the bed of the truck and it lands with a tinny clang, clang. The door handle is metal, long and curved outwards. I open the door with a tug, squeak, and a clunk. The interior is simple, hollow-looking, dirty and torn from wear. I scoot in one cheek at a time, shimmying myself behind the wheel. The stiff, vacant facade turns out to be quite cozy and comfortable. Mr. Hansen's straw hat, frayed and lifeless, sits in the passenger seat beside me. I bounce playfully up and down on the seat, hands on the steering wheel, feeling childish in my surroundings. I place the hat on to get the full effect of playing the role of old farmer headed to town.

The keys are in their hiding place, where anyone could find them. Two single keys on a flimsy ring come out ready and willing. With a slight lift and pull of the bar beneath me, the entire bench shifts forward, smoother than I expect. The steering wheel is thin, black and big before me with a small center for the horn. A stick shift protrudes from the center of the floor to my right.

Well, this should be interesting.

A rectangular clutch petal sticks out of the floor and is stiff when I press on it. I press the gas slightly while turning the key. The truck starts a rumbling, coughing series until it settles to a rough, putting purr. I grind the gears trying to find reverse. Popping the clutch sends me jerking backwards into the driveway. I turn the wheel just in time to keep me on the small inlet meant for this reverse exit. Now facing the main road, I stop with a small cloud of dust floating through the open windows. *Feisty old coot, isn't it?* I guess I was wrong, struggling does not seem to be in this truck's vocabulary and taming this bad boy may be a challenge in itself.

Makes me wonder a little more about the true Mr. Hansen.

I find first gear easier, but a release of the clutch again sends me forward faster than I wish. The truck lurches and hops forward several times until we reach the end of the driveway. I try to stay in control as I pull out onto the main road with another pop of the clutch and thrust of the gas. I am hoping it forgives me for my awkwardness before I reach my house, where I will pick up a few tools needed for this rescue. I can't help myself but test the horn as I pull up to my garage. The dog's howling amuses me for some reason as the goose-like sound surprises me, too.

Again, tools are needed: gloves, for obvious reasons, and a shovel for leverage and to coax the seedling into leaving the only place it has ever known. A wheelbarrow will ease the transportation and allow me to gather extra soil and stones to fill the hole and give the young tree a solid new start.

Here we go, Gigi, here we go!

I feel Gigi beside me, smiling at my hat and rooting me on as I shift gears and pick up speed in search of the life ahead of me. She is my co-pilot, my cheering section of one, and my force of inspiration. Together we are unstoppable.

Maybe it is the truck, maybe it is the hat, but I feel like a whole new person as I steadily move down the road. I know there is life out there waiting to be found, waiting for a chance to grow. I will find it today. It is buried in the darkness and screams to be seen. I will give it legs and clear a path for it to come into the light.

The child in me is coming out to play, seeing that this seedling will be found where my childhood thrived, where my happiness lived, where my soul met nature and flourished because of it. Now I will bring a piece of that memory back to my home and make it part of my future. I will gather it from the ground that knew me once; the ground that once felt the impact of my bare feet. The tiny bare feet of the child I once was, that loved the feel of nature beneath her and around her.

Here we go, Gigi, here we go!

Within minutes I pull onto the short dirt road that leads to the far end of the field. It, too, has narrowed over time and closes in on me the closer I get to the stone entrance. Few know of this pathway, though someone has kept it clear enough to recognize. Recently taken over by the adjacent church, with whispers of turning it into a local dog park, no one will consider my presence intruding. The truck creaks a few extra moans while toughing the terrain, but we arrive in one piece, ready for our mission.

My mother's house still resides a little more than an acre away. Hidden from my view, I am happy for the distance. She is likely to be home, but visiting is not on the agenda. My presence here today is for a much more important reason. My gloves slip on easily, and I instantly feel protected and confident in these surroundings.

The sun is hot somewhere in the sky, but only dampness lives here where the heat lingers, trapped and sticky. Nonetheless, I leave the hat behind, take my tools and rush into the woods with little knowledge or care for how it will play out.

The break in the wall is still apparent, inviting me in, but the underbrush is thicker than I ever thought possible. The wheelbarrow awkwardly rolls through the lowest pathway while the shovel and walking stick wobble loosely inside. The old fallen sticks and thick leaves crunch beneath my boots. Low hanging twigs snag my hair as I bob and weave away from them. With every tug, they entangle further.

I feel them trying to stop me, like they know I'm coming for one of their young. My good intentions push me forward through their assault on my senses. Come to find out, intentions are no match for the physical as a rock jumps out in front of me. I trip forward and the shovel handle catches me square in the gut. I lean over to accept my pain and curse the rock that broke my stride. It has drawn my attention back to the ground beneath me.

When I look down, the stone that had grabbed my foot is dislodged from the ground and lies there, still and innocent. A distinct line shows where the dirt and moisture owned it before. It is quite a nice rock, smooth and grey, too large to be pulled so easily with my step, so I pick it up and brush it off, feeling its weight and size. I balance it with both hands. This stone knows why I am here. It has brought attention to itself and is begging to be taken with me. I agree. It is too special to leave in the darkness, and I wonder how many others would like to come along. I throw it in the wheelbarrow with a loud clunk and watch my path for any others that may want to accompany me on my journey. The stones show themselves and are surrendering easily. The barrow is heavy and full, so without my seedling, a quick trip to the truck is necessary.

The day is passing too quickly, so I hurry back from the truck. It is a few hours past noon. I know any sunlight the trees are letting in will soon be blocked for the evening, so I wish to discover my treasure before my time is up.

I return to my search through the same path where the stones befriended me. The tree branches don't seem to care this time. They stay out of my hair and keep to themselves. The air gets cooler the deeper I go, and I realize the sun is completely hidden by the canopy of trees.

I can hear the wind whipping, rustling the branches and leaves above. The elder trees that control these surroundings aren't letting in the whispers from outsiders, showing their authority and control over the ones below. Maybe I am being paranoid, but I think this is for my benefit as they bring attention to themselves to prove their power over me while I'm here.

I can't help but look up at them wondering why they feel so threatened and insecure when they stand so strong and healthy.

What could they lose from others receiving encouraging thoughts? If nothing is below them, will they feel small? Are they not comfortable in their own, right? Do they not know that they are the strength, the protectors and the heart of nature? Do they not know that control, by limiting incoming influences, only creates false beliefs? They are only trees: Figures of nature, born in their place in this world, with their legs firmly planted in the ground. Right?

I stare up at them in awe of what they have endured to reach such heights and ask silently to allow me to save one of their own from the struggles of their path. I get no answer, just more whipping winds and rustling from above.

I forgive them for their attempts to scare me and enjoy the movement playing out above for this is the dance they know and they can't help themselves but to play along with nature.

They stare down at me silently in their own right; tall, vacant, and hovering. I feel their glare and watch them studying me, swaying in their greatness. I spin myself around to get a better view. Lightheartedly, I sway with them in a dazed hypnotic state. The motion feels free as my mind tries to catch up, and within a minute, dizziness and nausea set in. A low breeze chills me and knocks me off-balance. I start to fall, but my hand lands on a cold, mossy surface. I take it for the sturdiness it offers, leaning for just a moment.

My head clears, my stomach settles, and I realize where I am. I have landed on the large rock that was the centerpiece of the field. This old friend has caught me in my disoriented state. It seems so small now, but I am sure this is it. Here is where I use to sit and could see all around me. The one all the kids would meet at on those hot summer days. It was the meeting place, the rock that everyone knew.

I find myself pulling the brush and vines away. I climb up to sit down a minute and remember how special this spot was. It barely seems fair, that its significance has dwindled in time.

The view has changed, but I close my eyes to feel the wind and smell the fresh cut hay that once inhabited this area. The rock feels cold, not warm from basking in the sun like I remember. Its core is damp. *What else should I expect after all these years of neglect?* I wish I could dig it up, take it with me. My gloves come off so I can feel its texture once more.

I roll my hand over the moss with a soft stroke and watch it all crumble away. The rock's scars are revealed in familiar bumps and grooves. I remember now the shape so well, large enough to fit several scurrying children, jumping from its height. How large I feel sitting here, and I wish I could shrink to honor its significance, for it makes no excuses; it doesn't apologize or change for its surroundings. Time has passed and growth has surrounded it, but it still sits true to the world. I can feel the cool, wet surface beneath the green softness. Its strength reaches up and shivers through my spine, deep from its core, welcoming me back.

I apologize quietly for forgetting about it, and thank it for supporting all those memories for so long. Maybe someday, someone will clean up this lot and recognize this large stone for the beautiful landmark it truly is.

I relax a moment, not wanting to say goodbye to my old friend. I look around wanting to etch this moment into my memory, when a strip of sunlight reaches through the clusters of branches and shines directly on the rock beside me.

A hazy strip of light sparkles and flickers like an old movie trying to project its image. It dances beautifully before me, capturing a piece of my childhood and rendering me helpless in my present moment. The light finally lands steady, thick enough to touch as a little girl appears ghostlike, but as clear to me as the summer day she lives in.

Humming lightly, she braids together a collection of flower stems. The small white- and yellow-petaled heads stick out here and there from the small rope. I can tell her mind holds no worries and I admire her innocence. I feel the urge to speak to her, but her peacefulness is hard to disrupt. Watching her illuminates something deep inside me.

The sun shines on her from somewhere through the canopy and flashes of light shimmer in her long blond hair for she lives in the sunbeam and nature has allowed her to visit as a gift from the past.

The calmness she reflects takes my breath away. I am afraid to breathe for her light and airy appearance may blow away too easily. I study her every move, watching her little fingers weave each stem slowly and delicately. Her little black patent-leather shoes with tiny buckles tap against the stone. Her white tights lead up to a white crinoline dress with black polka dots.

I remember those special occasions when we had company, when the best part was wearing that dress. It would flare like a parachute when I twirled fast. The tights were uncomfortable and the shoes were slippery, too slippery to climb on this rock, but on those days in my favorite dress, I would sneak out of the crowded noise and find my way out here to be with nature and its silence.

I want to reach out and touch her, hold her, tell her it will all end well even when times get tough. I want her to know that these days are the ones she will always remember, that these memories are the ones that will ground her and connect her to nature.

I have so much I want her to know, to understand, to watch out for, but it doesn't seem fair to disrupt her peaceful, magical place.

Why tell her life is hard, that people will disappoint her, and heartache will come with the pleasures? Why explain that the simplicities that she knows now will feel like illusions she will seek out later in life?

I look away for it is too hard for me to watch and not want to be her again. Her loveliness makes me want to jump into the sunbeam and disappear into her world forever.

I want her to know this moment fully for all its pleasures because there will be times that these moments will be what she clings to so that all else is tolerable. This will be her foundation for what truth, happiness, and simplicity really are.

With this thought I watch her in amazement, as she looks my way. I hear her small voice say, "Do you like butter?"

"What?" I choke out from beneath my held breath.

"Do you like butter?" she repeats and holds up a small perfect yellow buttercup.

"I don't know. Let's see."

As I lean forward into her light, I can feel and smell that summer day. The birds are chirping and the wind blows in my face. The sun feels warm and I can hear distant chatter and laughter from the company at the house. I close my eyes and lift my chin as she places the buttercup under it. A yellow glow must have reflected on my skin when she twirls it because her soft voice says, "Yep, you like butter!" and she giggles softly.

She continues to weave the buttercup into her flower string. A tear slips from my eye as I watch her wrap it around her head like a crown fit for a queen.

"How do I look?" she says with a smile that shows off her dimpled cheeks.

"Beautiful! Can I tie it for you?"

"No thank you. I can do it," she says in her tiny, polite voice. "There, how's that?" She puts the crown on her head and shakes it lightly to see if it will stay.

"Perfect!" I tell her. "You are perfect!"

She then links her fingers together, stretching her arms out straight, takes a deep breath and drops them to land on her lap in a shy sort of way. Her ankles are crossed as she lifts her legs, knocking her heals against the rock. Noticing her black patent leather shoes shining in the light, she separates her feet and asks, "Do you like my shoes?" Her heels touch and her toes tap together with a clicking sound.

"Very much. They are beautiful."

I watch her bring one shoe up to her hands. She begins to unbuckle the small black strap. "They aren't very comfortable, but they go with my dress. Isn't it pretty? It's my very favorite."

She fiddles with her shoe, removing and throwing it as far as she can toward the house. She throws the other one too, and they both land softly in the sprouted tall grass.

"Do you want to see how far I can jump?"

She stands up with little effort and I wonder about her white tights and how dirty they will get. I know my mother hated me getting my tights dirty, but her toes grip the rock so gently, the thought leaves me.

"Sure. Is it too high for you?"

"Oh, no! My mom doesn't like me to jump in this dress or those shoes." She leans in and whispers, "That's why I took them off. They're too slippery up here. She will scold me later for getting my tights dirty, but it's worth it."

She balances herself, then turns and says, "Come on, jump with me. Its lots of fun."

I stand up slowly, balancing myself on the slippery damp rock beneath me. I feel the enormity of my adult size compared to this precious little girl and the rock that has shrunken over the years. My boots feel bulky, awkward and misshapen, unable to grip the surface.

I can't resist her tiny fingers as she reaches out for my hand. We blend as one as the sunbeam widens to engulf us both. I can fully sense the moment she lives in, a quieter time, a peaceful place, solitude at its best.

"Ready?"

Without waiting for me to answer, she swings our arms back and forth, counting as she goes, "One, two, THREE!"

I close my eyes to capture this carefree moment. Through the air we fly, soaring in a fearless, faithful leap into the plush tall grass. The smile on my face reflects the giggles that stay echoing in the sunbeam, fading to a near distance.

My landing is not in the dry, tall grass of a friendly field, but rather in the mushy wet leaves of a forgotten forest. The sunbeam has gone and has taken the memory with it. The squishiness beneath my feet awakes me to my time and place. It was the plunge I needed to bring me back to earth, but for a short moment, I was stripped of adult worries.

I open my eyes, a little sad to be back. I look around, now worried that someone may have seen me in my happy illusion. I see mostly trees, brush, and moss around me, but one shimmer of light catches my eye. Another beam of light reaches down through the crowded brush, just beyond my rock.

Are my eyes tricking me again? Teasing me with delusions? Not this time. This time it spotlights the perfect little tree.

There it stands; tall, lanky, and thin like a teenager who grew too fast, it slumps over slightly, feeling the weight of its own growth. It seems to weep from the lack of light, but somehow, has managed to survive. A few green leaves grow sporadically and hang limply off its awkward branches. In my surprise, I dash to its side.

The area is full of weeds and brush with no path directly to my little tree. However, in my excitement I do not think beyond or before my focus. Instantly as I jump into a patch of thickened ground cover many thorny, wiry tentacles reach far and long to attach themselves to my pant legs. I try to make my own path, somehow believing it will be easy, but they are quick, sharp, and determined to take control.

We have gone nowhere and neither will you. We have you now and we won't let you go this time. A dark dismal place is where you are comfortable. We can feel it. You know it and you can't fool us. A place of light is an illusion you will never have again. Your place is with us. Time will pass without sunshine, without warmth, and we won't do it alone anymore.

I fight to remove myself from this dense familiar area. I panic, as I believe in this moment that they are right, that a path out is impossible. *Who am I to rescue someone else when I can't save myself from myself?* They will pull me down, hold me here for eternity and I will never see light again.

I entangle myself further in thought and pain. Deeper and deeper, I feel them pull me in like a conversation I wish I never started. With every move, with every word, with every thought, I am pulled down further. It is not until my blood is drawn that the pain is all too familiar and I feel my escape is absolutely necessary.

A last burst of confidence, with a few twists, turns, and a slight kick in the right direction, I find myself clear of the obstacles that deterred me from my purpose. I trip slightly, balancing on one foot, stumbling backwards. I instinctively grab at the closest object I can reach to break my fall. The young tree is my savior as my hand clenches it tightly. Catching me, it bends to the call of my rescue. It leans over completely with my awkward grasp. I release it as soon I realize I have pulled it down with me. It springs itself upright in a resilient stand.

I don't bounce back so easily.

I stand slowly, pulling at the old leaves that have embedded themselves in my hair. I take a breath for my narrow escape. I fumble to regain some composure before examining the seedling.

There it stands bowing to me in a sheepish way. I lift its head to see nature's untarnished perfection. I feel its rubbery texture that supports its small leaves. I look over every inch and feel its thickness that enters the ground in a perfect design.

I brush away the leaves that cover the roots and run my fingers along the thin spidery toes that reach in, searching for nutrients, searching for and gripping onto any support it can find. I grab the trunk and rock it gently to see if a shovel is needed. One more time through the thicket is all I have left in me. Then, as if this innocent life is begging to survive and can read my mind, it moves slightly, giving into my offer of coming to a better place.

It relinquishes its grip on the ground, so easily, I wonder if it was holding on for just one more day.

Isn't that what we all do during those rough times?

We hold on, thinking tomorrow will be the day. The day life will start, the day everything will make sense, and our view of the world will finally be fearless. We hope for that moment that someone or something will transplant us to a place of clarity and balance. Life is just one more day, but those days add up and life is what we get, willing or unwilling.

Ironically, here stands my savior, as I believe I am rescuing it. The lonely child in the thick of the woods has met its rescuer, and time stands still. It releases its resistance and comes willingly in hopes of a brighter place. The seedling lands in the wheelbarrow with raw roots, exposed. I fill the barrow with soil from the surrounding area. The soil is welcome and comforts the small tree in its transition. Like a baby's favorite blanket, it covers the rawness and soothes the severed nerves with warmth.

Time and time again, I repeat the path back and forth to the truck, finding more stones and soil along the way. The path no longer fights back. I trample all thorns with no thought of them by the last barrow full. *How small my obstacles have become?*

Proud of my find and rescue, I finish loading the truck. My tree sticks out of the pile leaning helplessly to the weight of itself. I promise it a safe trip and a new home where the sun shines daily, where the dogs are frisky, and the birds are friendly.

The straw hat waits patiently on the seat. I place it back on my head and become farmer Lizzi once again. The truck starts with the same coughing and sputtering, and shoots off with the slightest encouragement.

My journey home is quiet. The sun has dwindled to a dull shine, allowing shadows to grow in the wake of its heat.

CHAPTER 31:
ALONG THE WAY

Along the edges of our journey grows the seeds of learning.

My journey home is filled with mixed emotions. I am excited for my beautiful tree yet tired and achy from the heat and hard work. I see the end of this project in sight, but have connected so deeply to this journey, that I feel it will be hard to move on.

What happens tomorrow when my foundation is solid and my world begins to grow?

Nature has shown me this path, helping me to see and feel what I needed to, to move on. My journey home continues to inspire my thoughts.

Nature is the wonderful magical world we live in. It has the answers if we look, if we search, if we grow. We can only walk the path nature leads us down, and appreciate the details along the way.

Details are lessons in disguise. They are the lessons, or seeds, that are planted along our paths hoping to catch root. From the most enlightened journeys, to the simplest ones of going home, there are lessons along the way, waiting to be recognized. What we see may give us great insights to beautiful truths.

I watch the flowers and trees in blurs of color pass by my window. They are plush and fresh, renewing my energy. I take note of my journey so far and the little seeds that have been planted along this journey's edge.

I found my soul connected to nature through the pureness of my inner child. I was shown that memories are everywhere, from the stars above, to the roots below, and I was reminded that forgotten places may hold life to fill the emptiness.

Within these edges runs a stretch of road where I found peace and wholeness through a little hard work, thought, and a better understanding of family.

I have addressed my fears, laying them out for life to sort through them. They are out there for all to see. I am proud of the work behind me and look forward to the road ahead.

At the end of each road begins another, and I feel I have traveled far in my mind, body, and spirit with little physical ground covered, making me question the distance to a new life. I see now that some distances may be short, while the journey is long and challenging. All I can do is move ahead with the past behind me, the future ahead of me, and truth by my side. My journey has just begun, but home, here I come.

Gigi whispers in my ear, "Not too fast. Enjoy the travels between the challenges for these are the moments of rest and recognition."

I know she is speaking of the little girl in me that I must honor. I must recognize and accept that she is taken care of, respect her growth, and allow her to move forward.

That little girl deserves to be happy, to be innocent, and to move beyond the sunbeam even though it is tough out here. I will bring her with me and integrate her into my life. I am glad she is back.

I leave behind the obstacles and restraints of the past and let them stay in their darkness knowing I do not have to visit them anymore. I sigh, partially for the heat, and partially for the releasing of those burdens.

In slow motion, I truck down this road as solidness and hope weigh down the back. I take this moment to appreciate the edges of my journey home.

Shadowed light flickers over my windshield as the wind flows in against my dry, dirty skin. It washes away all my tension. I breathe a calming warmth as the day settles deep down in my core. I become aware of every flower, garden, and tree that blesses this road home with growth and beauty.

I also notice neglected areas of trees in large patches, overlooked by most commuters. They are thick and dense like the field of my past. They are crowded and broken down within themselves, some toppled over with no place else to go.

A family they are, as they were born from one another, affecting each other with their every move. The storms come and destroy the weak. The strong stand tall, flourishing in their time while the young try to survive, hoping one day to reach the sky. These families, these forests are overlooked; few onlookers notice the struggles they have endured.

Land or family, I pray for the life that is within them, for when one is destroyed there is a loss of connection to the past. I am urged to stop and clear out all the dead wood, all the bad words that have riddled them over the years, in order to show them they can all stand tall and beautiful again. But it is not my place, not my property, to intrude or judge what has become of them, so I move along in hopes that I can save just one tree, one life, from the devastation.

My new beginning starts as I round the corner and this path ends. I see exactly where I belong, where my children breathe, where my husband stands by me and my dogs run free. It has led me to the heart of my life. My journey has led me to the beginning, to my home, to me. This is where new life will grow.

CHAPTER 32:
GROUNDED

Life is grounded to the roots of the past while growing toward the light of the future.

Carefully, I pull the truck up over the lawn, backing it up to the hole. My arrival has brought on a sea of howls and barks as the truck door creaks open and slams shut.

The cool tone of the late afternoon air has slowed down the birds, leaving only the hardy to chirp sleepily. The hawk is nowhere to be seen. Maybe she is resting in the tall evergreen just observing for now.

With a quick jog to the patio door, I set the dogs free. In all their excitement for my homecoming, they bark and race across the lawn in attack mode at the large metal intruder that has invaded their space. I watch them in their silliness all the while knowing that if a real threat presented itself, that they would run tails between their legs. Their energy puts a spring in my step as I head back to the truck.

I smile for the happiness they give my days and the life they bring to the yard, which would be lazy, still, and drab every afternoon if it were not for them. They are the life that runs here, and I am grateful for their presence.

I sometimes wonder if they are happy here, not that they know any difference. But given a choice, *would they have chosen another caretaker?* I try to imagine where they would be, what kind of life they would have if I hadn't chosen them to take home, but maybe they chose me.

I believe we all choose each other, one way or the other. From the person we meet at the grocery store who strikes up a conversation, to the friend we've had since childhood, we are drawn together, connected through the common threads of nature. Whether it's through the roots and ground we share, the choices we make, the energy that surrounds us, or the energy we give each other to grow and be, we see a piece of ourselves in the other.

We plant ourselves amongst one another every day with good intentions, hoping for interactions of emotions, support, or at least a connection, so together we can grow and move forward. We are all part of one big forest trying to stretch our branches. Our lives intercept, some for one moment, some for a lifetime, but each interaction propels us forward into the future. *Where would we be without the other?*

We are grounded to one another as the push and pull of nature creates friction and energy. Caring for another living creature gives me purpose, grounding who I am. I find this every day with my four-footed furry friends. The simplest of actions, feeding, watering, and giving love grounds me in this world while their energy and returned love inspires me. I am excited to add my tree to the list of lives to care for and watch grow. Its beauty and life will stretch further than its branches, bringing joy to my surroundings.

I find myself moving across the yard with the energy of my animal friends beside me. I gravitate to the planting of this new element in my life, hoping to reset the balance and keep life flowing through my surroundings.

The truck bed hovers over the edge of the hole, which waits patiently for me. The tailgate releases in a grumpy rattling slam. I climb up. Looking down at my hole, I see all the hard work I have endured. It doesn't seem like much now that all is said and done. I feel a little embarrassed for the fuss I have made. I can see the smallness of it and wonder how I got so lost in the thought of the issue that it overrode my ability to see it clearly. I smile at it for I see that my struggles were more my own thoughts than its physical reality. But this one small hole has bridged two parts of my life thus healing the past with hope for the future.

I start to shovel the dirt into the hole, one scoop at a time. Individually specks of dirt fly through the air, landing lightly, scattering the bottom. I am finally laying it all to rest.

I see my words "Shoot for the Stars" scrolled in the dried mud below, showing through the first dusting. One more heaping scoop lands, covering it forever. Those encouraging words spiral up with each shovelful. One scoop at a time, my emptiness fills to a solid foundation.

With all the strength I have left, I scoop and throw, scoop and throw, scoop and throw. The emptiness fills up faster and faster, quicker than I would ever have imagined. The truck begins to empty. I feel a satisfaction for the work that has been done. Every heavy scoop portrays another epiphany. The sunlight filters through them as they land solid and aware of their place and purpose. Fulfilling my destiny starts here by filling my emptiness with solid ground.

At the top of the hole the ground levels off. The last of the dirt gives the ground a slight heaping fullness. I jump down to dance proudly on this new ground. This is where the past has met the present and the future will grow. Packing it vigorously with every step, I lock in the goodness intended for new life.

On my knees, a smaller hole is hollowed out with my bare hands. My lanky tree waits in the truck-bed leaning forward for the pile beneath it has disappeared. Only the collected stones and my walking stick keep it company. It appears scared and lonely. I feel sorry for it, because it looks pathetic and needy in a state of confusion. Ripped from the world it knew, finding itself exposed to new elements, and unsure of the future, it slumps forward almost begging for truthful answers to the questions we all ask at one time or another.

Where am I going? What will become of me? How will I survive in new territory? Where will my nutrients come from? Who will interact with me? How can this be good? Will I shine in the sun or just wither to the heat? Will my roots dig in deep or will the shallowness of life overcome me?

"Don't worry little one," I say softly. "Boundaries are here. Yes, boundaries and love. We can have both. We will have boundaries for those who cause pain and try to give us limits. Boundaries for those who are jealous and petty, trying to hold us back. We will grow to our potential and thrive in the sunlight. Because those who are no longer here don't get a say, don't get to intrude on our space, anymore. We have moved on, and grow we will, accepting all this space, with no one shadowing over us, controlling our sunlight, or limiting our growth. How wonderful and scary this will be."

I hear its concerns as I lift it gently from the truck.

Oh no! Here we go. Is this going to hurt? What is happening?

I gently place the raw severed roots—the nerves, if truth be told—into the center of the moist, airy soil. I can feel the comfort and relaxation that overcomes the whole tree. A tear falls, moistening my dirty cheek. I reach down, sliding fresh soil over the limply planted roots. I tuck it in with my tears dripping into the soil.

The soil easily lies over the roots soothing every raw nerve. A small mound gathers around the trunk like a crowd welcoming back a long-lost friend. They hug and cling, gathering closely, supporting the insecure, unsure, newcomer. I pack it firmly securing a strong new beginning.

My dry, cracked hands absorb the moisture from the soil, and the essence of the young life before me. I can feel the pulse of the ground with every beat of my tired heart, and I know with every deep breath we are drawn together because a part of me has been planted here ready to grow with every passing season.

My little tree stands straight and tall holding its head up high searching for the sun. I feel its confidence build as I step away to admire its beauty. We smile together knowing this is where we belong, where there is room to grow so we can become the beautiful entities we were born to be.

Soon people will admire its strength, its courage, and its beauty. They will want to be a part of its growth and will want to stand alongside it just to feel its presence. It will be their shade when it is hot, their strength to lean on, and their peaceful place to rest under. Its beauty will remind them of the good in the world. It will be all this and more for me.

I rake around the sapling to smooth out any rigidness left behind while delicately shaping the surrounding foundation to a perfect circle. It drinks aggressively as the hose spouts out cold, refreshing water. I have made it full circle in the planting of this tree. From tears of sadness, to tears of hope, I found my way.

CHAPTER 31:
STONES OF LIFE

May our character guide us through life, like stepping stones paving the way.

I stand back in honor of the day. The sun has dropped heavily while shadows are cast, long and thick. The breeze is brisk against my skin. Flowers and trees alike welcome the early evening for they have tired in the burning sun and look forward to the view of the sparkling stars. The morning will come soon enough bringing the heat once again, but for now, time is washing away the day.

Well, Gigi, what do you think? Perfect, isn't it?

She answers me the only way I knew she would: with a breeze so cool and strong that the leaves and blades of grass are blown together in tiny claps of applause. The faint chatter of squirrels and birds create whispers of hoorays while the wind whips low and steady through the stones of the wall, bringing whistles and cheers from all around.

Thank you, Gigi! I couldn't have done it without you. And, yes, I agree, Auntie El will love it, too.

My view has changed, my landscape has too, as I stand proud, tired, and happy in the evening air.

A little concerned for the newness of it all, I feel support is in order to balance any insecurity it may have. One day it will know its power and live strong on its own, but until it knows what it is capable of, it will need something to hold on to, something sturdy to brace it from the winds, from the harshness of nature's way. It could use a friend to help it grasp the idea of the goodness that is about to come. It will need a supporter to ease it into the freedom of standing alone until it can accept its position of bringing happiness to others. Without a second thought, I think of the one that has walked this journey with me, the one that held me up when I needed it, the one that stood sturdy and tall for me, digging in when times were rough. Truly, a friend indeed, it is perfect.

It will withstand nature at its worst, for that is where it is from. It will hold up when leaned on. It will weather the storms, bask in the sun, and see it through, hand-in-hand. My walking stick will be all it is needed to be until this little tree can root to the soil and take a stand for where it belongs.

A short trip to the house puts my colored wires to good use. I knew I needed them. A few long stands of each, and a few snips with the wire cutters, they wrap around the tree and walking stick in a colorful display. I tie them gently together, twisting and wrapping. Immediately, the little oak leans in with a sigh and a thank you, resting on our friend.

Stones lay in the truck bed and in the grass waiting impatiently, all looking for attention like excited children waiting to participate in a fun new game. I picture them in my tired imagination, wide-eyed and excited, all yelling at once, *"What about us? Yeah, what about us? What can we do? Yeah, what can we do? I want to do something! Me too! Me too! Where do we belong? We want to help! Yeah, we want to help!"*

I amuse myself with some internal banter.

Oh, I have plans for you, little ones, don't you worry. Your job is an important one and you won't let me down.

I reach for them one by one. *"Pick me! No, pick me!"* they scream.

I see many have soaked up the sun and dried to a perfect, dusty white while others lie beneath the pile waiting to shed the dampness they have known for so long.

"What? What? What are we going to do?" they call out.

"You are my supporting qualities, the characters in my foundation that will hold me up and see me through. You will remind me what is important. You will hold me

steady and firm helping me create boundaries and security for the new life that grows here. You will connect to one another in power and strength, solidness and beauty, giving wholeness to our wonderful life."

"Really? We? We are important?"

"Yes, you. Some of you come from deep in the earth where the ground gave up, and some of you from the path of my cluttered past, but all of you will join to surround this beautiful creation. Are you ready?"

The ease in which they are lifted tells me of their willingness to do their part. Each stone is placed just so in honor of their position. The solid earthbound features are named for what they are and what they will bring to my future.

I start with the largest rock I can find and place it down gently at the edge of the grass where the dirt begins. I name this stone Strength for that is what has brought me through. It lands, proud and solid, claiming the first position among the many to come. Next are Light, Clarity, Balance, and Guidance for these qualities are necessary for a successful journey. Protection, Support, and Nourishment signify the three basic needs for survival while Desire, Honor, and Purpose awake my Spirit with Happiness for living.

Each stone is as unique as it should be, and they plop down into the soil like heads hitting a pillow. With every trip back to the pile, I feel the excitement for what is being created and know my life has changed forever.

I continue with the stones of Love and Passion for they surround my Heart with Peace, Serenity, and Harmony. Then I name Creativity, Nature, Enlightenment, and Beauty for the cornerstones of my spirit, while they bring Laughter and Healing to my Mind, Body, and Soul. Hope, Faith, and Prayer triangle my belief in the higher power, reminding me I am not alone during times of question. I do not forget Positive Energy and Wholeness for embodying the essence of all the qualities that are dear to me.

One last seat in my circle and one last stone left to place down. I reach in the back of the truck with one last ache in my body. It is the final piece to connect them all. I kneel before it and know there is only one name to be given: Growth.

The stone Growth connects all the stones together with a common thread for life's purpose. Growth is the reason we are here. Growth has guided me through this journey with Spirit and Beauty; Growth is the reason I Pray and Honor Nature; Growth is the reason we seek Enlightenment and Wholeness;

while Positive Energy is the Nourishment for the growth process as Creativity, Passion and Love for life bring Happiness and Laughter to my heart.

There can be no Growth without Desire or Purpose to drive us; while Faith, Hope, and Healing energies allow us to grow with Harmony, Serenity, and Peace. Our Mind, Body, and Soul grow with a strong Heart while Support and Protection help us stand tall and safe. Clarity and Light keep us Balanced on our journey giving the Strength and Guidance we need to grow toward the future.

The final stone of Growth snuggles down between Wholeness and Strength, slightly touching each stone. It glows lightly at first, but then a light of energy shoots through the circle of stones in both directions, one by one, until each and every one is radiating. The circle completes—beginning and ending with me. From beginning to end, end to beginning, we are one source of energy, connected and tied together forever. They all glow in one last burst of light as they settle down to their new home. This circle of life is complete, and the energies that flow from it will spiral upwards for a bright and healthy future.

I sit back on my knees trying to relieve the aches and pains of the day. I look up in amazement at the individual beauty that is planted before me. This was the journey that was set forth for me and has led me to a destination I never knew existed. Like chasing a butterfly into the woods without a care of where it was going, I got lost and struggled to find my way back. Instead, I have found my way through to the other side in order to sit beneath this beautiful creation. This will forever be a magical moment that reminds me to live free with an honest heart, a true soul, and a full life.

I am at my journey's end. I am strong, enlightened, and one with nature. My tomorrows and destinations will be many, and my journeys diverse, but for this one, I can look back, see my footprints, and know this is exactly where I am supposed to be.

The night is coming, but the sun refuses to relinquish its power so easily. It will be light a little while longer, so the evening sky will have to wait its turn. The handy old truck has done its duty and deserves a good night's rest.

I scoot the dogs back into the house, and with a slam of the tailgate, a sputtering start, and one last chance to wear the straw hat; the truck and I putt our way over the lawn, away from the tree. We enter Mr. Hansen's garage and with a turn of the key the truck mumbles and coughs as if it is letting out its last breath. I gently pat the steering wheel, thanking the truck for all its help and hard work. The straw hat is rested on the passenger side; it sits unaffected, floppy, and arrogant, taking all the credit for making me look good. The keys fall lifeless under the seat. The garage door pulls down submissively, and I feel like I am abandoning a new friend.

A trip through Mr. Hansen's house reveals Brutus has emptied the tin dishes of food on the porch, so I refill them before I leave. A last look at Mr. Hansen's photos reminds me of how much life I have been missing right in my backyard. He could be a friend. I would love to hear the stories behind those photos someday. Yes, someday, but for now, I have a great idea.

I leave the porch light on this time so I can see it from my kitchen window. I never realized how comforting it is to know he is here. On the nights I cannot sleep, I don't feel as lonely when I can see the light across the way. The darkness has traveled too far these last couple of nights. Strange, how his absence has connected us. I never knew how much I counted on his presence. I wonder if he notices us as much.

My house seems active as I cross the stone wall. The dogs' barks echo in excitement, which tells me the boys are arriving home—all three of them—gathering in the kitchen. A few steps into my yard, something lightly balances on the sharp blades of grass. A feather, long, striped in brown, white, and mahogany-red gently hovers low to the ground, trying its hardest not to blow away. I look above to see if the hawk is near, but the sky is clear, the birds are quiet, and all I hear is sweet Gigi saying, *"For you, Lizzi. A gift for you!"*

CHAPTER 34: REFLECTIONS

May the sparks of light that brighten our lives wash over time and space to eliminate the dull, shadowy moments of the past.

With a few restful days, Friday evening comes quickly following a beautiful day, hot, not too sticky, with blue skies and little clouds. The Fourth of July marks the calendar and the season with full beaches, brightly lit nights, and grass green and thick. Birds are nested, children are playing outdoors, and the season glows with activity. For me, no matter what the weather brings—storms, rains, cold snaps, or chilly nights in prior weeks—rain or shine, by now, summer rings true.

Tonight, the sky will reflect the essence of celebration with brilliant fireworks and explosions echoing into tomorrow. Dusk is just over our shoulders, and as a family, we load the cooler, and carry the sweatshirts, blankets, and chairs to the sandy land along the water. We are one of many who will appear with the evening, and stay until the darkness arrives, then leave as the crowds fade away.

The short path through the sea grass narrows to single file as the sand gets heavy. My sandals are lifted, swinging from my fingertips. There is more sand than people right now, but that will change as blankets checker the beach, spectators gather, and screaming kids collect on the water's edge.

I walk along the shoreline where the waves break gently on the silky clay, and my footprints are stolen by the thirsty ocean. I find a spot close enough to hear the ease of swaying waves, but far enough away that the sand has dried to a whitish tan. The boys drop the cooler before the blanket is unfolded and they run off with friends.

"Be back before dark."

"Okay."

"Oh, let them be. They'll be back," Jeremy scolds me for being too much of a mom.

I say nothing, for I am happy he is here with us, and I don't wish to argue. Besides, he is right. It is a mom thing. Better to say what is on your mind than to wish you had.

I set up the chairs while he breaks out the wine. We sit in a cozy silence of relaxation as the crowd thickens. Many people we know pass by us, some we gesture hello through a simple wave, others are stopped for a quick conversation and a few laughs to brighten the night, and many others are strangers in familiar faces from around town.

I pay little attention to the details around me. The sun goes down as smoothly as two glasses of wine. My conversation with Jeremy is simple and easy, melting us into the comfort of each other. It is not the words that are spoken, but the softness and direction of them that keep me connected to him. When our conversations are light and smooth, I know he is truly with me. This time with him tonight is fleeting, but I feel closer to him still.

Jonathan and Justin come out of the dark, plopping themselves down on the blanket, scattering it with sand. They toss the cooler for snacks and soda, settling down as the first whistle shoots up the edge of the sky, bursting into a white spidery sizzle. The crowd quiets down to a filtered muffle after the first cheers wave across the beach.

My toes dig into the sand until they are damp and cold. I watch sparkles travel upward like Gigi's popcorn flying from the pan in overlapping whistles as they burst into beautiful, colorful blooms like Auntie El's flowers. They fall brilliantly while another explodes, capturing the hearts of all. Mesmerizing, they continue one after the other in a wonderful display, serenaded by collective booms leaving only puffs of smoke behind.

I see my journey played out before me in the sky above, explosively emotional and forever overlapping with twinges of magic. My journey has brought me to this day of independence.

I think back over the last few weeks, months, and years, resolving with all the struggles of memories and pains. It all brought me to the weakness in my foundation that couldn't withstand the pressure anymore as I recognized its call for help and a wish to be whole again. I dug out the goodness trapped inside through sweat, tears, and pain. Nature supported and guided me to grow as an individual. Words of encouragement were built on while holes rooted to the past were filled in with nourishing layers.

I found my inner child within the thickness of the forest while surviving transitional obstacles. A connection to a fallen branch and forgotten boulder reminded me of true hidden characters within me. Today is the destination of my journey as I sit strong, happy, and independent of the past.

Beauty bursts out above us, capturing moments of light. I turn to see my family watching intently, happy, healthy, and safe as the world bursts wide open.

If this is where my life, my journey, my family experiences have brought me, who am I to complain?

The fireworks light up the sky time and time again. Each individual light is thrown into the sky destined to brighten our view. All stars fade away, much like my past, to the brightness and happiness of the now. So be it. These shining sparks are so bright that nothing else can be seen. In the crowd of many, we could be the only ones here. I take Jeremy's hand, hoping he will know my appreciation for the life and happiness we have created together. He squeezes my hand lightly in agreement.

I have my family beside me, before me, in the glowing light of color across their smiling faces. They are the bright individuals who have entered my life, bursting with promise across my horizon. Shining so brightly that all else fades away. With them I find myself, independently happy and independently strong.

I soak up the sky and all its glorious moments, thankful for the lights that shine in the darkness, thankful for this day of love and recognized independence.

CHAPTER 35:
A PASSING YEAR

A year is a day in the life of nature, awakening with the sunrise of spring, living through the momentum and inspiration of summer and fall, while slumbering by the night of winter. A lifetime is reflected in the seasons of the year, being born by the spring light, aging through the growth and changes of summer and fall, only to settle into the wisdom and maturity of winter's calm. Nature is the gift of life, the beginning and the end of a day, a season, or a lifetime.

Another year has passed in the blink of an eye. The boys have matured that much more as my little tree has grown to its own surprise. My awakening to growing with them has gathered in my foundation solidifying the life we have. After last spring rose like the morning with planting and new beginnings, the summer began to burn in like high noon, heating up with activities, picnics and the usual refreshing days at the beach. The boys absorbed the sun, darkening their skin to a deep tan. Their hair shimmered in sandy blonde spikes. Their smiles were contagious in the light of the outdoors.

I loved my coffee-strolls with the new addition to my view.

The season continued with no permission or regrets. The hot mornings had soon turned into scorching afternoons, and the grass struggled to hold on to its color, day after day. The nights gave little relief, and seemed too far away during long days with little clouds and winds as hot as the air. Stillness overcame the season, as energies were reserved and all retreated to the indoors, beaches, and pools during the brightest hours. The siesta time of the year as people lounged more often during the midday sun.

With the heat, nature delivered us rich colors full of life. As baby bunnies with tails of white, and fawns, small, spotted, and fragile, fed from their mothers, striped skunks and masked raccoons wandered the night. My trees and flowers stayed thirsty in the mid-day sun. The stars brighten the sky night after night. The sea grass rose thick and tall around the pool while the hydrangeas puffed in blue and white, ready for the picking.

Busy birds, bees, and critters alike stirred as the monarchs fluttered by in velvety orange and black, all living for the moment. Chipmunks, small, quick, and fluffy, tails in the air, rushed over the stone walls. The hawk circled daily, screeching and searching from above with little concern for her survival for meals came easily. The summer played out like the active child, curiously growing around every corner.

The liveliness of summer slowed only to welcome the maturing of the year, with a few chilly mornings, the passing of flowers, the curling of the sea grass, and the thinning of the crowds on the cooling beaches. Spots faded off the young ones as nests were abandoned and the breeze off the water turned crisp and forceful. Shortly after, falling into the evening hours of the year going by was easy, and with maturity, came sophistication in every earthly tone.

Weeks passed. Autumn slipped in with earlier nights and a serious calm that washed over the season. The year came into its prime as colors of blues, reds, and yellows mixed to create an established landscape of the sky, leaves, and grasses. All things earth-toned were alert and awake as pumpkins, orange, round, and quiet, sat on doorsteps, and busses, yellow, rectangular, and loud, rolled down the streets. My little tree joined in with the turn of its leaves and the shedding of the season gone by. All of this, marking the season as a time of recognizing the changes we must all go through to grow, learn, and mature.

Leaves fell and danced across the dying grass as the wind and weather forced them to move on. The geese clamored in groups, pointing the way to warmer weather. Creatures were productive, preparing for the senior months of endless cold and long nights.

The winter season faded in like the night hours while nature drifted into its final stages of the year. Rhythms of slumber, wisdom, and reflections set in, seizing time. A shimmer of moonlight, and the whiteness of snow against the blackness of night exposed nature in a flash. An X-ray of the season stripped it to its bones; trees bared it all with shadows casting in milky gray. In a chilly frost, winter iced over, leaving only the anticipation for life to begin again, waiting for the morning spring to awaken our world.

Snowcaps and burning fires complemented each other as friendly foes, while the icicles and flames both burned hot and cold, snapping and crackling at the sight of the other. My guardians in green stood ruggedly handsome, fending off the cold while capturing and balancing all of winter's white beauty gently in each hand. They watched over the little one, standing proud and sturdy out in the open cold.

The air settled into a fresh transparent veneer, reaching out in nips and pinches until cheeks were red, rosy, and crisp. The beaches were left lonely, with only the shells and sand staying true to their waves. The empty nests were long forgotten, while seeds awaited spring below the hardened ground to birth a new year with new life again.

The morning of a new day arose as spring entered our world, once again, by breaking through the icy waters and melting away the year before. Life poked its head up from the ground, to be crowned with light and a welcoming warmth; each sprouted seed breathed its first breath and cried out to the world "Spring."

Once again, colors busted out in baby steps as the grass softened like a newborn's blanket spread out for all to see. The birds returned home as the trees budded in harmony and the sun reclaimed its hours. A year has whispered by in the passing of the seasons. My heart is lighter, my tree is stronger, and the sun insists on rising every morning, bringing hope with new days. The freshness of flowers once again inhabits the gardens, and my little tree stands independent with clusters of leaves hiding its many awkward branches. I feel the changes all around me, and within me, as a year has moved us all to a better place while staying true to its own patterns and gifts to be given and received.

Yes, the year has passed in a blaze of color and light with deep shift changes for all to experience, and today it will all be a beautiful backdrop for a special Auntie El visit.

I water my tree, feeling it settling into the ground, declaring its own space with every deepening root. The leaves have doubled in a lustrous green. I imagine every root mirroring the growth before me. My walking stick has been removed and decorated in honor of the warrior it is.

Mysti pokes the edge of the stones. Crossing over them, she lays down in the cool hose water gathering around its trunk.

"Silly girl. You will be all muddy."

She ignores me for it feels good on her belly and allows her to be by my side. The others sniff around the stone wall in search of chipmunks that have run into the cracks hiding from their large noses.

"Leave those chippies alone," I yell, but that just excites them more, for now they know they are on to something.

I stand in the morning sun finishing my chores with hopeful thoughts for the upcoming months. The summer is here but plans for the fall have already started rolling. During the winter cold I took a chance of planting a seed or two of my own.

I felt the separation of family continue as the holidays came upon us with no plans for a large gathering; only private family functions were organized and attended. The following months brought no shift in our disconnection, and communication was at an all-time low. As my conviction to strengthen my surroundings for my children as well as myself grew stronger, I took the chance on calling cousin Jake for a heart-to-heart sit down, hoping to reconnect some severed ties that hung in the balance. He met me without questioning my motives saying he looked forward to catching up.

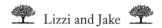 Lizzi and Jake

I arrived at the coffee shop first wanting to get a quieter table than usual so we could speak freely and honestly. I ordered my coffee and headed to the corner table by the window. Icicles hung and melted outside in the early March sun. Jake entered a few minutes later. He waited in line for his coffee as I wondered what I would say. I waved him over when he looked my way. He is taller than I am by several inches. I find it hard to reach my arms up and around his broad shoulders and bulky winter jacket. We solidly embrace longer than a quick hello, squeezing each other lightly for it had been too long since we had connected. Our interactions over the last couple of years had dwindled to chance meetings in town or the quick text message. I had internalized this as more family division, taking it personally until his greeting made me feel at home in his presence. His warm brown eyes and laugh helped me feel at ease and more comfortable by the minute about bringing up his father. We filled each other in on our children and laughed at how old they are getting and how old that made us.

The conversation shifted to the extended family when he asked, "How is Auntie El doing? Do you see her often?"

"Yes, I try to call her at least once a week and stop by as often as I can. Especially with the winter months, it is hard for her to get out of the house. You should stop and see her. She loves company."

"I know. I will soon. Your mom? How is she?"

"Good, hanging in there. Some minor health issues but nothing serious."

"Glad to hear it. I can't believe how busy I've been. With work and the kids. I haven't seen anyone in quite a while."

"I know, it is hard to stay connected to everyone these days. Have you talked to Chris lately?" I asked.

"No, he hasn't been my biggest fan since all this stuff with my father came up. And you know he and Emma aren't on the best of terms either these days."

"Yah, it's too bad this whole mess has gotten so out of hand."

There was a moment that seemed to hang in the air with the subject of family so I dove in. "How are things with your dad these days? Any better?"

He looked out the window a moment, clearing his throat with a stare of annoyance. "You know Lizzi, that man is as stubborn as they come."

I smiled and let out a short chuckle for the truth of that touches a piece of our whole family. "Well Jake, we have all known that for years. A trait that runs deep through our bloodline."

He laughed a little, but I could tell that this time the stubbornness that showed up was no joke. "Listen Jake, I wanted to talk to you about something, but I don't want to overstep."

"Oh, I see, this wasn't really an 'I miss you Jake' coffee. You have an agenda."

"Well, no that's not true." I felt defensive. "It's kinda both really."

"Okay, I'll bite. What's up?"

"I want to have a birthday party for Auntie El this fall. She will be ninety. And I was wondering how you felt about that?"

"I think that's great, Lizzi. What's the problem?"

"So you would come. Bring Emma and the boys."

"Yes, of course, why wouldn't I?"

"Well because of you and your dad for starters. Are you still not speaking?"

"Yah, That's a tough one. He doesn't seem to want to bend at all about seeing my boys. I am really not sure what to do."

"I hate to ask, but why won't you let him see the boys? You know he loves them."

"You think this is all me, Lizzi? Is that what you think?" He looked at me with a glare of disappointment and instantly I felt ashamed for asking.

"No Jake, I didn't say that. I didn't mean that at all. You know I know better than that. But this has been going on for so long and the whole family is completely separated over taking sides about it."

"There is no side to take here, Lizzi. That's not what I intended, anyway."

"Well, everyone seems to think there is apparently. Since my last picnic Aunt Betsy and Aunt Lil have barely spoken a word to me."

"This isn't your issue, Lizzi. Don't let them make it."

"It's hard not to when my mother feels so deeply for your father."

"I am sorry for that. I certainly don't mean to hurt anyone, but I do have a family of my own to look after now."

"I am sure it hasn't been easy for you and Emma either." I offer, "But do you think you will change your mind about him being able to spend time with the boys?"

"That's what everyone doesn't understand, Lizzi. I never said he couldn't see the boys. He just makes it so difficult. Emma and I had decided that he couldn't come take them anytime he wanted. That he had to plan and call first, and that wasn't ok with him. He started accusing Emma of keeping them from him. Started being disrespectful to me in front of them. At first it was a simple miscommunication. Emma forgot about a play date she had scheduled at his house; the next time one of the boys was sick. He took it personally. He said Emma was doing it on purpose. I was just trying to draw some boundaries when he came over in a rage one day. Demanding to see them. Yelling and screaming in front of the kids. They were scared. So we told him to give us some room, some time. That's all."

"It's been almost three years, Jake. Don't you think that's long enough?"

"We tried," he responded quickly, "we really tried. A few months went by and we called, we did. At first, he didn't return our calls, to make a point I guess. We tried to set times for him to come over, but he would have none of it. He only wanted to spend time alone with them. He wanted me to drop them at his house for the weekend. That wasn't going to happen. It was all or nothing with him. What was I supposed to do? Besides he has made it clear that he wants nothing to do with Emma which just makes it worse. What am I supposed to do with that, Lizzi? You tell me."

"I am sorry I didn't know," I offered in understanding.

"Nobody knows because nobody thought to ask. They only took his word for it. Your brother called me once but only to tell me how much of an asshole I was being to my father. I don't need his shit either. I have a great family and my boys don't deserve to be exposed to the same chaos and bullshit we were brought up in."

"I'm with you there, Jake. I have been keeping all this from my boys, as well. They, too, are starting to ask why we don't see family as often anymore"

"I was hoping my father would be at your picnic a couple years back, take the opportunity to see the kids there, maybe break the ice a little. But neither him or your brother showed. I was really disappointed and since then all I have heard from friends and family is that he is bad-mouthing us. I don't know, Lizzi, he has made it pretty easy to stay away."

"What can I do?" I asked, hoping there was an answer.

"There is nothing you can do. Maybe it will work itself out. The boys are getting older. They ask about him lately, especially around the holidays. We only see Emma's side and they are starting to get curious."

"Well, it might be good for them to get to know their grandfather a little, right? I mean none of our parents are getting any younger."

He looked at his watch. "Listen Lizzi, it's been nice seeing you but I have to go. Plan Auntie El's party. I am sure Emma would help. Call her. She would love to hear from you. She thinks everyone in the family hates her now. We should all get together with the boys."

"That sounds nice. I will call Emma and make plans."

Jake pulled his coat from the back of the chair and slipped it on. We said good-bye with another hug. As he zipped his jacket he nodded his head in thought, then added:

"I hope my father goes to the party. It might be just what we need."

Just a month later I took a more carefully planned approach to my brother Chris and Uncle Teddy. One Sunday morning I found myself at a diner twenty minutes away, where they often meet for breakfast. A tidbit of information I got from my mother.

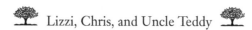

Lizzi, Chris, and Uncle Teddy

The restaurant was busy beyond my expectation. A line formed from a small hostess desk out the entrance door to a small breezeway standing area. I excused my way through the crowd with some remarks and dirty looks on cutting the line. Once inside I scanned the main dining room looking for any sign of Uncle Teddy or my brother, Chris. Nothing. Then I noticed an archway leading to a smaller back room. While crossing through I must have looked confused because a waitress stopped me asking if she could help. "No, thank you," I replied without looking at her. "I am just looking for someone." The smaller room held five or six booths and a few round tables for two. I spotted my brother immediately to the far right sitting across from Uncle Teddy in a tall red booth. I marched over to them before I could lose my nerve and stood at the end of table between them. Chris had a rugged look with a flannel shirt and dirty ball cap. They looked like father and son together. I hadn't seen Uncle Teddy in a long time, but I would know him anywhere, for he and my mother had grown to look alike, with their short grey hair and stocky build. Chris looked up and took a double take as if he was expecting their waitress. Either way, I was the last one he thought he would see.

"Lizzi," he said, surprised and almost choked on his bite of food. "What brings you here?"

"Actually, you guys do. May I have a seat for a moment?" I didn't wait for an answer. Scooting Chris over, I ended up sitting across from Uncle Teddy.

"Hi, Uncle Teddy. How are you?"

"I am okay, and you?"

"Pretty well, thank you."

Chris jumped in to cut off the niceties. "Why are you here, Lizzi? And how did you know we would be here?"

"I want to talk to you about something, and Mom told me where you two would be."

"Remind me later to thank her for that. Would you, Chris?" Uncle Teddy said snidely.

Chris smirked at his wittiness and waited for me to react.

"There is no easy way to bring this up so I am just going to say it," I started. "I know your relationship with Jake is strained right now, but..."

"Strained? Is that what you call it. That ungrateful little shit has written me off like old trash and you call it strained."

"Lizzi!" Chris jumped in with a cautionary tone. "You don't want to do this."

"Actually, Chris, I do. And I want you to listen as well."

Chris threw up his hands as if to say "you're on your own now, sister" and Uncle Teddy sat back. He took a napkin, roughly wiped his face, and threw it on his plate. His finger came across the table. "Look. You have no idea what it is like to not see your own grandchildren for almost three years, so don't think you're going to waltz in here on a whim and tell me how it is."

"I am not trying to be disrespectful here. I can't image how hard it has been for you. I just don't see how anyone is making it any better."

Chris took a breath, ready to jump in again, but I stopped him. "Before you say anything else will you please hear me out?"

They both sat still and quiet. Suddenly my nerves got the best of me and I forgot why I was there.

"Well, out with it, little girl. I want to hear this," Uncle Teddy finally said.

"Okay. This is my thought. Auntie El is going to be ninety in the fall."

"Yes. So?" Uncle Teddy gruffly responded.

"I want to throw her a surprise birthday party and I want to know that both of you are on board."

Silence and stares were all I got.

"More coffee, anyone?" A waitress stood over us.

"Not now," Chris replied more harshly than necessary. The shy young waitress sheepishly walked away.

"Well?" I continued after she had gone.

"What do you mean by on board?" Uncle Teddy questioned.

"I want to know that you will come. Both of you and your family." I looked Chris' way.

Chris just looked at Uncle Teddy. After a few moments of silence, he finally responded, "If he is ok with it, I will be there."

"I don't know, Lizzi," Uncle Teddy said while looking away from me. "I love Auntie El, but you're asking an awful lot here."

"Yes, I can see that. And I wouldn't if it weren't important."

"What about Jake and the boys?" he continued.

"I already talked to Jake. He and Emma and the boys will definitely come. It's now up to you to decide."

Again, silence stood between us, strong and uncomfortable.

"Okay," I said. "I said what I came to say. I will let you get back to your breakfast. I hope you will think about it." I stood up to leave, and with my hand on Uncle Teddy's shoulder I added, "Just in case it helps your decision, Jake said he hoped you will take this opportunity to see the boys at the party."

I felt his body relax as he gulped back a feeling or two. I left with a pit in my stomach and a small wish that I knew what was said after.

That was almost three months ago and I haven't heard from either of them, or a word about my ambush, not even from my mother. Silence is golden in my family and they certainly know how to play that card. This morning I stand in my yard watching all the beautiful colors hoping those exchanges will grow roots of their own.

For today, I am looking forward to Auntie El's visit. She would be shocked to know I spoke to them. Maybe a little proud but I can't tell her for it will ruin her surprise. So the story is that I am having a family reunion and the only surprise she thinks we are getting is to see who shows up.

She arrives on time for our mid-afternoon iced tea date and I am proud to show her my walking stick. She admires my crafty handiwork as we sit on the back porch. She smiles between sips as I explain the symbolism of each embellishment. The handle is wrapped in colored wire, beaded with crystals and strips of leather that dangle the hawk's feather loosely by its side. It symbolizes the strength in nature, the freedom of the hawk, and my life's journey.

On this afternoon, the sun is hot and the sky is clear. Auntie El's dress is aqua blue with white large flowers blooming wildly across it. A matching fabric belt hugs her tiny waist, and her sandals are white, heeled and toeless. She sits with her tea in one hand and a pink flip-out paper fan in the other, waving it before her like the dainty lady she is. If her hat were any bigger, the table umbrella would feel inadequate, but size is not everything for the floral print is putting my flowerpots to shame. She is a sight, and I love her for her flare, but we are a mismatched pair today with me in my flip-flops and worn-out, plain pool cover-up.

The ice in the tea melts quicker than we can drink it. My tree, small, bushy, green, and proud is straight in our view. She has approved my choice and blessed my caretaking skills so far, although she believes the stick should have stayed a little longer.

I assure her of the strength and independence it has grown to achieve over the last year and that it can stand on its own through any weather.

We watch a robin fly back and forth from the tree.

"A nest? What do you think, Auntie?"

We walk to see what she is up to, hoping not to scare her off. Mysti gets up to follow us but her movements mimic Aunt's in a fragile way. They both wobble across the yard, Mysti achy and stiff, Auntie El the same, but in heels.

"Are you okay? Please, don't fall."

She waves me off, annoyed I would even suggest such a thing. "I'm fine. Keep going. I'll catch up."

As we walk closer, my pride grows larger. I smile happily for the wonders of nature. I would never have found the strength to move on, or have such appreciation for my world, without that journey. I found growth would come when the time is taken to appreciate and nurture its existence. I know I can dig out of the holes that life creates and fill in the darkness with life. This tree is my reminder, my symbol for the life I can create. It taught me that life comes from the deepest of our feelings, from the roots that feed us, and a great foundation. I know my journeys in life will be many, great and small, long and short, but it is those journeys that life grows from that give us solid ground.

I can't help but reach out and touch the trunk and know the thickness of how it has grown.

"Very nice, dear. It really is a perfect spot. Right in the sun with plenty of room to grow."

I peek behind a patch of leaves. "Look!"

Within the fork of two small branches, a perfect round nest sits comfortably. A robin's nest with three eggs, perfectly blue, safe, and secure in the arms of the nurtured, which has now become the nurturer, the supporter, the protector.

She has found a home for her babies in the new tree.

"We should leave her to her eggs," Auntie El says.

We leave the tree to do its job as the momma bird returns to her nest.

"Amazing, the wonders of nature and how it all plays out," I offer in passing.

"Yes, nature is forever unfolding, showing us new ways to appreciate life," Auntie answers in her peaceful, understanding voice. "I am proud of you for what you have done here."

"You are?"

"Yes, I know this meant more to you than just planting a tree. I know the courage it takes to stand up for yourself, stand-alone in your beliefs, to work through the past. This is proof that life will come from good intentions, that nature will use that life energy to its advantage."

I pause a moment, then ask the silent question that still remains to be seen, "Do you think they will come?"

"Did you send out the invitations yet?"

"Yesterday."

"To everyone?"

"To everyone!"

She nods her head slowly in approval. "A family reunion! You can count me in. I'll bring my famous oatmeal raisin cookies."

I smirk to myself knowing the truth. A guilty way to force their hand, but so be it. Sometimes we all need a perfectly good reason to gather with the ones we love. A reunion it is to her, and I am proud to honor her life, celebrate her with one special day.

"And Auntie?"

"Yes, Lizzi?"

"I have one request."

"What is that, dear?"

"Wear that hat, too. It brightens the place up."

We laugh together in our own ways, finding room for our differences to keep us close. I only hope that the family that connects us can do the same.

CHAPTER 36:
JUST A HUNK A' WOOD

When we care for, connect to, and honor another's past, our kindness transcends time to ease the source of their sorrow.

In late August, it finally arrives. I open the package and hang it quickly. My little tree is finally big enough to support it. A long overdue idea has finally come to fruition. All I can do now is wait anxiously for him to notice.

As I finish the evening dishes, I see him, Mr. Hansen, walking through the tall-grassed field holding a wooden bowl full of his last summer vegetables: yellow squash, cucumbers, peppers in red and green stacked high. His elusive cat, Brutus, walks the stone wall ahead of him, meowing loudly for attention. Our encounters have been friendlier and more often in the past year, making this a special treat. Our corresponding alone times, me in my yard and him in his garden, are more likely to be broken with purposeful conversation than not, and his demeanor has shifted as the distance between our homes has been marked with a well-beaten path through the connecting field.

Brutus even shares in our meshing of energies with his daytime appearances this summer. Although he has not yet let anyone touch him without a spit and a hiss, he is no longer the phantom kitty that only leaves behind empty tins and dead mice on the porch doorstep. A rolled-up blanket wrinkled and covered in orange cat hair lies under the step where he sleeps, almost out in the open. The sunlight is his friend and taunting my dogs is his favorite pastime by strutting back and forth over the stones of the walls. He can disappear into thin air as quickly as the dogs are released for the chase.

Today is no different as Brutus' incessant meowing perks their ears and entices them. They gather at the door howling and scratching to be let out. I refuse, for it will just cause chaos.

Mr. Hansen hears the dogs calling. He involuntarily smiles while leaning down to place the bowl on the flattest stone he can find. Brutus takes this opportunity to lean in for a chance petting.

The taunting for affection is short lived. Brutus allows a full brush of Mr. Hansen's hand over his head, down his back, and up his whipping tail before he turns to take a swipe. Mr. Hansen pulls his hand away just in time to avoid a large-clawed paw ready to break skin. He is still pleased how far this feral cat has come in the last year.

Standing upright again with a slight arch to his back to remove a kink, Mr. Hansen catches a glimpse of my small tree, just beyond the wall. Full of green leaves, healthy and strong, he sees it as proof again that a little nurturing of a wild thing can go a long way. With a closer study from his distance, he leans in and squints, noticing something hanging loosely just beneath its green cluster.

Curiosity wins him over. I watch intently as Mr. Hansen crosses the wobbly stones easier than ever before. Upon his slow approach, there is something familiar about the strange object suspended from the young oak. A large piece of wood dangles from the lowest branch. Strung up by braided colored wire, it knocks lightly against the thin trunk in the cool evening wind.

Grabbing it by the bottom corners he lifts it upward. Unable to resist a smile, his eyes wrinkle as a tear falls down the crease of his nose. So close to the real original image it sets his heart back a beat. It sits in his hands, flooding back a memory, he thought, only he could cherish. There before him is a large chunk of solid oak with a heart carved through it, an arrow piercing its lower side only to resurface at the opposite top, and deep in the center the words, *"Hank & Elsie Forever"* are dug into the middle.

He takes a moment and traces every letter with his finger, remembering the moment he hand-carved the same image himself.

From my kitchen window, I watch as he pauses and studies the simple sign. It makes my heart sing. I guess if life is cared for, connected to, and remembered, you never know when it will come back around to touch your heart and be a part of your future.

He looks toward my house and wipes away the slow-dripping tears, but he is smiling brightly as he walks home slowly with Brutus's tail tipping the grass beside him. Dusk settles in the corners of the field, and I know he is back in the comforts of his home when the friendly glow of his porch-light cuts through the distance connecting our worlds once again.

CHAPTER 37:
CHANGES

Life is grounded before me with encouragement to reach for the sun and the stars. Its future is strong in the midst of the air it breathes, and gives, flowing with the persuasion of the breeze, sighing with every release of its beautiful leaves, and smiling with every new bud it creates. With every interaction it has with another, from the birds that nest in its branches, to every leaf that falls, seasons move forward, and life grows on.

Summer is disappearing quickly. The days are smooth and gentle. Fall has taken a breath or two. The sun is blessing us with warmth, although the breeze can easily whisk that away. I breathe easier this morning than I thought I would for Aunt El's party has rushed up on me. The clock ticks tensely and refuses to slow down for anyone. I scurry with resentment for it because there is no one else to blame. Jeremy tries to calm me into believing all will be well.

"Do we have enough plates? Should I go get more? Are you sure the cake is nice enough?" I ask him, repeating myself frantically.

"No! I mean *yes*, we have enough plates. The cake is beautiful. She will love it! Please stop. You will make yourself crazy." He shakes his head as he passes me by with a bag of ice, headed for the closest cooler on the patio. "It will all be fine."

"What if no one comes?"

"It is for Auntie El. They will all come for her." He walks back through the open sliding glass door. "If they don't, shame on them and we will be eating hamburgers and hotdogs for the next two weeks." He laughs, cracking himself up, then turns and hugs me gently. "You have done all you can."

"What if nobody gets along? What if it's a disaster?"

"It won't be. They are adults. It's been how long since they have all been together? Over three years?"

"My point exactly. What was I thinking?"

"You were thinking enough is enough. You were thinking Auntie El deserves to celebrate her ninetieth birthday with her family. You were thinking from your heart. Don't question it. You have done the work. It is up to them now. Relax."

"Easy for you to say."

I hug him back, trying to be confident that he is right. That someone has to acknowledge our connections. I know everything needs nurturing and a chance to grow. I only hope we can all find that here, today.

They all arrive, one after the other, carrying goodies and dishes covered with foil shining in the sunlight. A picnic table with balloons and presents is placed strategically near the small oak tree in hopes that it will radiate good energy our way. This healing energy breathes happiness and grows life. I want that for us all today. After all, we are all connected whether we want to be or not, and I hope my own healing will shine through and be received today, finding a way to the roots of this family to at least help us feel our connection once again.

A rough start begins to worry me. Jeremy has left to pick up Auntie El for her later arrival and surprise entrance. All are here, but they remain speaking softly in small groups of their own comfort zones as the kids wait patiently to jump in the pool. I rearrange flowers, fiddle with tablecloths, and check the coolers too often to count.

Jeanie finds me, knowing my mental panic. "Are you sure I can't help with anything?"

"No, Jeanie, but thank you. I am just a little nervous."

"I can tell. Relax it will all be great. She will love all of your efforts and so will everyone else, even if they don't admit it."

"God, I hope so."

"Come with me, you need a glass of wine."

Before we can reach the kitchen, I hear Jeremy's car coming up the drive. I finally take a deep breath with Jeanie's hand lightly patting my back.

"She is here!" I anxiously scream much louder than necessary over the already quiet crowd keeping to respective conversations. Jeremy and Auntie El enter through the kitchen, exiting to the back porch where we all wait silently. Her hat is large and her dress bright yellow. Just the sight of her brightens up my drab thoughts. Before she can grasp the scene of birthday balloons and streamers, everyone shouts "Happy Birthday!"

She grabs her chest, startled beyond words as she tips backwards on her heels. Jeremy places a hand behind her, fearing she may actually topple over.

"Oh my! What are you all doing? You will give an old girl a heart attack!" She laughs her Gigi laugh and we all laugh with her. One by one, we wait in line to hug her tightly.

I am last. I stand back and watch the family gather for her. She begins to cry. With broken joy, she says in my ear, "Family reunion, my old ass!" The tears of laughter flow easily for both of us.

"Come sit. I have a special chair for you, if you can make it over the grass in those heels."

"Oh, you just stand back and watch me young lady. These old bones have more life in them than anyone knows."

"Oh, I believe you, Auntie El. I believe you."

We walk together, arms linked for love, not support. We pass by family already resumed to their comfortable common areas. The kids are splashing loudly in the pool.

The specially-decorated, yellow lawn chair with streamers and balloons sits right next to the tree and the picnic table full of presents. She sits carefully with a little help and I tell her that she's beautiful.

"Oh, stop," she waves her hand in a blushing motion.

But I mean it full-heartedly. She sits as a beautiful reminder of how life should be: bright, fun, and happy. From her dress full of sunflowers, to her wide-brimmed straw hat that sits stiff on her head wrapped in a fabric bandana, she is a reminder of all that is good. I know nothing else matters at this moment more than to bring the family together, if even for a day to share in what was, and what can be.

I watch as activity and mingling loosen up. As small groups of women gather, the kids play joyfully in the pool, and the dogs watch intently for any treats thrown their way. Jeremy is laughing heartily at the grill amongst my uncles who have joined him at his cooking post.

All seems well, though Uncle Teddy, cousin Jacob and my brother, Chris, have respectfully ignored each other thus far. I may never know the depth of their pains or the truth that lies between them and that is okay, for today I can only know how far I have come and try to express that the best I can. I can only know the depth of my roots and hope they will find theirs and we can all connect again someday. I can only rest in the separation that has helped me grow and know that this is where it begins, here with me as an individual. I hope my home and intentions radiate that growth, giving them a safe place to be together if only for today.

One more guest joins the party. Mr. Hansen stands at the wall carrying a pie. Jeremy waves him over with the long-handled spatula while sipping from his dark-bottled beer with the other hand. I can see Mr. Hansen's smile beneath his straw hat, and I am so delighted that he chose to come. All feels well.

I stay busy restocking, collecting dishes, and shooing the dogs away, afraid if one motion stops all of this will prove to be a moment of grandeur and hallucinations. I convince myself that the children's laughter rings so true and lively that it has to be real. My family is gathering, and talking, and eating. Giggles and chatter carry us through the afternoon. No matter what got us here or how the future will turn out, now is the moment I will cherish.

I pause for only a moment from my hostess duties, scanning the yard, and taking in every action of the day unfolding. The sun burns hot, the drinks sweat and drip as they are pulled from the cooler, burgers are flipped in the haze of their own heat, towels and flip flops leave pops of color throughout the yard, and the air is calm just accepting the life of the day. I breathe easier, knowing there is little more for which I would ask.

With that thought, I watch my brother, Chris, cross the far side of the yard and extend a hand to our cousin Jacob. They shake hands a minute with stern expressions, and then break into tolerant smiles. They turn and walk the length of the yard together where my mother, Uncle Teddy, Auntie El, and Mr. Hansen are relaxing in their lawn chairs. I hold my breath as they pull chairs into the half-circle. Jacob calls his sons over to say hello to their grandfather for the first time in years. Uncle Teddy ruffles their hair, smiling at how big they are. My mother glows in her own passive way. Mr. Hansen and Auntie El's hat rims brush up against each other, making a wonderful pair. A sight they all are as the small oak stands steady behind them.

A nice start.

I can finally join in. The fear of it all disappearing has subsided in my tiredness. I walk across the yard where Aunt Lil and Aunt Betsy sit with Jeanie. I feel the solid ground beneath my feet with every step. I hear their voices. Their laughter is magnetic and contagious, like an old favorite song from the past. As I sit among these women, these women of my past and hopefully my future, I know I belong. A hominess of long lost comforts swarms us through the words of an old story being told. I scoot my chair up closer, and Aunt Lil leans in to nudge me with a shoulder.

"What a great idea. I don't know why we don't do this more often. This is just what everyone needed."

I look at her sideways, squinty-eyed and smiling. She smiles back, and we laugh to one another in our own secret way. Deep down I know we share the belief that this, like so many other things in life, just takes time; time to smooth over the jagged edges so that one day they can be tossed back down on the shore as a beautiful memory waiting to be found.

I smile devilishly, looking to my little tree shimmering in the early evening sun. I feel its strength and know its heart has rooted here within us. I thank it silently. A breeze gently bustles its leaves in acknowledgement of my gratitude, and one small leaf stands out amongst the many. Streaked with yellow and a hint of red it tells me that, yes, fall is coming and there is change in the air.

Do you see this, Gigi? Do you see this?

And I can only think that when one changes, others will follow.

I look up to the sky. There are no clouds in sight, and the hawk sits silent in the large evergreen, watching intently in her own perspective. The weather holds. No storms today. The horizon is clear.

CHAPTER 38:
KINDRED SPIRITS

Kindred are the spirits that recognize the journey of the soul.

Deep fall came with the trees stripped of their green and the air of its warmth, but the change in the season also came with a clearing of another kind. A long-awaited agreement turned the wooded area of my childhood field into a town park for hiking and dog walking. This clearing out of the deadwood, weeds, and briar patches was led by a church group called "The Gentle Gardeners." I volunteered and immediately put my wheelbarrow, shovel, rake, gloves, and boots to use once more. It was a collaborative effort, and proved to be productive. The space became welcoming with every passing day. With many hands and good intentions, the old field has found a new life.

The large trees still house wildlife and stand strong in their own right. The forgotten and neglected land is now both their home and the reason for their existence. Honoring their space while bringing in the light gives them the respect they deserve. We only changed the environment around them, not removing them, as others would have. Trails were marked for all to follow, thus showing them the way.

One main path leads straight to my large rock, a focal point of this sanctuary. It basks in the mid-day light once more. Owning my heart, for many reasons, I personally took on the task of unburying it from the moss and decaying debris. I would not have had it any other way.

Now it is my favorite place to visit, which I do as often as I can. I find it comforting and a nice place to rest, sketch, or journal. Chillier days of November are setting in, but today I take the time for a casual walk to enjoy this gift of nature. The air is crisp and fresh preparing for winter's calm. The trees have complied with the weather, shedding their leaves, beautifully embracing the season. This newness of change is in the awareness, whether for a moment, a season, or a complete clearing of old vibrations. Life waits for us to notice. I am here today with a new perspective, with life before me, and around me, as Buddy strolls by my side, blessing every moment. Buddy is the hardy one these days as time has taken its toll on Mysti and Penny. At twelve and thirteen now, their stiff legs and aching joints tire them quickly and make for painful evenings. Day-Z finds new smells distracting and wanders off too easily.

The sun makes its way through and around the trees, allowing the whole area to breathe happiness. The sadness has evaporated. Only happier memories of the field that once was remain. In the forgotten and neglected, growth occurred and became something new and special, both in spite of, and because of, it. Nature grew so that one day it could be recognized and appreciated for what it truly is.

Life itself.

I reach my rock, sitting a moment to appreciate all that is and has been to get me here. Family comes to mind. No aftershocks from the party. All seems quiet. Perhaps we can gather again soon. Buddy paces nearby, and my walking stick leans beside me. I breathe a sigh of relief and embrace the comfort of calm.

A rustling in the leaves behind us surprises me, causing Buddy to perk up with a nervous howl. A woman appears with her German shepherd close by her side.

Her approach is casual and unthreatening. From under her ball cap, she appears to be older than I am by quite a few years, but I cannot be sure. Her eyes are kind and her face pleasant and accepting. I have never seen her before, but there is something very comforting about her stance and features. I wonder where she came from. Buddy is smitten by his new dog friend immediately and disobeys my command to stay.

The woman giggles a familiar yet friendly laugh, assuring me it is fine as they bounce around the rock together as fast friends.

"They must be kindred spirits," she says in a tone all so insightful.

"Must be," I agree as we both enjoy the playful interaction before us.

"Great place, isn't it?" she offers with a smile.

"Yes, it is. The trails are a little rough right now, but they get you here," I say almost apologizing, but secretly, I am grateful that another has found my special spot and is enjoying nature to the fullest.

"They really aren't that bad. Besides, over time, things will smooth over. I am sure of it."

She turns to leave, but my stick catches her eye.

"Nice walking stick."

I am flattered by the compliment. "Thank you, it is quite special to me."

"I know," I think I hear her say, but before I get a chance to make sense of it, she calls her dog from Buddy's playful bounces.

With a slap to her thigh, she calls out, "Let's go, Gi-Gi!"

With a knot in my throat, a tear in my eye, and a wave of gratitude, I watch Gigi bounce through the thicket making her own path to catch up with her owner.

"No wonder you like her, Buddy. She seems very special."

Buddy and I watch them fade behind a large tree. Feeling a strange connection to them, we both are tempted to follow but sometimes a gift is better left as just a gift, like chance meetings, a sign that someone is watching, or a moment of knowing I am on the right path.

I look up to the trees, knowing they are watching and listening, too.

Thank you, Gigi, for letting me know you are here, for walking my path beside me, and for sharing every special moment.